LARCENY

This is a work of fiction. It is not meant to depict, portray or represent any particular real persons. All the characters, incidents, and dialogues are the products of the author's imagination and are not to be constructed as real. Any resemblance to actual events or persons, living or dead, is purely coincidental.

Published by Triple Crown Publications
2959 Stelzer Road Suite C
Columbus, OH 43219
www.TripleCrownPublications.com

Library of Congress Control Number: 2004106284
ISBN: 0974789550

Edited by: Kathleen Jackson
Graphics Design: www.ApolloPixel.com

Printed in the United States of America

ACKNOWLEDGEMENTS

"For my son"

Everything I do, I do it for you...

Live by the Jewels that have

Been handed down to you...

And I assure you that

There will never be any room for error...

Love Always,

The one who has given you life...

"DAD"

Also I would like to thank Vickie Stringer, Triple Crown Publications and Kathleen Jackson for all of their help and assistance.

DEDICATION

This book is deeply dedicated to my most truest and dearest comrades...

James H. Fowler

Ishmael Ford-Bey

And

Ruben "Rat-Man" Bell, R.I.P.

Forever I shall remain "Loyal" even in my death...

J. Rock...

Special Dedication To:

My brother Eric "Fat-Cat" Poole

My cousin Michael "Six Pack" Modlin, R.I.P.

J. Rock...

CHAPTER 1

"When we met"

SONYA

It was a cool day in May of 1994 when we first met. As I entered the building most famous in Washington, DC for its political scandals and often seen on every news channel after 5:00 pm, I felt good.

For some reason, today seemed so good. I woke up this morning feeling more beautiful than ever. As I looked at myself in the mirror of my one bedroom condo on Connecticut Avenue in Northwest, DC, I must say that I was proud of the reflection I saw. I could tell that the low-carb diet that I've been on for the last month was doing my abs supreme justice. My stomach was almost flatter than Janet Jackson's and my ass was more shapely and fatter than a Las Vegas stripper. Thanks to my mama I had inherited one of her greatest assets. Also, I could see that the Palmer's Coca Butter that I use keeps my golden brown skin as flawless as Halle Berry's. If I was to compare myself to someone famous I'd say it would be "Toni Braxton", but slightly thicker in all the right places.

In most men eyes I'm considered a perfect ten, a "straight dime piece" is what they call it, and to my surprise not just men but women too, especially the ones who desperately want to sleep with me. I'm always getting indirect invitations from bi-sexual women, and to tell the truth, these women are gorgeous also. Although it may seem interesting letting another woman lick my pussy, I still decline. I'm not into that and I don't think I ever will be, I'm "strictly dickly".

I opened my bedroom windows this morning to get a feel of the summer's cool breeze. The weather was nice it was in the high 70s. As I opened my walk-in closet full of upscale business suits, casual tops and bottoms of the latest fashion; Guzzi, Versace, Donna Karan, Prada, Chanel and many more, I thought it would be perfect to wear my new cream Dolce & Gabbana short halter-top dress. I pulled out a pair of medium heel ankle-laced sandals by Joan & David, to show off my freshly pedicured toes. Since I felt so good, I planned to wear my hair back and let its tail fall down to crease of my spine, sort of how the famous singer, "Sade" wears hers, and no I do not have a big forehead.

I stepped into the shower and turned on the radio to the station that plays all the coolest jams. I turned the volume up as they played Tanya Blunt's new song, "Through The Rain". Tanya is also from Washington, DC and it's so good to see people from DC getting a chance to show their true talents.

When I got out of the shower, I hadn't realized that time had flew past so quickly. I had gotten in the shower at 9:30 a.m. and it was now it's 10:15, damn that shower felt so good I guess I had gotten caught up and lost track of time, sorta like lovemaking, huh? Anyway, I let the cool breeze from my bedroom window dry my golden brown skin off and then I lotioned my body with my Victoria Secret's Amber Romance body lotion and put on my clothes, pulled my hair back and looked in the mirror one last time. Oh, did I mention I'm also bowlegged.

Here I am, Ms. Sonya Chanell Dunkin, the Assistant Producer at B.E.T. Studios, with a lavish condo in the upper northwest and the proud owner of a new emerald green convertible BMW 325IC, and for the record, I'm single, sexy and free. I didn't have enough time to grab a bite to eat because my appointment was scheduled for 11:15 a.m., so instead, I grabbed a granola bar, got in my BMW and headed for 500 Indiana Avenue, NW, Washington, DC's Superior Court.

It was this day that I met the man of my dreams, the most gracious and perfect gentleman I've ever met in my life. This was the day I met the man I plan to spend the rest of my life with. As I entered the elevator and the door was about to close, it opened back up again and "there he was". There were two other woman on the elevator also, one who seemed as though she was a nervous wreck. I assumed she was an untrained court clerk getting the run around from her boss. The other one was an elderly woman with a pretty smile who wore the worst perfume I've ever smelled in my life. And there he was, just about six feet tall, caramel complexion, jet black wavy hair, which he wore semi-low, 1?" with the grain. He had a precise shape up, as though his barber had outlined it with a razor, and he wore a light, perfectly trimmed goatee.

It was as if I had x-ray vision because when I pierced my eyes through his clothing, it was obvious this man was in extremely good shape, he had a body similar to the actor Shamar Moore. His face was very handsome, it reminded me of Denzel Washington when he played "Malcolm X". As I glanced up and down at him, shoes first, I saw that he wore about a size 9 or 9 ? shoe and he had on a pair of black calfskin slip-on's by Salvatore Farrangomo with the silver buckle, a pair of thin black slacks by Farrangomo with a matching black belt. His slacks weren't tight nor too baggy, they fit him just right. When he stood still, the cuff of his slacks would lay over the top of his shoes and when he walked, the cuff would pop up, exposing the buckle of his shoes, which matched his belt. He had made sure that his outfit was perfect. He also wore a thin black long sleeve mock neck shirt, which enhanced his Movado watch.

On the other hand, he had on a plain "white gold" bracelet designed like a bicycle chain. He also carried a small notebook case and his walk was a gracious, cool superior walk, as if to say, "nothing or nobody can fuck with me!" It wasn't a thugged out, I'm trying too much to look hard walk, it was more of a glide with a sense of security, boldness and assurance.

The elevator reached the third floor and the doors opened. As I was getting off the elevator, I couldn't resist the sensational smell of his cologne. I imagined it might have been "Curve" by Liz Clauborne or "Blue Jean" by Gianni Versace. Before the doors closed, he leaped out of the elevator and followed me as I continued to walk down the hall.

"Excuse me Miss, may I please have a moment of your time?" He asked.

Although I knew he was talking to me, I still played it off. I looked up and down the hall and answered, "Are you talking to me?"

"Yes I am. Hello and how are you?" He said, his voice sounding smoother than he looked. "My name is Jovan Price and I normally don't go out of my way much, but for you I had to make an exception. It is obvious by my actions that I'm extremely attracted to you. Is there any kinda way that you and I can get to know one another better?"

Normally, I would have told the average brotha that I was either involved or engaged, but with him I respected his approach so I said, "Well, Mr. Price..."

"Jovan, please call me Jovan, Mr. Price is my father." He said, smiling.

"Okay then Jovan, my name is Sonya and it wouldn't be any harm in us getting to know each other a little better, but right now I'm running late. I have an appointment in about 60 seconds, I shouldn't be that long maybe 15 to 20 minutes."

"So Ms. Sonya, is it good to say that you'll have lunch with me?"

In my mind I'm saying, "Hell yes, with your fine ass!" But, as always, I'm too ladylike to be acting like my hood rat cousin, Trina, so I said, "Yes, I will have lunch with you."

"Good, then you can meet me on the first floor about 12:00 o'clock, which is a half hour from now."

"Ok, I'll be there."

"I'll be waiting Sonya."

It was now 12:00 o'clock, the busiest time in downtown Washington, D.C. As I stepped off the elevator anticipating my lunch date with Mr. Jovan, I maneuvered my way through the crowd of lawyers, District Attorneys, criminals awaiting trial and busy protesters who often frequent this building. I looked all around for a minute and I still couldn't find him, until all of a sudden I heard that full smooth voice, followed by that familiar sensational cologne scent.

"Excuse me Miss Beautiful, are you looking for someone?" Jovan asked.

There he was standing behind me. I didn't realize he was that close at first, and any other time, when someone crept up on me like that I would have been on some type of guard but with him for some reason, I felt a sense of security.

"Oh, there you are, so what's up?" I asked.

"Where should we go for lunch? Do you like seafood? I was thinking we could go down to Phillips Seafood Restaurant on the waterfront." Jovan said.

"Yeah, I could go for some shrimp and a salad." I said.

"Good then, are you driving?"

"Yes Jovan, I'm parked in the garage over on C Street."

"Well, I'm parked about 2 blocks down from you."

"We can take my car and I can bring you back to your car after we finish lunch." I said.

"Oh no, you don't have to do that, I'm not due back in court, the hearing is over with. How about we meet each other in front of the restaurant." He said.

"Cool." I said.

As I pulled my BMW out of the parking garage, I started to contemplate what I was doing. Should I go to lunch or just head on home as though I never met this man, I started thinking as I retraced every step from the moment we met in the court building. He seemed okay, very sexy, polite, he had good manners and was fine as hell, I would say the perfect gentleman, but when he told me he wasn't due back in court and that the hearing was over, my antennas immediately shot straight up.

Now I grew up in Trinidad N.E., one of the most treacherous neighborhoods in D.C., and there ain't too much you can get pass me. Most of the game niggas run on other bitches out here is so weak you can see right through it. I've done seen niggas talk a virgin into fucking on the first night, so whatever game a nigga's shooting at me, is getting batted down off the break. So I did what most people in my position would do, I took a chance because for one, he could be some type of criminal, which I doubt, or he could have had some type of lawsuit hearing or he may be some kind of lawyer, who knows. I'll never know until I go to lunch and find out more about this man Jovan Price.

As I pulled up in front of Phillips Seafood Restaurant, I could see that Jovan had gotten there first and was standing in the walkway of the restaurant waiting for me. There were four other cars parked at the restaurant, a black corvette, a blue MVP mini van, a 500SL white Mercedes Benz and a gray two-door Acura Legend. Since Jovan had gotten here so fast, I guessed that the black Corvette was his or maybe the Mercedes. Most guys I know from DC wouldn't be pushing a 500SL and wearing a Movado watch, they'd be rockin' a Rolex.

When I got out of my car, Jovan was a complete gentleman, he opened my door, grabbed my hand and helped me out. He even added in a little humor.

"Ms. Sonya, so glad to see you. For a minute I thought you had a change of plans." When he smiled, I just looked up at him and imagined kissing him on those pretty full lips.

"No Jovan, I didn't have a change of plans, I guess your car is just a lot faster than mine." I said, giving him the opportunity to tell me which one of those lovely cars was his, but he just smiled and positioned me in the direction of the restaurant.

CHAPTER 2

"The Paralegal"

Jovan

Around 9:00 o'clock this morning I got a call from my employer at his law office. There must have been some type of problem because usually he would be in court around this time trying to get one of his clients out of jail, or at least trying to fuck any district attorney who wanted to prosecute one of his clients. Here I was, Jovan Conrad Price, getting harassed by his boss at 9:00 in the morning, especially on my day off.

I work for Mark Rohon, an attorney who has the biggest criminal law firm in Washington, DC, Rohon & Robinson law firm. He is the leading attorney at his office and he's very well known for his many highly publicized cases. His legal skill attracts the biggest drug dealers in the city.

If anyone who's getting some type of papers in DC, or at least on trial for some murders and want to get off and win the case, then Mark Rohon is their man and believe me, his services do not come cheap. It's been said that Mark works so hard getting his clients out of jail that the Government wants to investigate him to see if there's some kinda way that he's involved with their criminal conduct. But like any other smart attorney, Mark always has a way of getting out of any scheme.

I've only been working for Mark for about 5 months, and the

more I work for him, the more I see how crooked lawyers are. But for me, a nigga from the streets of Southeast, I respect his game and besides, this ma'fucka is getting paid out the ass. Niggas come by his office everyday dropping off shoe boxes full of money, and out of all this money, this fucker only pays me a punk ass thousand dollars a week. Now I'm no lawyer, but most of the cases that are put in Mark's motions, come from my labor.

I took a paralegal course for 2 years and received my graduate diploma about 6 months ago. I knew Mark from paying him on previous cases for some good friends of mine. We connected well and became cool, and he always told me if there's anything he could do to help me legally he would, so when I received my diploma in paralegal studies I went straight to Mark.

At first he seemed a little hesitant about hiring me, but once I explained to him my position and the need for money to continue my education, he graciously obliged. I was more than happy to get the job, but for real, I was still fucked up financially. I not only needed money for school, I also have a lavish spending habit, I like the finer things in life, I'm used to having money.

All my life I've been getting that money, loot, dough, cash, cheese or whatever else you may call it, I have always had a lust for that paper, I crave for it like a junkie craves for a fix. It used to cross my mind to get back into hustling, but I always knew that it took too much risk, time and hard effort to achieve the type of bank I really wanted and besides, there was too much competition in DC at the time.

The summer of '94 was a booming year, everybody was getting it, doin' they thang. I often thought about kidnapping and robbing a few of these niggas out here getting that money, especially those punks who ain't suppose to have it. Nowadays, everybody's hustling, slinging them thangs, niggas who ain't put in any work or come up hard from rock bottom is getting money, pushing 600SL's, Lexus Coupes, LS400's and 850I BMW's.

When the notorious Big Silk was on the scene, none of these

niggas was flaunting their bank like that, let alone coming off their fucking porches, but as soon as they heard that this killer had gotten three life sentences, all of a sudden niggas started poppin' up with shit. Don't get me wrong, there were some "real" gangstas out here getting money when Big Silk was on the scene, but them punks who he peeped as variable niggas who wasn't fit to play in this game, definitely got what was coming to them, they were being robbed at will.

Now that I was changing my life, it was hard for me to get used to not having a lot. Often times I felt depressed, unfocused and just plain ole broke as hell. I knew I had to put a plan together, the perfect plan that I've been working on for the last two years, I call it the "Political Move", and all I need to make my plan work is a nice bankroll and a down ass bitch.

I considered a few females that I was dealing with at the time, like Barvette. She was one of the top flight broads in the city. Barvette looked good and she had a business head on her shoulders, but the only thing about her that I couldn't get with was that she fucked around with too many major niggas. She wasn't looked at as some freak ass hood rat, she's more like a female player who knows how to play her cards right. She's the type of female you can take anywhere and she'd adjust to the situation.

At one time we were considered almost an item, we had the most fun together. Although I still see her every now and then, I still can't put her down with my move. It's been rumored that she's now dating an NBA star who plays for the Washington Wizards. When I found that out, I just knew there was no way to fit her into my plans.

There was also Keda, who I call my gangster bitch. She had the total package, a pretty face, pretty eyes, nice body, nice job, education, good pussy, bomb ass head and was down for whatever. But there was one area Keda lacked in, she had two little boys from a previous relationship, and not to mention they were bad as hell and kids are not a part of this move.

Lastly, there was Peppa. Pep was cool, she fit all the criteria but only one thing, Pep was too much of a hood rat and loved the party life. She is the type female who would walk into a business meeting with a "Donna Karan" spandex suit and tennis shoes on, I definitely couldn't use Pep.

What I needed was a straight-up educated, but down for whatever, no children female. Face it, I needed a real live straight-up "bitch" like in Bonnie & Clyde.

Ring, Ring, Ring. As I got up off the floor from doing my daily routine crunches to answer the phone, before I could even say "who is it", I heard a panicky voice, "Hello Jovan, Jovan! Are you there?"

"Yeah, I'm here, who's this?"

"It's me, Mark."

"Damn Mark, I'm suppose to be off today remember?"

"Yeah, yeah I know, but right now I need you, it's urgent."

Damn, usually I'm the one telling a lawyer I need him. "Ok Mark, what's up?"

"Well Jovan, I need you to come down to the office and shephardize a few cases for me and help format this motion for this evidentiary hearing we got coming up. I'll be calling you from court giving you certain cases in between the hearings and you can fax them to me." Mark said.

"Damn Mark, why'd you wait so late to file this motion?" I asked.

"Because Jovan, the court didn't give the proper notice of service that one of my clients was just granted this evidentiary hearing on appeal."

"So you mean to tell me this is an appellate case?"

"Yeah Jovan and I've got these fuckers by the balls."

I laughed. "That's good then Mark. Oh Mark."

"Yeah Jovan."

"Who's the client you're representing?"

"His name is Bilal, Bilal Davis."

Sonya

As Jovan and me entered the restaurant, we were greeted by a young shapely white waitress.

"Hello and how are you, welcome to Phillips Waterfront Restaurant. Today's menu includes our lavish seafood buffet of grilled tuna, baked salmon, lobster bisque, filet trout and the soup of the day is sharp fin chowder. The patio will be open until 3:00 pm and we have a smoking and non-smoking section inside." The waitress said.

I wondered if Jovan smoked because that would be a complete turn off. I looked at his lips to see if I could see any traces of purple that most people I know who smokes have. My cousin, she has the darkest lips ever from smoking and every time we go out, it's a must that she cover them up with bright red lipstick. Since I wasn't able to detect any signs of smoking on Jovan, like the smell of his clothes, yellow stained teeth, purple lips and a need for a fresh pack of Newports, I assumed that he didn't smoke.

Jovan interrupted the young waitress as she continued to tell us about damn near everything the restaurant had.

"Excuse me, we would like to be seated outside on the patio if you don't mind." He said.

The young waitress looked at Jovan as if to say, why in the hell did you cut me off like that. I liked that in Jovan, a sense of aggressiveness. When we were seated, I thought I'd add a little humor to the situation.

"Thanks Jovan, for a minute I thought she was gonna tell us

how the place was built and give us a grand tour." I said.

We both laughed and then Jovan said, "You better be quiet cause here she comes with the menus."

"Shhh, I thought she already told us the whole damn menu." We both laughed again.

I liked that about Jovan he carried himself very well. I could see that we were starting to connect and feel a little more comfortable with each other.

Jovan

Bilal Davis, all I could do was think back and reminiscence on the last time I saw Bilal. It was the winter of 1985 and I had just turned 15 years old. He was from Northeast DC, over there on 6th & K, across the street from Wilson Elementary School, an area which would later be known as the gold mine that helped DC's most biggest drug dealer, "Ray Edmonson" rise to multi-million dollar status.

My grandmother lived a few blocks over on 9th & G, right across the street from Golden Elementary and Sherwood Recreational playground. This is where all the major players and future NBA stars played basketball, people like Sherman Douglas who played for the Boston Celtics, Curt and Charles Smith, Lawrence Morton, Michael Gram, and on weekends, some of the players from the "Georgetown Hoyas" would play against local drug dealers in exchange for certain gifts.

My favorite was to see "Big Fat" dunk on any and everybody that got in his way. Sometimes my big cousin Poochie and my Uncle Bobby would go over to play and I'd watch them, along with almost every pretty female from round the way. The playground was always packed with pretty females, but as usual, they were all too old for me, and besides, pussy wasn't the first thing on my agenda back then.

It was a cold day in November of '85 and I was at my grandmother's house bored as hell. No one else was there but grandma and me. My father was a smooth nigga and he wasn't around that much, he was mostly outta town on some type of business, at least, that's what I thought. As I got older, I came to find out that he was on the run for some bank robberies he did back in the late '70s. This is why when he came by grandma's to see me he wouldn't stay long, but he'd give me a few dollars, throw a couple of jabs at me to make sure I knew how to fight, drop me a few jewels and step off.

The one jewel that stayed with me the most was when he'd used to say, trust no one, master your condition and keep all suckers in the bounds of moderation. Of course, I wouldn't understand any of this shit until later on in life when it became reality.

Sonya

Jovan ordered baked salmon filet with sun-dried tomatoes and a side order of creamed spinach, along with a glass of freshly squeezed grapefruit juice. I could see from his order that Jovan is very alert towards his health, which is something that we both have in common. I wonder if he drinks occasionally like myself? That would be a plus.

When it was my turn to order, I got a seafood salad with bleu cheese dressing and a side order of steamed shrimp, along with a glass of lemon ice tea.

"Got a big appetite huh?" Jovan asked me.

"Yeah Jovan, I was in a rush this morning and wasn't able to eat a thing."

A slight grin came on his face. "So that's why you took my invitation to lunch, you wasn't even thinking about getting to know me better huh?"

Before I answered I blushed a little. "Look Mr. Smarty Pants, if I didn't want to get to know you I would have made the first right on Pennsylvania Avenue, headed home, fixed myself my own seafood salad and watched the daytime soaps. And for the record, I must find you somewhat interesting because I don't miss my soaps for nobody."

"Well, excuse me Miss."

We both laughed while looking each other in the eyes. I wondered if he's thinking what I'm thinking, does he feel like I feel and does he want what I want.

"Well Sonya, where are you from?"

"I grew up in the Northeast over in Trinidad, all the way up until I got in the 9th grade, then we moved uptown to Webster Street, NW."

"Is that where you went to school?"

"Yeah, I went to Roosevelt High and I stayed there until I graduated. I had a rough time in school mostly because my mother stayed in the hospital a lot, she had Cancer and died when I was in my last year of school."

"Damn Boo, I'm so sorry to hear that."

"It's cool. I've learned to deal with it, I can't let that hold me back from achieving higher things in life. In fact, I use it as motivation." I told Jovan.

"That's good. Do you have any brothers and sisters?"

"My brother is, hold up Jovan, I just met you, I shouldn't be telling you all my personal business like this."

"Sonya, your business only becomes personal when you hold it in, and when you hold it in too long, sometimes it may hinder you from getting what you really want in life."

At that moment, whatever he said sounded good and I thought about it for a second, especially when he said it may hinder me from getting what I really wanted in life, and right now what I really wanted was to get to know Jovan better, so I continued with his little interview and anticipated the wait for my turn to ask the questions.

"Ok Jovan, I have a younger brother, his name is Anthony but we call him Lil Tony. He's locked up down in Lorton, VA behind the wall. He's been in prison since he was sixteen and he's twenty-four now. He got 30 years to life for killing a guy who tried to rape me."

While telling Jovan about Lil Tony my eyes started to get watery even though it's been a long time since that day when Lil Tony heard me screaming in the alley on 16th Street and came to my rescue, only to see that the man he thought was his father holding my throat and choking the life outta me while pulling down my pants and trying to take my virginity.

Jovan

Bilal stopped over my grandmother's house to see if I was coming outside. He had his little brother, Jamal with him. Jamal was 8 years old and Bilal had nicknamed him Mal-Mal and he was the only true love Bilal had, everything Bilal did he did it for Mal-Mal. Their father was killed in a bank robbery shootout with the Feds, which left Ms. Cookie, their mother, a nervous wreck. She didn't know how to take care of her two boys because she had always been dependent on Bilal's Pops. To make matters worse, they both were dependent on heroin, so when he was killed that left Ms. Cookie, the worse addict that Northeast, DC ever had, to take care of her two boys alone.

Ms. Cookie never had any food in the house, so Bilal was the one who had to take care of Mal-Mal. He would go to the Safeway Grocery Market on 7th & H Street, NE and steal whatever kind of food you could eat without it being cooked because they didn't even have gas on in the house.

When Bilal and me used to go down to McBride's Department Store to steal, we would see Ms. Cookie on the corner of 8th & H Street nodding and scratching. I remembered once when he went up to her to tell her about Mal-Mal being sick, she lifted her head up real fast as if she was concerned and then said, "Baby, you got ten dollars so I can get my fix?"

Bilal began to hate Ms. Cookie, he used to say, "Jovan, one day I'm gonna be rich and I'm gonna take Mal-Mal to Disneyland, Sea World and all them other places parents take their children. I'ma get a real big house for Mal-Mal and me and that bitch Cookie better not ask me for shit!"

Although we both knew that Bilal was dreaming and it would never happen, I still had to add to it to keep his mind off of Ms. Cookie.

"What about me Bilal, whatcha gonna do for your boy?"

"Oh Jovan, I'ma get you a white Nissan Maxima, about 50 pair of New Balances and a fat gold rope like Run DMC. Yeah nigga, it just gonna be Mal-Mal, you and me."

Sonya
Jovan held my hand tight while I sat in silence for a moment, then he said, "Sonya, if you don't want to continue, we could move onto another subject. I understand how it is, believe me, and when it comes my turn to talk, you will hear things similar to your story."

For some reason, I kept feeling a sense of security with Jovan, as though his words were sincere and his heart was pure, the perfect gentleman, it was all too good to be true. I couldn't wait until it was my turn to ask him questions.

"Ok, now Sonya, is it alright if I ask how old you are?"

I gave a slight smile and said, "How old do you think I am?"

"Well, you definitely don't look old, in fact for a minute, I was kinda skeptical about asking you to lunch because you look so young." Jovan said.

I laughed. "Yeah right."

"No, but seriously Sonya, you are a very gorgeous women and also in tremendous shape, I wouldn't care if you were 60 years old, I'd still ask you to lunch."

I laughed again. "Jovan, now you're pushing your luck."

"Well, you know all I can do is try."

"Don't worry, you're doing a good job and baby for the record, I'm 27 and my birthday is April 3rd."

Oh no, did I call him baby? I hope he doesn't take that as a sign of weakness. I barely know this man and I'm calling him baby already, what in the hell has come over me?

"So you just turned 27?" He asked me.

"Yeah, but sometimes I feel like I'm 87."

"Damn sweetheart, you going through that much drama?" We both laughed and no he didn't just call me sweetheart, this little lunch date was going well.

"No, I ain't going through that much drama, but I do have a very difficult job."

"Oh, so you do work."

"Yes I do, why'd you say that?"

"Oh, because earlier you said something about watching the soaps."

"No baby," oops there I go again, "I watch the soaps whenever I'm off and sometimes when I'm at work, I tape them so I can watch them when I come home from work."

"Oh ok."

"I've been doing that for years."

"So, what type of work do you do?"

"I work at BET Studios, I'm the Assistant to the Producer."

"Damn, so you call the shots huh?"

"No, not really. What I do is run around like a mad woman for the man who calls the shots, remember I'm an assistant."

Again we both laughed. Damn, it feels good to be in a man's presence, a fine ass man at that. Little did Jovan know, if he keeps up the good work, then maybe this little lunch date could possibly turn into a dinner date.

Jovan

When Bilal and Mal-Mal came into my grandma's house, you could tell that Mal-Mal hadn't eaten, he was quiet and he looked cold. I went upstairs, got him one of my old sweatshirts and a coat I had back when I was young. Grandma always kept those types of things, she didn't believe in throwing nothing away. I then fixed us some oodles and noodles and steak-ums that grandma kept in her freezer for me to cook when she was gone. I made Mal-Mal and Bilal two sandwiches a piece and a bowl of oodles and noodles. Mal-Mal ate all of his food but Bilal didn't, he wrapped his sandwiches up just in case he wasn't able to find Mal-Mal anything to eat later. Bilal was taking on a big responsibility, because no matter what was going on, he always made sure Mal-Mal was alright.

While Bilal and me went downstairs to play video games, Mal-Mal stayed upstairs and ate cookies and watched cartoons. I was killing Bilal on Ms. Pac-Man, we played a couple more games and then we started to talk.

"Hey Jovan, let's go down to Hechinger Mall and steal some cologne and leather belts." Bilal said.

"What the fuck are we gonna do with cologne and belts?"

Bilal laughed and said, "We gonna sell 'em stupid!"

"To who?" I asked him.

"To the fucking hustlers on 9th & I and the ones on Orleans

Pl., they love that type of shit."

"How you know?"

Bilal dropped his head to his chest before he said, "Cause my mother's a fuckin' junkie and she do it all the time, that's how I know."

So we all walked down to Hechinger Mal and went into the Safeway Foods first. We stole enough food to feed Mal-Mal for about a week. So far our shoplifting spree was going good, no police were in sight and no one would ever suspect two teenagers with an 8 year old would be stealing like it's going outta style.

When we went into the Cavalier's Men Shop, this is where we used Mal-Mal's innocent looks to get what we wanted. The salesperson was a fat pudgy lady and she looked like she was in her 30's, she was the only salesperson on the floor at the time. Bilal must have done this before because he knew right where the belts and cologne were. "Go 'head Mal-Mal, do your thang." Bilal told him.

Mal-Mal went over to the lady to distract her from us and said, "Excuse me pretty lady."

"Why hello young handsome fella, how can I help you?" The saleslady asked Mal-Mal.

"My daddy's birthday is tomorrow, can you help me pick out a hat?" Mal-Mal said.

"Why I sure can little man, come on over here with me."

The fat lady took Mal-Mal over to the hat rack while Bilal and me opened our coats and each of us wrapped five Pierre Cardin leather belts around our bodies. Then we stuffed our inside and outside coat pockets with bottles of Ralph Lauren, Geoffrey Beane, Stetson and English Leather colognes.

When it was time for us to leave, Bilal went over to Mal-Mal and said, "Hey, you brought daddy a hat last year, why don't you get him something else."

"Ok, I'll be back. Hey pretty lady, when I come back can you help me pick out a pair of gloves?" Mal-Mal said, with his innocent look and whiney voice.

"Why I sure can little man, you just promise to come on back, you hear."

Damn, Mal-Mal did that shit too perfect, but I already knew where he got it from, Ms. Cookie used to make him do that whenever she was "ill", and trying to get her fix.

Sonya

"So Sonya, where do you live?" Jovan asked.

"Why aren't we getting a little too personal." I said, giving him a sexy smile.

"Oh I'm sorry, I'm just starting to feel really comfortable with you and I could sit here and talk to you all day long." Jovan said, as he leaned back in his seat studying Sonya's body language.

"Well Jovan, since you don't look like some kinda stalker or anything, I guess it wouldn't hurt to tell you where I stay. I live on Connecticut Avenue in a condo called 'The Saratoga'."

"Nice place, ain't it?" Jovan said.

"You've been there?" I asked him.

"Yeah, a few years ago. A friend of mine had a nice condo there. Do they still have those marble bathrooms?"

"Yeah they do."

"That spot reminds me of a hotel in Vegas."

"Yeah, which one Jovan?"

"The MGM Grand."

"I've never been there."

"You've never been to Vegas?"

"No silly, I mean I've never been to the MGM Grand, I went to Vegas a couple of years ago." I hoped Jovan doesn't ask me who I went to Vegas with, that would be the start of many lies, so to keep from lying I shifted the conversation into another direction.

"So Jovan, since I sat here and told you all my business, now it's my turn to ask the questions."

"Hold up Sonya, I've got one more question."

Jovan

With our shoplifting spree over, it was now time to drop Mal-Mal off and go try to sell our goods to the hustlers on 9th & I and Orleans Pl. On our way back, Bilal had a look of unhappiness on his face. I wondered what was wrong cause we had just stolen about a hundred dollars worth of shit, so why the fuck was he mad.

"Hey Bilal, what's wrong nigga?" I said to him.

"Whatcha mean what's wrong?"

"Man, you look like you just lost your best friend."

"Naw nigga, I got something on my mind and for future reference, I ain't never gonna lose my best friend. My best friend is right here and he ain't going nowhere, ain't that right Mal-Mal?" Bilal said, looking at his brother.

Mal-Mal looked up at his older brother all smiles and said, "Yeah Lal, we best friends for life. I can't wait til we get rich, get our big house, go to the movies, the park, play games and eat candy all day."

"Naw little nigga, you ain't gonna be eating no candy all day, but we is getting our house and all that other stuff."

Bilal grabbed a hold of Mal-Mal's head and said, "I love you Mal-Mal."

"I love you too Lal."

As I looked at them express their deepest love to each other, I began to think about my big brother and the pain grew deep in my heart. All I could do was block it out and hold it in until the day I would be able to release it.

Bilal was only 15 years old but he took life very serious, he knew that he had to do something to be able to raise Mal-Mal like he wanted to. Then he looked at me deep in my eyes and from the way he was looking at me, I knew that whatever was about to come outta his mouth was to be taken seriously. Bilal was a grown man trapped in a little boy's body.

"Hey Jovan?" Bilal said.

"What's up Lal?"

"Look man, you know it ain't nobody but Mal-Mal and me, you know he's my life and my only love, right."

"Yeah Lal, I already know that."

"Jovan, can you promise me something?"

"Yeah, what's up Lal?"

"Promise me slim, that if anything was to ever happen to me that you'll look out for Mal-Mal."

At that moment, I didn't know that my promise would mean taking on such a big responsibility so soon, but we were friends and all I could do was be loyal to our friendship.

"Yeah nigga, you know Mal-Mal's my little man, shonuff I'll look out for him."

"Thanks Jovan, you my only true friend." Bilal said, with all sincerity.

As we continued to walk down H Street, we saw Ms. Cookie coming in our direction. Today Ms. Cookie looked clean, she wasn't scratching or nodding, but she was getting very skinny.

"Hey mommy!" Mal-Mal yelled, with a big smile on his face.

"Mal-Mal, my baby." Ms. Cookie said.

Ms. Cookie grabbed her youngest son and hugged him as if she hadn't seen him in years. Mal-Mal was happy to see his mother and it wasn't often that he saw her in a healthy state of mind.

"Hey Mal-Mal, you wanna go over to Aunt Gloria's house with me?" Cookie asked him.

Bilal interrupted with the most serious look on his face I've ever seen. "Naw, he a'ight he ain't trying to go nowhere."

Ms. Cookie immediately snapped, "Look here Bilal, this is my son, I carried him for 9 months to bring him into this world so I can take him wherever the fuck I want to!"

"Lal, I wanna go with mommy over to Aunt Gloria's house." Mal-Mal whined.

Lal didn't want Mal-Mal to go, but he could see that Mal-Mal missed their mother, so he said, "Ok Mal-Mal, you can go, but Cookie let me tell him something first."

"Go ahead but make it quick." Cookie said, while coldly looking at her first born as if he were her archenemy.

Bilal took Mal-Mal's hand and whispered in his ear, "Look Mal-Mal, when you go over Aunt Gloria's house be good."

"Ok Lal."

"And if Cookie tries to leave you over there, don't cry cause I'll come and get you tomorrow, ok."

"Ok Lal."

"I love you, lil nigga."

"I love you too Lal."

"You my soldier?"

"Yeah, for life."

Then he hugged and kissed his little brother and said good-bye as if it would be the last time he'd ever see him.

"I wish your ass would stop acting like you his father, you ain't his daddy Bilal." Cookie said to Bilal.

"Well, when you start acting like a mother, then I'll start acting like his big brother, but until then, I'm his father and his big brother." Bilal said, giving his mother a hard stare.

Before Ms. Cookie could cuss Bilal out, I interrupted and said, "C'mon Bilal, we got something to do. See you later Ms. Cookie."

"Bye Bilal, bye Jovan."

Sonya
"Ok Jovan, what's your last question?" Sonya said, curiously.

Before Jovan opened his mouth, I could see that the expression on his face became very serious, his eyes had a mixture of boldness and bashfulness. He sat back in his chair, crossed his left leg over his right, put his left hand under his chin and asked the question that would change the whole tone of our lunch date.

"Well Sonya, I know this is a little too early and if I'm in anyway outta place, I expect you to let me know. Also, if you feel the slight bit of discomfort, I would like to apologize before hand."

After hearing him apologize, I became anxious and I was curious as to what he wanted to know.

"Ok Jovan, go ahead shoot your shot."

"My question is, do you have a man Sonya?"

At that moment, I was unbalanced and I knew that my future friendship with Jovan would reflect on my answer. Although I haven't been seeing anyone, I did have a very serious relationship two years ago and even though it's over, I know that I'm still in love with this man. But shit, that's been over two years ago and life must go on, and besides, I'm tired of playing with my pussy all the time, I need some dick, a good dick. I need someone to hold and cuddle me, someone to make passionate love to me while fucking my brains out at the same time. Even though my vibrator does the trick at times, in reality, I still need the flesh. Bad as I wanted to tell Jovan this I couldn't, he'd just have to stick around to find out for himself.

"Well Jovan, this is kinda awkward for me to tell you this, but I'm gonna give it to you in the raw. No, I don't have a man, although it would be nice to have one. I haven't had a man in over two years and to be honest with you, my body hasn't been touched by a man in over two years."

Jovan raised his eyebrows and I wondered what he was thinking, but then I remembered that I said I hadn't been touched by a man in two years, so I retracted and said, "And no Jovan, I'm not gay, I don't go that way."

"I didn't say that Sonya." Jovan said, smiling.

"I know, but in case you were thinking that, I just had to put that out there."

Jovan
Bilal and me were headed over to 9th & I and Orleans Pl., when all of a sudden something came to my mind. First of all, this is Bilal's neighborhood and I don't know any of the hustlers out

here. Although my Pops and my Uncle Howdy have a vicious reputation for being stick-up boys, I was still a little skeptical about going around there.

"Hey Bilal, hold up!" I yelled to Bilal.

"What's up Jay? What you scared nigga, ain't nothin' gonna happen to you." Bilal said.

"Nah, I ain't scared of nothing."

"Then what's the hold up."

"I just gotta go pass my Grandma's house for a minute."

"A'ight, we need to go put this food up anyway." Bilal said.

We walked over to my Grandma's house, went in and had something to eat. For some reason, every time Bilal came over, Grandma always offered him something to eat and Bilal never declined. While Bilal was downstairs eating, I went upstairs to my Pops old room.

Now, I've been creeping in and out of Pops room going through his shit since I was 9 years old. You could tell Grandma never went in there cause everything was always in its place. I knew where Pops hid one of his guns, the third shoebox to the left. I went into that shoebox and got the gun, but when I picked it up, I never realized that it was that fuckin' heavy. This was the first time I had ever touched Pops gun. When I was little I never touched Pops shit, I always just sat there and looked at it. Pops had a pretty ass nickel plated .357 Magnum with a rubber grip, which most gangstas called the bulldog. I looked into the revolver and saw it was loaded with six bullets.

I heard Bilal's voice from downstairs say, "Hey Jovan, c'mon man, we got things to do."

I tucked the bulldog down my pants and tightened my belt to make sure the heavy ass gun didn't fall out.

"Ok man, here I come." I called down to Bilal.

I put on my sweatshirt and changed my coat to the heavier one my Pops had gotten me, it was a blue north face ski coat. Bilal loved this coat, and since he only had one thin ass jacket, I told him I'd give it to him.

When I came downstairs and Bilal saw me in the north face joint, the first thing to come out of his mouth was, "Man, you're an Indian giver."

"No I ain't." I said to him.

"Man, yes you are, you said you was gonna give me that coat a long time ago."

"And I'm still gonna give it to you."

"When?" He asked, not believing me.

"Soon as we get back I'll give it to you and you can wear it home since my other coat is over in Southeast."

"Thanks Jovan, you the only friend I got besides Mal-Mal."

All the other kids around here was scared of Bilal, mainly because he was poor and the fact he always stayed in fights because people would tease him about Ms. Cookie.

"Hey Grandma, I'll be back ok."

"Ok baby, don't be out all night, you know I gotta take you home so you can go to school tomorrow." She said.

"Alright."

As Bilal and me were walking down the street he said, "Damn man, why can't you just move over here and go to school."

"Man, Moms won't let me."

"Shit, I don't see why not."

"I think it might have something to do with my Pops, I dunno."

"Whatever! Anyway Jovan man, we're about to get paid. We can sell these belts for 10 dollars apiece."

"What makes you think we're gonna get ten dollars when they only cost fifteen?"

"Shhhit, watch me work and we can sell the cologne for five dollars a bottle."

"Now I can see that, but the belts, I dunno."

"Ok nigga, like I said watch me work."

Bilal, for some reason, had hustling in his blood. He was determined that we were gonna sell those belts for ten dollars. Me, on the other hand, I wasn't too much on the hustling tip, mainly because my peoples took care of me. We wasn't rich or anything, but my Moms did have a job as a waitress at the NCO Club on Boiling Air Force Base and plus, whenever Pops came through he would drop off a few dollars.

Even though Bilal didn't know I had the bulldog on me, our positions were set, he had the goods and I had the protection. When we reached 9th & I, the first person we saw was Fat Jimmy. Bilal knew Fat Jimmy from his Moms, she used to deal with Fat Jimmy right after Bilal's Pops was killed, but when Fat Jimmy realized that Ms. Cookie was only dealing with him just to keep her habit up, he left her alone and that is what led Ms. Cookie onto the streets. She no longer had a man that could keep her with a steady supply for her habit, so she started going out stealing and tricking, selling her body to anyone who had some good dope.

"Hey Fat Jimmy!" Bilal yelled, as he saw the fat hustler exchange bags of dope to one of his customers.

"What's up man?" Fat Jimmy said.

"Who dat, Lil Bilal? What's up youngin, I ain't seen you in awhile. What, you looking for your Moms?"

"Naw man, she's over at my Aunt's house."

"Then what the fuck you doing on the strip little nigga."

"My man and me got some Pierre Cardin belts we trying to sell."

"Some belts?" Fat Jimmy asked.

"Yeah."

"Are they leather?"

"Yeah man, brand new joints, all different colors."

"Let me see 'em then."

Bilal opened his jacket and showed Fat Jimmy the belts.

"Damn youngin, where ya'll get all these fucking belts from?"

"C'mon Jimmy, what kinda question is that?"

Fat Jimmy smiled at Bilal. "That's right young nigga, you've been taught well, just like your father."

Even though Bilal's Pops was a dope fiend, he still had a lot of respect in the hood, he was known as a cold blooded killer and it's rumored that he used to rob a different bank every week. When people compared Bilal to his Pops, he would get a real sense of pride as if he one day would be reincarnated into his Pops image. That shit used to pump Bilal up.

"Who dat with you Bilal?" Said Fat Jimmy, while watching my every move.

"Oh, this is my man Jovan, you probably know his Pops too." Bilal said, pointing to me.

Now I wasn't too happy running around braggin' on my Pops and Uncle, cause I know they used to terrorize this hood back in the day. For all I know, they could have robbed Fat Jimmy.

"Who your Pop youngin?" Fat Jimmy asked me.

"My Pops name is Winkle." I said to Fat Jimmy.

"Who, Winkle Price, Howdy's brother?"

"Yeah man."

"Yeah, I know Winkle and Howdy, we used to go on capers together back in the day. How's your Pops doing anyway?"

"He's a'ight."

"He still on the run for that bank robbery?"

"Nah slim, my Pops ain't on the run for no bank robbery, he outta town on business." I said, defending my Pops.

Fat Jimmy looked at me as it to say "damn" he had let the cat out of the bag. It was obvious I didn't know about my Pops legacy in the gangsta world, so he quickly switched the conversation from my Pops to my Uncle.

"How your Uncle Howdy doin'?"

"You know he down in Lorton Max doin' 15 to 45 years."

"Yeah I know, I got word he down there doing hard time. Youngin you come from a vicious family, both ya'll do and I can just imagine how ya'll gonna turn out. Give me one of them belts Bilal, let me see if they fit."

Fat Jimmy tried on all the belts but he was too fat to fit them, so we ended up selling him three bottles of cologne for 5 dollars a piece.

"A'ight Jimmy, thanks man." Bilal said.

"Anytime youngin, whenever ya'll get some shit come see me first."

"Ok, we'll do that."

"C'mon Jovan, let's go over to Orleans Pl. and see if we can get rid of the rest of this shit."

Bilal and me walked from 9th Street over to Orleans Pl. When we entered the alley, there were so many customers I couldn't believe this spot was pumpin' this hard. Orleans Pl. was a powder coke strip, it attracted all kinds of people from prostitution to politicians, and the man behind all this that would benefit and become a multimillionaire was a young big lip kid with a 3 point jumper outta this world, Ray, who later in life would become the biggest snitch in Washington, DC's history.

Bilal and me approached our second customer of the day, he was laid back in the cut watching over all his workers as they ran back and forth through the alley handing him bundles of money, and when I say "bundles" I mean "bundles", this dude was collecting so much money that he'd call one of his Lieutenants over every time he'd get like ten thousand and tell him to put it up.

I would later find out that this Lieutenant's name was John. Now John was Ray's cousin and he had just as much or maybe more respect then Ray did. John was like an enforcer type dude, something I admired, and it was rumored that he didn't play no games and if you crossed him or anybody down with him, then you'd be dealt with immediately.

Bilal knew John from him coming around with his Pops back in the day and John also liked Bilal. He knew that Bilal was the only one taking care of Mal-Mal like a man and he respected him for that. Bilal used to ask John could he hustle for him but John always lived by strong principles. Even though he knew Bilal needed money to take care of Mal-Mal, he still kept to his word that he would never employ juveniles in this drug game. So instead, he'd get Bilal to run a few errands to the nearest carryout or something and give him about 25 dollars for it, shit 25 dollars just to go get him a 5 dollar fish sandwich, John was a good dude.

"Hey John, what's up?" Bilal said.

"Who dat?" John said, as he squenched his eyes trying to see the two youngsters in the dark alley.

John didn't permit kids into his alley because it was way too dangerous. If anything was to ever happen to them he'd feel responsible, so to avoid all the trouble, he made strict rules, the alley was off limits to juveniles.

"It's me, Bilal."

"Bilal, what I tell you 'bout coming in this alley."

"Ah man, my man and me here just trying to sell these belts and cologne we got."

"Some what, belts and cologne?"

"Yeah man."

John had a slight grin on his face. "Let me see what you got."

Bilal showed John the goods and when John looked at the belts and cologne, he laughed so hard that Bilal and me felt a little ashamed.

"Why you laughin' John?" Bilal asked.

"Cause man, I don't wear this cheap shit, I wear two hundred dollar belts and cologne! This shit ain't nothing, I can't do anything with this. Damn man, tell you what, ya'll go head and keep your shit, I'ma give you fifty dollars anyway cause I know you gotta take care of your lil bro. Take this stuff down the alley to one of my runners, they might buy it, they some Bammas anyway."

"Ok thanks, John."

"Yeah, it ain't nothin'."

"You better start taking your butt to school Bilal, both you and your man here."

"But you don't even know me John." Jovan said.

"Yeah, but you hangin' with Bilal, so I know you ain't going to school either."

"Ok thanks, John."

"Yeah, now hurry up and get your asses out of this alley." John said.

"A'ight." Bilal said.

When Bilal and me walked down to the end of the alley, we bumped into this hard faced, dark skin dude with beady hair and pimples. He didn't look like no runner to me, he looked more like a fiend.

Bilal said, "Hey man, you wanna buy some belts and cologne?"

The guy looked up and down the alley nervously before he answered, "Where they at and what you want for 'em?"

"Ten dollars for the belts and five for the cologne."

"Let me see 'em."

Bilal pulled out the goods and showed them to the dude.

The dude said, "Shorty, these ma'fuckin' belts cost 15 dollars and this cologne cost 8 dollars, what ya tryin' to do, get over on me?"

"Naw man, we ain't tryin' to get over on you, we just tryin' to get paid." Bilal said.

"These fuckin' belts ain't worth no 10 dollars." The dude said.

At that moment I said something that I shouldn't have said. "Look slim, if you don't wanna pay what we want then give us our shit back."

"What you say! What you say, you little bitchass nigga! Nigga, I'll take this shit from ya'll!"

Bilal then jumped up and said, "Man, you ain't taking shit from us!"

"What you gonna do huh?" The fiend said, as he still looked up and down the alley. "Nigga, this shit mine now get the fuck away from here for I beat the shit outta both ya'll!"

Bilal reached for the goods and outta nowhere this ma'fucka hit Bilal in the face and kneed him in the stomach. Bilal went down on his knees, crying throughout all the commotion. I didn't know what I was doing, but for some reason, I didn't feel nervous or scared, I felt like what I was about to do was justified. I looked at Bilal on the ground, and although I was angry, I still didn't replace logic for emotion. I knew that something had to be done and fast, so when the fiend turned towards me, I already had the bulldog pointed at his chest. I didn't hesitate or panic, I waited until his body was positioned directly in front of mine and then I pulled the trigger two times, "boom-boom", the impact of the bulldog damn near lifted me off my feet.

Bilal looked up at me in a state of shock and said, "What the fuck you do Jovan?"

I never answered because it was obvious I was protecting us by any means necessary.

"Where the fuck you get that gun man?"

"Shut up man, get the shit and let's go."

At that moment, everything in the alley stopped. The fiend was lying there dying in his puddle of blood then we heard some voices saying, "Hey, what ya'll doing?"

As Bilal and me took off running down the alley, we heard a woman scream and say, "Hey, come back here, what ya'll do? They shot Boo-Boo, call the police!"

We ran faster until we reached Sherwood Recreational Park where we sat down and caught our breath, then came the question.

"Man Jovan, why the fuck you ain't tell me you was strapped?" Bilal said.

"I dunno man, you probably would have told me I was scared and to take it back." I said.

"How the fuck you gonna know what I'ma say if you don't ask."

"Man, the shit just happened, that nigga violated us and he got what he deserved."

"What if he dies?"

"Then that's what he deserves."

Bilal was silent for a moment then said, "Ok, where the fuck you get that gun then?"

"I stole it out my Pops room."

"Your Pops got shit like that laying around the room?"

"Naw man, I was sneakin' through his shit and found it."

"When he find out you got it, he gonna whip your ass."

"No he ain't cause I'ma put it back tonight."

"A'ight, then let's go put that shit back cause it's getting late."

"Hey Bilal, you think anybody saw us?" I asked, scared that someone might have seen us.

"Man, them ma'fuckas don't know us, they coke heads remember."

"Yeah right." I said, as I thought about what I'd just done.

"Hey Jovan?"

"What is it now Bilal?"

"Hey, thanks man for not letting that ma'fucka stomp my head in."

"Slim, you my man and I fuck with you from the heart, I ain't gonna never let nobody do nothin' to you and get away with it."

"Visa versa nigga."

We both gave each other a hug and went into Grandma's house, which was directly across the street from the Park. Soon as I came through the door, Grandma got right in my ass.

"Boy, where your ass been at? Didn't I tell you don't be out too late, I gotta take you home."

"Yeah Grandma, but it's only 9:00 o'clock."

"9:00 o'clock my ass, next time I'ma leave your butt standing out in the cold. Act just like your damn daddy, don't listen for shit."

"I'm sorry Grandma, you know I love you baby girl." I said, hugging her tight.

"Go upstairs and get your things with your silly self." She said, giving me a light smile.

"Ok." I said, heading upstairs.

"Hey Grandma Price, can I use the phone to call my Aunt before I go?" Bilal asked.

"Yes Bilal, go ahead baby."

Ring, Ring, Ring, "Hello." Aunt Gloria answered.

"Hey Aunt Gloria." Bilal said.

"Who's this, Bilal?"

"Yeah."

"Hey Bilal, your momma ain't shit, she left Mal-Mal over here all fucking day and you know she ain't coming back, and baby I got to get up and go to work in the morning." Aunt Gloria said, pissed the fuck off at Cookie.

"Ok Aunt Gloria, I'ma come get him right now."

"Where you at Bilal?" She asked him.

"Right around the corner."

"Hurry up cause these kids getting on my last nerve."

"Ok." Bilal said, hanging up the phone.

I went upstairs to put Pops bulldog back and pack my things. When I came back down, I had the blue north face coat in my hand.

"Hey Bilal." I said.

"What's up?"

"Didn't I say I was about my word."

"Yeah, so what's up?"

"Here nigga, this coat still new so don't fuck it up." I said, handing him the coat.

"So it's mine now?"

"Yeah, it's yours."

"Then I can do what the fuck I wanna do with it."

"Give me my shit back nigga."

Bilal and me were joking with each other as if nothing happened earlier.

Grandma then yelled from the back of the house, "Hey, I hear you two out there, ya'll better stop that damn cursing in my house!"

"Ok, sorry Grandma."

"Sorry Ms. Price." Bilal turned to me before he left and said, "Man thanks, Jovan you the only friend I got."

When Bilal told me that, you could see the sincerity in his eyes as if he was about to shed a tear.

"A'ight man, see you next weekend."

Bilal left and was on his way to pick up Mal-Mal from Aunt Gloria's house which was on 12th and Wyle, a few blocks up from where the murder was put down. Just before Bilal could hit the corner of 12th Street, two police cars closed in on him. Both officers got out with their guns drawn.

"Freeze Goddamnit!" Said one officer.

"Don't move and put your hands in the air!" Said the other officer.

Bilal was scared and confused as he placed his hands above his head, praying that they wouldn't shoot.

As one officer began to frisk Bilal, the other held him at gun-point. Bilal almost fainted when he overhead the dispatcher on the officer's radio say, "Calling all cars, we now have the full description on the two suspects involved in the homicide on Orleans Pl."

The officer holding the gun turned the volume up on his radio, while the other officer was still searching Bilal.

The dispatcher called out, "Suspects are two young black males between the ages of 14-16, medium height, one of the males was wearing a blue coat with writing on the sleeve, blue jeans and tennis shoes."

The officer frisking Bilal yelled out to the other office, "Does he fit the description?"

"Yeah that's him, lock his ass up!" The officer said.

Bilal was arrested and charged with murder. There was one witness who pointed out Bilal and stated that there were two people, but the one with the blue coat pulled the gun. After hours of interrogation, Bilal never broke he kept his silence, he remained loyal and was sentenced to a juvenile facility up until he was 21 years old.

This was the first time that the reality world Bilal was living in became completely visible to me. Bilal took the murder charge for me, something that niggas nowadays would catch diarrhea in the mouth if they were caught, and I will remember this and forever remain loyal.

Sonya
"So now Mr. Jovan, whatever your middle name is, Price." I said to him.

"Conrad sweetheart, my middle name is Conrad."

"Ok Conrad, it's my turn now to interrogate you."

As we looked each other in the face, I still couldn't believe how strikingly handsome he was. I hoped Jovan didn't have a girlfriend, wife, kids or anything else that would make me get up and leave this place immediately.

"So now sir, first how old are you?" I said, with a devilish grin.

"I'm 24 years old, but I'll be 25 next month."

"Um-um-um, so you're a youngin?"

"C'mon Sonya, you only got me by less than 2 years, you act like you 'bout 40 something." We both laughed.

"Naw Jovan, I'm just joking with you. So when is your birthday?"

"June 3rd." He said.

"Oh, June 3rd, that's my bro Tony's B-Day."

"Yeah, he must be a good dude like me then huh."

"Whatever Jovan, you're sweet now but you're probably a Lil Devil after someone gets to know you."

"Naw Boo, what you see here is what you get." He said, as he looked me in my face, letting me know that he meant every word.

Damn, I hope Jovan ain't playing no games cause if this is what I get, then I wouldn't want for nothin' else. Jovan Conrad Price was the perfect gentleman, a handsome, sharp, smooth, smart and intelligent young black man.

"Ok, so Jovan do you have a job?"

"Good question Sonya, you know most women nowadays don't even ask that question."

Shit, what did he mean most women? I hope he's not taking other bitches out to lunch on a regular basis.

"Now I've been questioned like this by a lot of women, but most of the women my friends date never even ask that question."

Whew, I'm glad he cleared that up!

"Well Jovan, that's a very important question because if you and a person are to become friends and later on, who knows, you may end up falling in love or something, it's only right that each person know what they're bringing to the table."

"I totally agree. Well first of all, yes I do have a job, I work for Rohon & Robinson, a law firm in the city, I've only been working there for a couple months but I love it."

"What type of work do you do, I mean are you actually a lawyer?"

"Well Sonya, yes and no. When I say yes, I say that because most of the leg work on cases are done by me. I find cases of law, place them in a motion and format certain facts for the motion, then I give it to my boss who is the actual attorney. He'll look over the motion, make a few changes and bring it before the court and argue it." I said to her.

"So you saying, you're the brains behind the machine?" She asked.

"Naw, I wouldn't call it that, you can say that I'm part of a team and my position is unseen. However, I'm no lawyer yet although I plan to finish Law School, I only have two more, one year courses to take in order to take my bar exam. Right now, I'm employed as a Paralegal at the firm."

"What's a bar exam?"

"It's a test you have to take and must pass in order to get your Bar License to be able to practice law in certain cities or states."

"So I guess you're taking yours in DC?"

"No I haven't really decided yet, shit I gotta finish school first."

"Are you still in school now Jovan?"

"Naw Boo, I took a rest so I could get a job and pay for my next two courses. I just got out of school 6 months ago, I took a two-year Paralegal Course."

Damn, it was so good to see a nice young black man with an education and intelligence, and to think of it, he ain't even the preppy nerd type, this brother was smooth. You can tell that at one point in time he was a nigga in the streets but had enough sense to get his ass up and get an education and a job so that he wouldn't suffer the pains of death or prison like most of our young black males today. The world needs more people like Jovan.

"So Jovan, is that why you were in court today?"

"Yeah Boo it was hectic. We have a client who has come back on an appeal from 30 years and the Government wants to proceed with the case without giving us proper notice in time so that we could prepare briefs, so today my boss had to go and ask the Judge for an extension of time in order for our firm to prepare and file briefs. I was just there as a backup to make sure that the Judge and Government act according to the law."

"Is that why you had that black notebook?"

"Yeah."

See I knew he wasn't a criminal, I knew I made the right choice in coming to lunch with him.

Jovan
When Bilal was sentenced to juvenile hall, I was crushed because my true friend and comrade were gone for what seemed like forever. Since Bilal and I both were juveniles, there was no way that I could visit him, but at times, I would send him flicks of me and other bitches at the latest Chuck Brown or Rare Essence Go-Go Club. To me it felt like I couldn't do enough for Bilal, the person who was doing time for a crime I had committed and only three people knew about, that's Bilal, God and me.

As Bilal continued to do his time at Cedar Knoll Youth Division, I continued to keep the vow I made to him 2 years ago and that was to take care of Mal-Mal. Every time I went over Grandma's house, I would go get Mal-Mal, take him to play video games, to the movies and get him a outfit and new Knicks.

I was 17 at the time and was hustling, and for a 17 year old, you could say I was getting it good. At that time I was selling PCP in DC, we called it boat, love boat to be exact. There were also other nicknames for it like "John Hinkley", the fool who shot Ronald Reagan, or the most famous of all, "that butt naked".

I was hustling on one of the most pumping and vicious strips in DC, Whaler Place, Southeast. Sometimes I would go on Galveston Street, SW and hustle with my man, Rose, or over in Maryland up around Glass-Manor with my boys Lil James and Ek-Dre.

Barry Farms was one of my spots also, but a nigga had to be real careful hustling in the Farms cause people were getting killed and robbed almost every other week. I made sure that whenever I went into Barry Farms, I was always strapped but it was cool though cause I was mostly dealing with one of my brother's old comrades, Lil BB.

Lil BB was a little brown skin dude who went to school with my big brother, they was real close and when my brother died, Lil BB used to always look out for me. Lil BB had a blue 190E Benz and he used to come pass Galveston, pick me up, take me down Georgetown and we'd get outfits for a nite at the Go-Go Club on Atlantic Street.

At that time I was pumping good, I had just brought my first car, a burgundy Nissan Maxima with burgundy sheepskin seats and five star rims. At times, I used to go pick up Mal-Mal and take him out because Ms. Cookie was still on it like the brown hornet. Every time I saw her, she was getting smaller and smaller. At one time, she had lost so much weight that you could see every bone structure in her face.

Bilal was transferred from Cedar Knoll to Oak Hill Youth Center, which is a more treacherous joint then Cedar Knoll. When other dudes I knew would come home from Cedar Knoll, I'd ask them about Bilal and everything I heard about him was good. They'd say, "Yeah slim, that nigga Bilal ain't goin' for nothin'! Slim go hard as a ma'fucka, he's on the boxing team down there, he run the store, he big as shit!"

Niggas used to jock Bilal so much that I stopped asking about him cause I already knew what they were gonna say. When Bilal was transferred to Oak Hill, we lost contact and the fact that I was out here getting money, fucking bitches and going to Go-Go's didn't help either. I also began to lack in my efforts in looking out for Mal-Mal because at times, he would page me and it would take me a few days just to get back to him. But whenever he needed something, like video games, toys, etc., I was the one who got it for him. The only thing about it was I was too busy to spend time with him, my world was moving too fast and I couldn't see what was to come next.

In July 1988, I stopped hustling love boat and moved onto a more profitable drug called "Crack Cocaine". At the time, crack in DC was at its all time high, the demand for it was ridiculous. I was coping from my boys Ek-Dre and Lil James, these two brothers was getting it and they both had a good reputation all over. Dre was a smooth nigga who loved to dress, he had all kinds of Polo, MCM and Gucci shit.

James was the hard one, more like the leader among his crew. They were some good niggas and was getting some major paper on the hill. I was getting half a brick at that time, breaking it down in half ounces and ounces. I had runners up Glass Manor, Galveston Pl., Wayne Pl., Parkland, 4th Street, Condon Terrace and a few lames from Alexandria, Virginia.

I traded my Maxima in and brought a 1988 Nissan Turbo 300ZX with cream leather and put some white deep dish classic rims on it. My car was one of the tightest joints in the city, at least on the Southeast side, cause them uptown niggas and them niggas on R Street, NE was pushing 500EL Benz and Convertible BMW's and shit. The type of bank I was getting was considered play money to them because the niggas from around Bilal's way was super getting it. The Orleans Mob had 944 Porsches, Convertible Jags, 300CE's, Range Rovers, the new Acura Legends and anything that cost more than 50 thousand.

On the 4th of July, Mal-Mal paged me and I called him back.

Ring, Ring, Ring, "Hello." Gloria said, answering the phone.

"Yeah Gloria, how you doing, this Jovan. Is Mal-Mal in there?" I said to her.

"Oh hi Jovan, yeah his lil bad ass here. You coming to get him?"

"Naw, not right now, but I promised him I'd buy him some fireworks for tonight and I'ma come pass and drop them off and come back later and light 'em with him."

"That's good Jovan cause I gotta work tonight and Cookie said she was gonna be here but I ain't seen her ass yet." Gloria said, then she yelled, "Mal-Mal!"

"What?" Mal-Mal said.

"Boy, don't what me." Aunt Gloria said to him.

"Yes ma'am."

"Get you butt in here, somebody on the phone for you."

"Who is it?" Mal-Mal asked.

"Answer the phone and find out."

Mal-Mal came running to the phone and said, "Hello."

"Mal-Mal, what's up youngin?" I said to him.

"Hey Uncle Jay, what's up man. I thought you was gonna bring me some fireworks and light 'em with me tonight."

"I'm still gonna do that Mal-Mal, I'm on my way over there to drop the fireworks off to you."

"You gonna stay Uncle Jay?"

"For a little while, then I gotta go do somethin', but I'ma come back and light 'em up with you though."

"A'ight Uncle Jay."

"Ok young soldier."

As I was driving to 12th and Wyle NE to go see Mal-Mal, I

got a page from this little freak broad out in Bowie, Maryland that I was staying with at the time. I didn't call her back right away though. When I pulled up onto Wyle Street, Mal-Mal came running out the house.

"Uncle Jay, Uncle Jay." Mal-Mal said, running up to my car.

"What's up youngin?"

"Man Uncle Jay, this your car?"

"Yeah, that's my joint."

"Man, this joint is tight! I bet it's fast ain't it?"

"Yeah, it's fast."

One of Mal-Mal's little buddy's came running outta Gloria's house, he was there to see the fireworks. Mal-Mal was always bragging about his Uncle Jay so much that his buddies would be just as happy as he was to see me pull up, but this particular kid was a little too grown, he always felt he was in competition with Mal-Mal, so when he noticed that Mal-Mal was fascinated by my car, he felt the need to say something just to make him mad.

"Hey Mal-Mal, that joint ain't all that, my Uncle gotta Benz and his joint is way tighter than that!" His friend said.

"Shut-up punk for I bust your nose again! That's why you ain't playing wit my fireworks." Mal-Mal said to his friend.

"So, I don't care."

"Me either punk."

That shit was funny, seeing two youngins ready to wreck. If I wasn't in such a hurry, I would have taken both of 'em around back and let 'em fight. I was almost certain Mal-Mal would whip his ass because Mal-Mal was 11 years old now and big as a house, and to add, he was also bad as fuck.

I kept getting pages from that broad out in Bowie, Maryland, this bitch was blowing my shit up with 911-911-911-911. She used to page me so much when I was out with other bitches that I ignored it when she put in 911 because most of the time, she'd just be calling trying to find out if I was with another bitch or not. Damn, she was getting on my nerves, but at the present time, I needed her. She had a nice apartment in Bowie, which was 20 minutes away from the city and she had a nice job working for the Department of Labor, so I needed her credit.

She's the one who co-signed for the 300ZX, and when I get my bank right, she was gonna sign for a Mercedes 300CE for me, plus she was a stone freak in bed, she loved sucking my dick and I loved it too. But one thing about her I didn't like, she was a bamma ass broad, she talked loud, she couldn't dress and she wore cheap shit. Even when I'd try and buy her some fly shit, she still looked fucked up in it, she couldn't even rock it right. And to add to all this, she had a 2 year old daughter by some punk ass nigga that used to beat her ass.

As I looked down at my pager while Mal-Mal was still arguing with his buddy, I figured I'd use Gloria's phone to call her back. As soon as I entered through the front door, I could tell that Gloria was in a rush, she was running back and forth from the bathroom to the living room, as if she was in a hurry to go somewhere. She was fixing her hair and ironing her clothes at the same time.

"Hey Gloria, can I use your phone real quick?"

"Yeah, go ahead Jovan."

Ring, Ring, Ring, "Hello." A female voice said.

"Why the fuck are you blowing my pager up like that!" I said, with an immediate attitude.

"Jovan, somebody broke into the apartment!" The female on the other end of the phone yelled, hysterically.

"What?" I asked, not sure I had heard her correctly.

"They came in through the balcony."

"Is there anything missing?"

"I dunno! The furniture is all ripped up, the TV is broken, it doesn't look like they were trying to steal shit, it looks more like they vandalized the place. Jovan, I'm going to call the police." She said.

"No! Hell no! Don't call the police I'm on my way." I said, quickly.

"Jovan please hurry up, I'm scared."

When I hung up the phone Gloria could see that I was mad as hell.

""Is everything alright Jovan?" She asked me.

"Yeah Gloria, I'm cool. Look, I gotta go right now, I got something to do."

"Alright Jovan, you sure you're ok?"

"Yeah, yeah I'm ok." I said, walking out the door.

When I came outta Gloria's house and walked towards my car, Mal-Mal came running down the street.

"Hey Uncle Jay, where you going, I thought you were gonna stay and light the fireworks with me?"

"I'll be back Mal-Mal, right now I've got something to do."

"Can I go with you?" He asked me.

"Naw man, this is important but I'll be back." I told him.

"Hurry back Uncle Jay cause it's almost dark now."

"Ok youngin."

As I pulled away from Wyle Street, I saw Ms. Cookie walking towards Gloria's house, she was walking real fast, I rolled down the window and said, "Hey Ms. Cookie."

"Oh, hi Jovan baby. Where you going?" Ms. Cookie asked.

"I've gotta go do something. Look, I brought Mal-Mal some fireworks and I don't know if I'ma make it back in time to light 'em up with him. If I don't get back in time, can you light 'em up with him?" I said to Ms. Cookie.

"Yeah baby I'll do that, I'm on my way to Gloria's anyway."

"Ok then Ms. Cookie, see you later."

"Jovan, hold up for a minute."

"What's up Ms. Cookie?"

"Baby, you got ten dollars so I can get Mal-Mal something to eat from the carryout?" Ms. Cookie said.

"Yeah, hold up." I said, reaching into my back pocket where I kept a knot of ones and peeled off twenty dollars, because I knew if I gave Ms. Cookie only ten, she'd just go cop a dime of blow, but with twenty she could get Mal-Mal something from the carryout and do whatever with the rest.

As I got on the highway to Bowie, all I could think about was my money, I had fifty thousand dollars over this bitch's house. My mind was racing, who the fuck did this? I never brought anybody over there and when I came home, I'd circle the parking lot a couple of times before I got out. I was always cautious and careful not to put my bank in any danger. The more I thought about it, the madder I got and the harder my foot pressed on the gas.

As I turned off the highway onto the ramp, I reached under my seat and pulled out my black Barretta 9MM. I always kept my pistol with me, especially when I was in Southeast, cause on that Southside niggas ain't have no picks, they were always trying to kidnap and rob anybody who was getting some money.

Although the city was in an uproar around this time, I never had to use my Barretta, no one had given me a reason to. No one violated me like that dope fiend did back in '85, but tonight I felt violated and whoever did this surely deserves two to the head. I've killed before and I will certainly kill again.

As I pulled into the parking lot, I didn't circle the block, I felt there was no need for my routine. I jumped out of my car holding my Barretta, hoping and wishing that the perpetrators who did this were still around, Damn, all I could think about was my fifty thousand dollars, that's all I had, fifty thousand and my car. With that fifty thousand, I was going to cop two bricks and flip them over so this bitch and me could go to the nearest Benz dealer to cop my 300CE. When I opened the door to the apartment, I saw that the place was a complete mess and I knew my fifty thousand was gone. I ran towards the bedroom where I kept my money.

"Dee-Dee, Dee-Dee! I'm here, it's Jovan, you a'ight?"

"Yeah I'm fine, they just fucked my house up." Dee-Dee said.

When I went into the bedroom to check the vent where my money was, I saw that it was busted open. I knew my shit wasn't there, but I still reached my hands in to make sure. As I took my hands out the vent, my whole fucking world was crushed and instantly, I had developed a supreme hatred for all cruddy niggas in the game. From this point on, I was going to make it my business to know of all the niggas in the city known for robbing and kidnapping. I was also going to make it my business to know where they hung out and who was down with their crew.

Around 8:15 p.m., I got a page and when I looked at it and saw that it was Mal-Mal, I remembered I had promised him I would light the fireworks with him. Even though I was fucked up and my money was gone, I still had to keep my loyalty to Bilal. I promised him that I'd take care of Mal-Mal, so I figured I'd go light the fireworks and sit over Gloria's for a minute and get my thoughts together. I didn't call Mal-Mal back I figured I'd just pull up and surprise him.

"Dee-Dee." I said.

"What Jovan?" She said, in a snappy way.

"Here, here's fifty dollars, take a taxi over to your Grandmother's house." I said.

"For what? Where you goin'?" She asked.

"I've got something to do."

"Jovan, how the fuck you just gonna leave after something like this?" Dee-Dee asked.

"Just do what the fuck I said! Damn, your ass is always trippin' and getting on my fuckin' nerves!" I said.

"Well Jovan, if I get on your nerves that bad you can just move the fuck on and don't ever come back!" Dee-Dee yelled.

That was all I needed to hear. My fifty thousand was gone, the apartment had gotten broken into and my 300CE was nowhere in the near future, I realized I didn't need this naggin' ass bitch no more. After all I was only 18 and she's talking about settling down, shit I haven't even began to live my own life yet, plus I'm broke again and I gotta get back out there and grind on the corner, and the last thing a nigga who's trying to get his grind on need is a broad who don't understand. So, I did what any nigga in my position would do, I packed my shit and left.

As I walked out the door, Dee-Dee called me a million no good ass ma'fuckas, "You ain't shit Jovan, you too weak to have a strong women like me! Fuck you nigga, I hope you have bad luck all your life, you no good dirty bitch!"

As I got into my car and pulled off, I had a smile on my face. Although I was mad about my fifty thousand, I was happy as hell to get Dee-Dee outta my life. On my way to see Mal-Mal, all I could do was think about how I was going to get back on. For one, I didn't want anybody to know that my bank had gotten taken, also I didn't want to get fronted nothin', I liked to pay for my own shit. I wondered if I would have to sell my car and jewelry because if I did, then niggas would put it out in the street that I was broke. Shit, I didn't know what to do, I needed some time to sit back and think.

As I pulled up onto 12th Street, I saw a bunch of flashing lights and a lot of people standing around, some were crying, others were just being nosy. The crowd was so thick that I couldn't make my turn onto Wyle Street, so I got out my car and walked up the street, it was obvious something was wrong. When I hit the corner, all I saw were fire engines and ambulances, Aunt Gloria's house going up in a blaze of flames. I was determined to know what had happened.

As I walked up, I saw Ms. Cookie on the ground crying her heart out screaming, "My baby, my baby!"

Instantly, I knew Mal-Mal was in that fire. Man, what the fuck had happened?

"What happened Ms. Cookie, Ms. Cookie what happened?" I said, as my heart pounded inside my chest.

No one could hold me back. I was mad, mad at the world, mad at Ms. Cookie and mad at myself. Later, I found out that Ms. Cookie never went back to Gloria's when I gave her the twenty dollars. She went around Orleans Pl. to cop her some blow and Gloria had to go to work and left Mal-Mal and his cousin, Gwenee, at home by themselves.

Mal-Mal wasn't but 11 years old and Gwenee was only 12, anybody in their right mind would know you can't leave an 11 and 12 year old home by themselves with a bunch of fireworks on the 4th of July.

When the fire marshals finally put the fire out, they went into the house to investigate what had happened and to see if anyone was alive in the house. Ms. Cookie was still crying, trying to pry her way through the police and fireman, but they held her back with all their strength.

"Get the fuck off me, my baby's in there! Oh my God, Mal-Mal! My baby, my baby! Oh no, please God not my baby!" Ms Cookie screamed.

That's all I could hear, Ms. Cookie screaming. As for myself, I just stood in the middle of Wyle Street with no expression on my face, I had no feeling in my body, I don't even remember if I was thinking or not, I was in a complete daze, my whole system had shut down.

The first body they brought out was Gwenee, the fire marshal had her in his arms and her body was limp. She didn't have any burn marks on her or anything, so I took it that she must have died from smoke inhalation. Lil Gwenee was Gloria's only child, and when Gloria arrived on the scene and saw the fireman holding her dead child in his arms, she went off.

"Give me my child, give me my child!" She screamed, fighting with the police and fire marshal who were trying to hold her back. She cried in pain for her child and then her cry became an angry blame.

"Cookie, what the fuck did you do to my baby! What the fuck did you do!" Then she fell to the ground, scratching and kicking the police screaming, "Get the fuck off me!"

The fire marshal then brought Mal-Mal out, and when I saw him, the only way that I knew it was him was from the new Jordans he had on because I had gotten them for him last week. His body was burned from head to toe. I was so fucked up at what I saw that all I could do was fall to my knees right there in the middle of the street and cry the loudest pain that I ever felt in my life. Ms. Cookie fell unconscious and had to be hospitalized for a few days. All I could think about was Bilal and how would he take it.

I paid for Mal-Mal's funeral and wake because I had a little money from the niggas who still owed me in the street. I sold my 300ZX but kept my Rolex and I had about twenty thousand to work with after the funeral and everything.

After we buried Mal-Mal, Ms. Cookie went into rehab and I continued trying to get some money. I always felt in my heart that my life was indebted to Bilal for taking my murder rap and I also felt somehow responsible for Mal-Mal's death. If I had only been there to help light those fireworks Mal-Mal would never have tried to do it himself.

Sonya
"Ok now Mr. Lawyer, tell me where you're from." I said.

Jovan started smiling and for a minute, I thought he was blushing.

"Well Sonya, I grew up all over Southeast, when I was young we used to live in the Farms."

"You mean Barry Farms?"

"Yeah sweetheart."

"Jovan, that's a rough neighborhood isn't it?"

"Yeah it's rough, but it was cool coming up because that's where I learned how to fight, how to pick and choose real friends, how to survive and peep the game. It's also where I learned how to express certain talents."

"Like what type of talents Jovan?"

"Music, I'm one of the original members of the 'Junk Yard Band', I used to play the buckets."

I immediately started laughing. "For real Jovan?"

"Yeah sweetheart, I was the man on the buckets back in the day."

"Did you ever graduate to real instruments?"

"Yeah, I took up trumpet and piano in school."

"Damn, I never met a guy who knew how to play the piano." I said, impressed.

"There are a lot of things I know how to do that might surprise you." Jovan said, smiling.

"Stop being fresh Jovan, remember this is our first date."

"So, you're calling this a date? That must mean I got a shot at seeing you again huh?"

"No, I didn't mean it like that Jovan. I meant this is our first meeting and if this goes well, who knows what may happen." I said, smiling back at him.

"Now you're the one being fresh." Jovan said, laughing.

"So, where else did you live?"

"Oh, we moved from the Farms to the Valley."

"You mean Valley Green?"

"Yeah sweetheart."

I wish he'd stop calling me that because right now it's turning me on.

"Living in Valley Green was real rough, but somehow my mother found a way to keep me outta trouble. She sent me to the No. 11 Boy's Club after school, that's where I played basketball, football and took up boxing. On the weekends, she sent me over Northeast to my Grandmother's house and I liked going over there, cause that's where my best friend lived."

Triple Crown Publications presents

CHAPTER 3

"The Lawyer"

Ring, Ring, Ring, "Law offices of Rohon & Robinson, may I help you?" Cindy said.

"Hey Cindy, this is Mark. Is Jovan there yet?" Mark asked her.

"Yes, he's in your office waiting for your call."

"Good, plug me in." Mark said.

"Jovan?" Cindy said.

"Yeah Cindy, what's up?" Jovan said.

"Mark's on line one."

"Ok, thank you." Jovan said, pushing line one. "Hey Mark, what's the deal?"

"Well, it took you long enough to get there, I've been calling all morning." Mark said.

"C'mon Mark, you called me at home at 9:00 o'clock and it's now 9:35, I came as fast as I could." Jovan said.

"Damn, hope you brushed your teeth." Mark said, laughing.

"Good joke Mark."

"Ok Jovan, enough of the funny stuff, let's get down to business."

Jovan liked that in Mark, he knew when to joke and when to take care of business, Jovan guessed that's why they were connected so well.

"Look, I need you to find me some cases on conflicts of interest, ineffective association of counsel and illegal search and seizure."

"Are these the issues your client is putting forth?" Jovan asked Mark.

"Yeah, but not right now I just need the cases beforehand in case the Government wants to argue then I'll already have my guns loaded."

Mark always stayed two steps ahead of the Government, cause whenever they presented something in the cut, he hit 'em right back with it.

After Jovan got off the phone with Mark, he went into Mark's private law library and looked up the cases that would fit his argument to a tee, and the fact that this new client was his best friend, he worked even harder. He shepherdized case after case, updated them and faxed them straight to Mark. After he faxed Mark the cases, he called back again.

Ring, Ring, Ring, "Law offices of Rohon & Robinson, may I help you?" Cindy said.

"Cindy, plug me into Jovan again." Mark said.

"Jovan line one, Mark again." Cindy said.

This time Jovan didn't pick up the receiver, instead he sat back in Mark's chair, placed my feet up on his desk and pressed the intercom button.

"Yeah Mark, what's up." Jovan said.

"First of all, get your ass outta my chair, when you legally become a lawyer you'll get your own desk and chair." Mark said.

"Yeah right, besides yours huh?" Jovan said, laughing.

"I don't know 'bout that one buddy." Mark said.

"Hey, were those cases any good?"

"Yeah, they were damn good, the Government's mad as hell." Mark said, with a chuckle.

"What's next?" Jovan asked Mark.

"Well, my client only has one hang up."

"What's that Mark?"

"The Government still has the statement from a witness during the Grand Jury testimony and they're saying that this witness is still willing to testify." Mark said.

Damn, Bilal's shit was looking fucked up so Jovan asked, "Did the Judge grant a new trial?"

"No, not yet but we do have some good news."

"Yeah, what's that?"

"Come to find out the officers who arrested my client never had a legitimate warrant for his arrest, they just had a personal vendetta against him, so they got some information from an informant and put together a bogus warrant and illegally searched his home."

"So, does he now have a good argument to drop all the charges?" Jovan asked, hopefully.

"Yeah, but there is still one thing that fucks it up."

"What's that Mark?"

"If the charges get dropped, the Government is gonna re-indict my client for conspiracy and they will use the witness that was an informant for the police to testify against him and his Grand Jury statement, which I'm reading right now."

"Is his statement bad?" Jovan asked, needing to know.

Jovan just had to know because his best friend's life was on the line.

"Yeah, it's very bad, it says here that my client sold him at least five kilos of coke a week."

"Damn, they got him in a bind huh?" Jovan asked.

"Yeah, this will fuck him up for good."

Bilal was Jovan's best friend and he had to do something, he had to find some way to get him out of this bind.

"Mark, how much time do we have to work on this case?"

"I'm gonna ask the Judge for an extension of time, I'll call you back and let you know how it goes." Mark said.

When Jovan got off the phone with Mark, he was in a state of confusion. How in the hell was he gonna get his man outta this situation.

Jovan
After Mal-Mal's death in 1991, I chilled out for a while but I eventually got back into the swing of things. By the summer of '91, I was coping at least four bricks a week. My connect was from New York and sometimes he would bring it down to me, but most times I had to go get it myself.

After a few months of dealing with my connect, we became real cool. He put me down on a lot of things in the drug game and he taught me how to whip up bricks. I would take 2 bricks and cook them up with B1 Vitamins and baking soda and it would make 3 bricks out of 2 bricks. The coke would never come back Grade A, but on a scale from 1 to 10, I'd say it was a 6?. I wouldn't sell these bricks to the niggas I fucked with regularly, I always kept them with good coke so they could make their money fast and buy more bricks from me. What I would do was serve it to them Virginia bammas because they would buy anything as long as it was coke.

Virginia was pumping like that, them bammas would cop like 2 bricks a week from me, straight money not a dollar short, that's what scared me about those niggas. So when I served them, I made sure they brought their asses across the bridge to Washington DC because if any funny business was to happen, as far as the police was concerned, I'd have a better chance of getting away.

My connect also told me about the hydraulic stash spots, that James Bond shit. So what I did was went to the nearest Mazda dealer and brought myself a brand new MVP van. Then I sent it up to New York and my connect had his man make me a spot that could hold at least 8 bricks, that shit cost me 10,000 dollars, but it was worth it. I also bought a new silver 535 BMW with chrome BBS wheels.

At the time I was renting a townhouse out in Clinton, Maryland, 10 minutes outside the city and everything was going good for me. I was anticipating my man, Bilal coming home and whatever I had was going to be broken down 50-50, half of this shit was his. We'd both be getting money together, doing all the shit we dreamed about, but for right now, I was the man of the hour. I traded my old Rolex in for a new one, an 18K Presidential with a diamond bezel and diamonds flowing through the middle of the band, bitches would go crazy when they saw me rocking that joint. I also had a 3-carat earring that I rocked on occasion and a plain Rolex band bracelet.

My style of clothes also changed. It was no longer Polo, I had switched to Gianni Versace, Gucci, MCM and Ferragamo, I was getting too much money to be dressing like I was still some corner hustler. The more money I made, the less sweat suits and tennis shoes I wore. I started going to all the main events: fights, lavish parties and social functions, and I was fucking the baddest broads in the city. I had more clientele than I could handle, I was holdin' around a hundred thou plus assets.

At the time, I was involved with the prettiest up and coming youngin in the city, her name was Barvette. She was brown skin with a milky complexion, nice hair, a nice body and a walk that made her look sexier than she really was, and to add, the pussy was on one thousand. It was Barvette that hipped me to all the finer Restaurants in the city, she also hipped me to all the Boutiques on Wisconsin Avenue, Neiman Marcus, Genfranco Feree, Versace, Gucci and Everett Hall. In fact, I think the first time I ate at the Cheese Cake Factory was with her, or was it with freaky Tracey, I don't know cause I was fucking both of 'em at the same time.

We also went on trips together to Negrill Jamaica, Vegas, Cancun and a couple of other places. Although she wasn't officially my girl, we were still cool as shit, so if there was anything I could do to help her out, I didn't have a problem with it until she started asking for that Chanel shit. Now that shit was costly, they wanted three thousand for a pocketbook, so instead of breaking her off a nice bank for that Chanel shit, I broke off the relationship. I hustled too hard to be giving up that much bank to a broad who wasn't officially my girl.

Damn, I wished Bilal would hurry up and come home. All I keep thinking about is how comfortable it's gonna be for him when he gets here. Right now, I'm Bilal's only family besides Aunt Gloria and she was at the St. Elizabeth Mental Hospital. After Lil Gweene died, Gloria wasn't the same and Ms. Cookie passed away last year.

When Ms. Cookie went into rehab, she discovered she had full blown Aids from shooting dope. I saw Ms. Cookie after she got out of rehab, she looked bad because the disease was killing her. I used to take her to the doctor's and to the Pharmacy to pick up her medicine, and sometimes I'd take her to lunch and we'd talk about Bilal and Mal-Mal. Before Ms. Cookie died she finally, for the first time, went to visit Bilal. I don't know how that visit went because right after that Ms. Cookie was hospitalized and she went into a coma, and then two weeks later she died. I paid for the funeral and had her buried right next to Mal-Mal.

CHAPTER 4

"Only The Worst Could Happen"

It was October 1991, and Bilal was due to come home next month and Jovan couldn't wait, but what he didn't know was that all his plans to welcome Bilal home would soon come to an end. In early October, there was a coke shortage and Jovan was still getting bricks but not as many as before. The prices were ski high and Jovan's connect had to divide whatever he could get with all his major clientele. The city was at its lowest point, only a few niggas had bricks stashed and they wasn't servin' nobody who wasn't in their crew.

The only nigga out here who was still on top was Big Head Larry. Jovan didn't know Larry personally, but Bilal and he went to school together and they were real cool back in the day. At the time, Larry was hangin' out with this New York nigga named Po and Jovan didn't like Po because he came to his city when they were vulnerable and used it to his advantage. He got up under the most feared nigga in the city at the time, a nigga by the name of Big Silk. He knew he had to get Big Silk on his team cause if he didn't, those niggas out there would have tore his ass to pieces. In Jovan's eyes, Po was a bitch, he turned friends into enemies, he used real niggas for protection and he hid behind a mask, but when that mask was pulled off, it was too late. Jovan found out that Po was down with the Feds and this bitch ass nigga emptied his brain to the Government and turned State's evidence on all those who held him in high regards. To Jovan, Po had committed the ultimate sin.

Niggas out here were hungry, ounces were going for eighteen hundred a wop and you couldn't find nobody selling anything for less than that. Then came the break Jovan needed, at least that's what he thought, his connect called him and told him he was back in action.

"Ok slim, I'm on my way up!" Jovan said, excited to hear from him.

"Naw money, you ain't gotta come up, I'm on my way down there cause I got a few more people I gotta see." Jovan's connect said.

"Shit cool, c'mon slim I need you." Jovan said, needing to cop bad.

He told Jovan that he only had a few bricks and that he should try to cop as many as he could get. The price Jovan used to pay wasn't happening, it was a little higher but not as high as niggas were paying out here. He was going to give 'em to Jovan for twenty-six, out here they were going for thirty or better. Jovan went to his townhouse in Clinton to count his stash and all Jovan had was a hundred and eighty thousand. He usually never coped with all his bread but this time he had to, because he was gonna make a killing during this drought. He had enough to cop seven bricks and his plan was to break 'em down to ounces and sell 'em for sixteen hundred apiece, two hundred lower than the going price out here.

Four hours later, Jovan's connect called him and said that he was staying at the Ramada Inn in Virginia across from Pentagon City.

"Ok slim, I'm on my way." Jovan said, about to hang up the phone.

"Yo, hurry up money, they're going like hot cakes, I can't hold 'em for too long."

"A'ight slim, I'm on my way." Jovan said, hanging up the phone.

Jovan packed the hundred and eighty thousand in shoe boxes and placed them in two big ass Banana Republic bags, got into his MVP and popped the hydraulic stash. He placed the money in there and headed to the hotel where his connect was staying. When Jovan reached the Ramada Inn, he didn't bother to park his mini van because he was so anxious to be coping that he just pulled in front of the hotel, put his hazards on and jumped out.

As he was walking into the hotel lobby, his pager was blowing up like shit, everybody was trying to cop before the first of the month. Jovan was all smiles because this was going to be his big come up. All he could think about was the money he was 'bout to get and how right his bank was gonna be when Bilal came home.

When Jovan got off the elevator and knocked on his connect's room, he heard two voices. Now, whenever Jovan used to cop from this dude he was always alone, although sometimes he would mention his partner, Shorty, he still would do business with him by himself.

When Jovan heard the two voices, naturally he was on his guard. He put the two bags that he had his money in into his left hand and kept his right hand free close to his side, as close to his Barretta 9MM as possible. He prayed this nigga wouldn't try and pull no move on him because he already had a hate for cruddy niggas, and if they even thought about violating him, he guarantee there would be two niggas in the hotel dead and he wouldn't be one of 'em. He's killed before and will kill again if necessary.

When Jovan's connect opened the door, he had a smile on his face the size of Texas.

"Yo money, what's up!"

"Ain't shit slim, still doin' my thang."

As Jovan entered the hotel, he got a glimpse of the other dude sitting on the bed counting money.

"Yo Jovan, this is my partner Shorty, Shorty, this is Jovan."

"What up money, I heard a lot about you." Shorty said.

"Yeah and visa versa." Jovan said.

After the introductions, Jovan's connect and him got right down to business.

"Yo Jovan, what you trying to get, you know I ain't gonna be in town that long."

"Slim, I'm working with one eighty."

Jovan connect's eyes got as big as shit when he told him how much he had. Usually he copped only 4 or 5 bricks at a time, Jovan guessed the sound of extra money excited him.

"Yo Jovan, this is what I'ma do, I got 10 bricks left, I'ma give you eight and you can owe me the difference until the next time you cop."

Damn, that was a sweet deal. Jovan immediately handed over the money and placed four bricks in each bag. He stood there for a second so that his connect could count the money but it looked to him as if he was getting ready to pack up.

"You gonna count that?" Jovan asked, curiously.

"Naw money, I've been dealing with you for 6 months now, you ain't never been short, your bank has always been right." Jovan's connect said.

As Jovan left the hotel, he felt like nobody in the city could fuck with him, all he kept thinking about was how much money he was gonna make. His pager was still blowing up like crazy as he headed back to his townhouse as fast as he could to cook up and move this shit like a fat turkey on Thanksgiving.

Jovan then started counting figures in his head. He had 8 bricks at sixteen hundred an ounce, that's gonna come out to at least three hundred and eighty thousand. He had his 535 BMW worth forty-two thousand and his MPV van worth twenty-five, all together that was four hundred forty-seven thousand. His jewelry was worth about four hundred eighty thousand, and with the little money he still had out in the streets that niggas owed him, he figured he was worth about a half a million dollars, he'd have more than enough when Bilal come home. He wish that bitch Dee-Dee could see him now, he thought smiling to himself.

When Jovan got to my townhouse, he pulled his van in the garage, popped the hydraulic stash, retrieved the bricks and went into the house to start cooking them up. But first he called all his clientele back and told 'em he'd be ready in a little while. Then he got the ceramic pie plate and baking soda out to cook the coke. He didn't bother to whip it, he wanted this shit to be Grade A butta! He wanted the city to know he had that bomb shit, and plus, he was selling it 200 dollars cheaper than the going price.

When Jovan busted open the first brick, he could see that it wasn't the good shit he used to get, he didn't see them icy looking snowflakes and the smell was dull. When he placed the coke in the pan and waited for it to dissolve, the shit fell straight to the bottom. He stirred and stirred it, but it still never came together. Instantly Jovan started to get mad and he grabbed the phone and was 'bout to page his connect but decided not to, he thought maybe it was just one bad batch outta the eight. So Jovan went back into the kitchen and popped open the next brick, it was the same shit, and after opening all of the remaining bricks and seeing they were all the same shit, he came to realize this ma'fucka had sold him eight bricks of cement. This bitch ass nigga had violated him and he already hated cruddy niggas and now it was his time to express that hatred.

Jovan grabbed his Barretta 9MM, jumped in his BMW and headed straight back to the hotel where those bitch ass niggas were staying. He was going to kill both of them whores right there in the hotel. He was so mad that he was running red lights, speeding and not bothering to turn on his blinkers. As Jovan got on the 495 highway he was still speeding, dodging in and outta traffic and the only thing that was on his mind was murder, murder in the first degree, and to him it was going to be justified. They had violated him and they deserved what they were soon to get, just like that fiend in the alley on Orleans Pl. back in '85.

As Jovan dodged from the left lane into the right and back to the left, he didn't notice the red and blue lights flashing until he finally, for the first time since he had gotten behind the wheel, looked into his rear view mirror. Damn, the fucking police and as bad as he wanted to out run them he couldn't, anyway all he was doing was speeding. Plus, if he gave them a chase he definitely wouldn't make it back to the hotel in time to kill those bitch ass niggas, so he went ahead and pulled over, put his pistol under his seat and grabbed his license and registration from the glove compartment. Jovan planned not to argue with the police, he figured he would just take his ticket and then go kill those bitches before they left town.

When the Officer got out of his car, Jovan could see through his side mirror that he was saying something into the radio. After he finished talking into the radio, he unsnapped his holster and put his hand on his gun. When he reached Jovan's window, he asked him to turn the car off. Jovan did as he was told and when he turned his head back to ask what he was being pulled over for, all he saw was the barrel of the officer's gun.

"Don't move, put your fuckin' hands up!" The Officer said to Jovan.

As Jovan was literally being arrested while still sitting in his car, another cop pulled up and blocked his BMW in.

""Get out of the car slowly." The Officer said.

Both of these crackers had their guns pointed in Jovan's face, and for a second, he thought they were gonna shoot him right there on the spot. When Jovan got out the car, one officer put his hands behind his back and handcuffed him while the other one searched his car. They found his Barretta, which he didn't have a license to carry and that gave 'em more reason to go through his car. They sat Jovan in the back of one of their cars and continued searching his car for drugs or whatever else they could find. Jovan sat there for about an hour watching those crackers rip his BMW apart, they even called in drug sniffing dogs.

When they finally saw that there was nothing else in Jovan's car, they transported him to the DC jail, and since it was an Interstate Highway he was on, they had jurisdiction to charge him in Federal Court. Here Jovan was in the DC Federal Court being sentenced to 5 years for carrying an unlicensed firearm and his man Bilal had just came home two weeks before his sentencing.

Sonya

Jovan's answers to my questions were interesting, but what I really wanted to know about Jovan was his family.

"Ok now Mr. Lawyer, tell me about your mother." I said, because if he has a lot of respect for his mother, then I know he has respect for women period.

Before Jovan could open his mouth to answer my question, the waitress came over and asked, "Excuse me, would you two like anything else? Some dessert, a glass of wine or champagne maybe."

"No!" I snapped.

The waitress turned and walked away with a serious attitude. Jovan looked at his Movado watch to check the time.

"Hey Sonya, why were you so mean to the waitress?"

"Cause she keeps interrupting my interview."

Jovan smiled and looked at his watch again.

"Hey Jovan, do you have something to do?" I asked.

"Naw sweetheart." Jovan said.

I wish he would stop calling me that.

"It's only one-thirty, I've got all day. What about you?" He asked.

"I'm cool, I'm chillin' and if I get bored, I'll let you know."

We both laughed and then I went right back to my question.

"So Jovan, tell me about your mom." I said again.

"Well, my mother passed away when I was in school." Jovan said, with a sad look coming over his face.

"Oh my God, I'm so sorry Jovan." I said.

"It's ok Sonya, although I don't talk about it much, I do feel comfortable talking about it with you. I was in school taking my Paralegal course from October 1991 up until December '93, a little over 2 years. When I went to school, my mother was diagnosed with Diabetes and she never told me. I don't know why, but I guess she didn't want me to mess up my education worrying about her condition. When she passed, I was at the end of my course and I knew she would have wanted me to finish, so even though her death fucked me up, I still finished the course. She was a good woman but I always thought she worked too hard. She was a waitress at the NCO Club on Boiling Air Force Base. She was loyal to my Pops even after they divorced, I never saw my Moms with another man."

Damn, Jovan Moms musta been strong or madly in love with his Pops. I said to myself.

"She used to take me places and buy me all the latest gear. Even though we lived in the hood, Moms always had enough to get me the things I wanted, I mean I wasn't spoiled but I wasn't neglected either."

"Do you have any brothers and sisters?"

At that moment when I looked at Jovan, I could sense something was wrong. I grabbed a hold of his hand and said, "Hey Jovan, we don't have to talk about it if you're feeling uncomfortable."

Triple Crown Publications presents

CHAPTER 5

"The Lawyer"

Ring, Ring, Ring, "Law offices of Rohon & Robinson, may I help you?" Cindy said.

"Cindy, Mark, plug me in." Mark said.

"Jovan, Mark's on line one."

"Thanks Cindy." Jovan said. "Hey Mark, tell me something good."

"Ok, get your ass outta my chair."

"Man, I'm not even in your chair, I'm walking around here pacing trying to figure a way out for Mr., what's his name again?" Jovan asked, playing stupid.

"Davis, Bilal Davis."

"Yeah that's right. Mark, I think I got something."

"Yeah, what?" Mark asked.

"Look, if you can get an extension for at least one week and get me a legal visitation pass, then I can interview this guy and possibly get some info on his witness that could contradict his testimony and maybe get an affidavit that could free him."

"Well Jovan, I've got good news and bad news, which one you want first?" Mark asked.

"Give me the bad first." Jovan said, not really wanting to hear it.

"Well, I can't get you that pass because you must be a licensed lawyer."

"Damn." Jovan said, disappointed.

"But I can get you in with me on a temporary pass being as though you're my assistant and anyway, I'll be interviewing another client at the same time, so you'd have at least an hour alone with him." Mark said.

"Shit, that ain't no bad news Mark but I think I'm a little scared to hear your good news now." We both laughed.

"Jovan, let me put you down on some inside law shit."

"What's up?"

"As long as you know the law, how to work it, how to get around it and fuck it the right way, you'll never have any bad news. Bad news to a lawyer is another language for saying it's time to lie."

"So what's the good news then?"

"Jovan, good news will always be good news." Mark said, laughing.

"Ok, I will ask you once again, what's the good news?"

"Hey man, I got the extension a half hour ago."

"That's great Mark, you're always two steps ahead of the game." Jovan said, proud to be working with Mark.

"Thanks and you're getting good at it too Jovan, you're also on the right track, keep it up and when you become a lawyer, you'll always stay two steps ahead also."

CHAPTER 6

"School of Hard Knocks"

Jovan
I was sentenced to five years in Federal Prison with no outside support from no one. I had a few broads that used to come and see me every now and then, but I wasn't focused on them. My main concern was how was I going to get back home and get a lawyer to do my appeal because once again I was broke, well not flat broke.

When I got locked up, I had Keda who was my female gangsta at the time, go pass my townhouse and get my jewelry and the MPV van and take them over to my Grandma's house before the landlord found out he wouldn't be getting his eleven hundred dollars a month no time soon.

My BMW was forfeited by the Government because it was used in a crime. I could have went to court and tried to get it back, but I didn't want to risk the chance of them investigating how I paid forty-two thousand dollars cash and drove it straight off the lot, so I just took it as another loss. The only person I was in contact with the whole time I was locked up was my Grandma. I used to call her a lot but since my father was nowhere to be found, I knew that Grandma couldn't keep paying for all those collect calls on her Social Security check, so I slowed down on the calls and wrote letters and sent her cards occasionally.

Soon after I was sentenced, they transferred me to Lewisburg Federal Penitentiary. As the bus drove up to what looked like Castle Gray skull and two of the biggest iron doors I've ever seen in my life opened, the first thing came to my mind was how the fuck did I get here and why are they putting me in a maximum facility with niggas serving three life sentences? I would be lying if I told you I didn't care where they sent me, shit I only got five years, I wasn't supposed to be in here.

After being processed and given my federal prison number, 20518-016, I was given a bedroll and sent to "J" block. When I got to my cell, I didn't bother to look around to see if I recognized anyone because I was so tired that I just made up my bed and went to sleep.

The next morning when I woke up and went to the chow hall, the first nigga I saw was my man Mack from R Street. I knew Mack back in '88 when he had a convertible BMW, he was always cool with me. We never did business with each other but we always acknowledged each other's presence.

"Hey Jovan, that you?" Mack said.

"Yeah, what's up Mack." I said.

"What's up Joe."

When Mack spoke, he always expressed the word "Joe". To the homies, "Joe" is our slang in DC for main man or slim, dude or whatever. For DC niggas, it's different doing time in Federal prison than doing time back home, because we made sure that we all got along with each other. It wasn't anything like our State prison (Lorton), where homies robbed, killed and stole from each other. The homies in Federal prison stick together mostly for territorial reasons, so whatever beef a homie had with another homie that wasn't outside the limits of death, was immediately squashed once they entered Federal prison. We held back on any serious aggressions until it was time to go to war with others. DC had an image to protect and homies rolled with homies no matter what.

Mack came over to me and gave me five and a respectful hug that is only reserved for real niggas.

"What's up Joe, why the fuck you down here? Last time I saw you, you were pushing a BMW with a bad ass bitch beside you going down Georgia Avenue."

"Yeah slim, that same BMW got me these five fuckin' years." I said.

"All you got is five years?" Mack said, with a surprised look.

"Yeah man."

"Damn Jovan, what the fuck you doing in Lewisburg, you're supposed to be in a camp or at least a low security facility man!" Mack said.

"I dunno what type of games these people playin'."

"Yeah, you got to holla at your counselor about that tomorrow. Anyway, c'mon so I can introduce you to the homies."

Mack introduced me to all his co-defendants first. Some I already knew, some I didn't, but as I grew to know these niggas, every last one of 'em was real. He also introduced me to Lil Nut and we became super cool. Nut, Mack and me worked out regularly, it was these niggas what helped me get this six pack, triceps, biceps and a chest that needed to be in an Ebony Magazine centerfold. After 6 months in Lewisburg, my body went through a complete change. I lifted weights, not heavy weights, just light reps. I did pull-ups by the twenties and dips by the thirties, I did 500 crunches in the morning, 500 at count time and 500 before I went to bed. I turned myself into the ultimate physical machine and then it was time to work on my brain.

I read all kinds of literature and books, mostly by Dr. N. Akbar and I read a few by J.A. Rogers, Dr. Francis Creswelling, Carter G. Woodson, Jerome Bennett, Noble Drew Ali, Elijah Muhammad, but my favorite one of all was, "The Holy Quran".

But there was something else missing in my life that I need-ed bad, real bad. It wasn't a female friend, I had plenty of those to call if I wanted to get freaky and tell 'em to play with their pussies while I listened, but I was beyond that. It wasn't money, although I could use some, it was something else that was hold-ing me back and when I passed the library I knew just what it was, I needed to learn how to get outta here. I needed to learn the law, the same law that gave me five years, I needed to learn about because who knows, I could one day give it right back to someone else.

By the end of the first week of trying to learn the law I was frustrated, it seemed like every book I read didn't make any sense or went straight over my head. I stopped working out with Mack and Nut and focused all my attention on my legal situa-tion. I still would do a thousand push-ups and crunches every-day to keep my body toned, but mostly I was reading the Federal Criminal Code and Rules book.

One morning on my way to the law library, I walked by some new inmates and I didn't look any of them directly in the face, I just glanced at them as they walked by me with their bedrolls, headed to their new blocks. As I turned towards the library, I took another glance and suddenly I saw someone very familiar. I looked one more time to make sure my eyes wasn't playin' tricks on me, yep that was him, that's that nigga Shorty, one of the bitch ass niggas who had violated me and now it was his turn to be violated. I bent my head down and walked by again just to really make sure it was him but after I heard someone yell his name, I knew for sure that this was my man.

"Yo Shorty, you in that block over there." Said another inmate.

"Ok, thanks money."

Same name, same accent, finally I would get a chance to get my due justice. I went straight to my cell, I didn't move fast, I just acted normal and calm. I sat in my cell and began to put my plan together. I thought about the time I had, only 5 years, but this nigga had violated me, I had to get him but I also had to get away with it, think Jovan, think! The only way I could get this nigga was to get him in one of the TV rooms when nobody was there, or at least, when a lot of people was in there cause it's dark as shit in them TV rooms and when that joint gets packed, you can't see or move.

It was Friday, the day they showed the latest movies, so this was my chance to give it to a nigga who really deserved it. When my cellmate, Parker-Bey, came in the room it was almost time for the movie. My celly was from Detroit and he was in the Moorish Science Temple, he's the one I used to get all the positive literature from.

"What's up Jovan?" Parker-Bey asked.

"Ain't nothin." I said.

"You gonna go up tonight and check out the movie?" He said.

"Naw, I think I'ma lay back and finish reading this damn law book." I said.

"Yeah, you doin' the right thing trying to get outta jail, something a lot of these unconscious brothers should be doing, but instead, they'd rather stay in jail and kill each other." Parker-Bey said.

I'm thinking to myself, yeah, you got that right, well at least part of it, cause I'm definitely trying to kill a ma'fucka, but I ain't trying to stay in jail.

"I'll holla at you later Jovan, I'ma check this movie out."

"Ok Parker-Bey." I said, turning back to the law book I was pretending to read.

When Parker-Bey left, I waited a good five minutes before I started working on my plan. Damn, I pray this shit goes right, it's a must that I kill this nigga, but it's an absolute must that I get away with it.

First thing I did was put on my khaki uniform and black boots, then I put my gray sweatshirt on over top, making sure you couldn't see the uniform underneath. I looked at myself in the mirror, but the more I looked, the more I felt I needed a better disguise, so what I did was put on one of my celly's gray kuffi and a pair of those shades they sell in the commissary. As I looked at myself in the mirror again, I was now completely happy with what I saw, I looked like am militant black panther type dude. No one would know who I was, no one would be able to identify me and no one would know how vicious a killer I was but me.

I reached into my mattress and pulled out the eight-inch flat blade that Mack gave me when I first got here, tucked it in my pants, took a deep breath and headed to the TV room to kill my second victim, a nigga who truly deserved it. As I walked down the hallway, I could tell that I had on the ultimate disguise because when I walked by Mack and Nut, they didn't even recognize me.

As I walked by I could hear them talking. Mack said, "Man, where Jovan at, I ain't seen him in about a week?"

"He's probably in the law library working on his case, Slim must really be trying to go home." Nut said.

"Yeah, I can respect that."

When I entered the TV room it was just like I pictured, dark, loud and smoky from the cigarettes and black & mild cigars, the atmosphere was perfect for my plan. I walked to the back of the room and saw Shorty and another dude sitting there, talking and kicking it about old times. He probably was telling his man how he got a free hundred and eighty thousand back in DC, but little did he know that 180 thousand was gonna cost him his life. I took a seat directly behind Shorty. There were three other dudes sitting in my row with me, they didn't talk loud, to me it looked like they were minding their own business like all convicts are supposed to do. Sitting in Shorty's row, was Shorty, his man and two homosexuals sitting together.

As the movie was about to start, I reached in my pants slowly, making sure no one saw me and held the knife in the palm of my hand so tight that it felt as if I had dipped my hand in super glue, I wasn't scared or nervous, I was calm and collective. I peeped my surroundings one more time and then came the golden opportunity I was waiting for, the TV went blank for about 5 seconds. I reached my left hand up under Shorty's chin and pulled back with all my strength, exposing his whole neck and throat to the blade. My first blow was vital, but my second blow was much more vicious. I drove the blade so hard through Shorty's neck that the tip of the blade was poking out the back of his head. Shorty died instantly, he didn't have a chance to scream or fight back, he didn't even get a chance to tell on me, he was through!

When the TV came back on, Shorty's friend was quiet and I could see that he was involved with one of the homosexuals sitting next to him. When he was finished and looked over at Shorty and saw that he was dead, he never looked behind him, he just got up and left. In prison, when someone just gets up and leaves without saying a word, that means something just happened or was about to happen and if you're not involved, then you get up and leave also. So once Shorty's man got up, everybody else got up.

While niggas were trying to get outta the TV room as fast as they could, I laid back for a second, took off my sweat suit, balled it up and left it in the corner along with the knife. I folded my celly's kuffi up and put it in my pocket and threw the shades in the trash. Now I looked like the average inmate with khakis ironed and pressed, boots shiny and shirt buttoned up and tucked in.

When I came back to my cell, I saw that my celly was already in there.

"What's up Parker-Bey?" I said.

"Hey, what's up young brother, I thought you were staying in tonight to work on your case, you wasn't up in the TV room were you?"

"Naw, I went down to the law library to read up on a few things."

"Good." Parker-Bey said.

"Why you say that?"

"Cause I think something happened in the TV room tonight, I was just making sure you were a'ight."

"Oh you ain't gotta worry 'bout me, I only got 5 funky ass years and I'd be a damn fool getting into some shit." I said.

"That's right young brother, your main concern is to get home to your loved ones." Parker-Bey said.

"Yeah right and that's exactly what I plan to do."

CHAPTER 7

"Welcome Home Bilal"

While Jovan was in Lewisburg trying to get these 5 years up off me, Bilal was at home doing his thang. Jovan always knew that Bilal would be the perfect hustler, he had it in his blood, plus he was alone with no family and no place to go.

In February of 1992, Bilal Davis had the whole city on lock down. When Bilal first came home, he got with a Spanish nigga he was down Oakhill with named Carlos Gonzales. Carlos and Bilal became good friends while they were locked up and they always promised each other that they would get together when they got out. Carlos fronted Bilal two kilos of powder for twenty-five thousand as a coming home present and he went right back around his old neighborhood and started hustling. Niggas knew Bilal from when they were little, but mostly, they remembered him killing Boo-Boo in the alley back in the day, at least that's what they thought he did.

Bilal took over the Northeast with an iron fist, Orleans Pl. was abandoned after John got locked up and the fiends wasn't on powder no more, they wanted crack. Bilal did the first thing that came to mind, he got together the most vicious youngins from around the way, Lil G, Cat, Soup and Shortdog and he paid them to take out every major nigga that was sellin' crack. That way, when it came time for him to open shop, every dime in the Northeast would be his. Bilal cooked both kilos up raw because he wanted his shit to be the best coke out there. Although it was the only coke out there, he still wanted to attract customers from other neighborhoods.

When Bilal opened the alley back up on Orleans Pl., it was jumping even harder than it did back in the day. It was rumored that Bilal was making at least thirty thousand a day selling dimes. After about a month, Bilal had more money then Carlos, but regardless of that fact, they remained partners and they put their money together, copped 30 kilos from one of Carlos' uncle and then Bilal had shit on almost every major strip in DC. The last spot Bilal re-opened, the legendary Hanover Pl., NW, was the spot that was going to put him into multi-million dollar status. It was rumored in prison that Bilal collected at least a hundred thousand a day from Hanover Pl. alone.

As Bilal's organization grew bigger, his stash grew just as big. Carlos and Bilal went to Mexico to meet a new connect because Carlos' uncle could no longer meet their demand for more bricks, so he ended up introducing them to his connect in Mexico. They went to there and ended up with the deal of the century, the connect agreed to sell Bilal and Carlos 90% cocaine for seventy-five hundred a kilo, but under one condition. When they purchased, they had to buy no less than 200 kilos at a time. Bilal and Carlos immediately agreed and started doing business with the Mexican one week later.

Here Jovan was stuck in Lewisburg Penitentiary with 5 years and no way to get in contact with his man, his true friend, comrade for life, Bilal Davis, "The New King of DC".

CHAPTER 8

"Come on Home"

As the months went by, Jovan spent every free hour that he had in the Law Library, he wouldn't go to chow, watch TV, get on the phone or anything, all he wanted to do was learn about the law. The more he stayed in the Law Library, the better he got. He also met some real niggas while working on his case that helped him out, some showed him how to format motions, others showed him how to read cases. Big Linwood, Cashwell, Cookie and Young Rico aka Ali Katabb, all taught him how to fight the Government with its own weapon. After he learned as much as he could about the law, he became known around the prison as "Jovan the Law Fiend", "Jovan Cochran" or "The Jailhouse Lawyer".

Jovan had been locked up for almost 2 years now and the Judge finally answered his appeal. At the 4:00 p.m. stand-up count, Jovan's Counselor told him to come into his office and sign the priority mail book.

"What's up Stevens, what somebody sent me some money priority mail?" Jovan asked.

"I don't think so Price." Stevens said.

"Then what is it?"

"I think it's some legal mail here for you, just c'mon down and get it after the count." Stevens said.

During the whole count time, Jovan couldn't stop from wondering what this legal mail was. He paced the floor back and forth, trying to figure out what it could be. He was hoping it was the answer to his appeal that he had put in about eight months ago. He didn't ask for a new trial, he asked that the whole charge and indictment be dropped on the basis of illegal search and seizure and racial profiling.

The officer on his case never said he pulled him over for a traffic violation, he never wrote a ticket, he just placed him under arrest and searched his car without his consent. He also did not have any reasonable suspicion to search his car, he just saw a young black man driving a BMW doing about 70 in the left lane. The only thing he was supposed to do according to law, was give him a ticket and go on about his business.

After the count was clear and the cells popped open, Jovan raced to his Counselor's office.

"Stevens, you got that mail for me?" Jovan asked.

"Yeah Price, it's right here but first sign the log stating that you received it."

Jovan signed the log and grabbed the mail, he couldn't wait to read it, so he opened it up right there in Stevens' office. It read:

The United States District Court

For the District of Columbia

In the instant matter of the United States vs. Jovan Conrad Price, the District Court grants appellate's motion, reverses the conviction and drops all charges.

The Petitioner is to released from

Federal custody IMMEDIATELY

At that moment Jovan almost fainted. He rushed to his cell

to retrieve all of his personal belongings and went to call his Grandma to tell her the good news.

Ring, Ring, Ring, "Hello." Jovan's Grandma said.

"This is a collect call from Jovan, if you wish to accept this call please press 5 now." The operator's voice said.

Grandma pushed 5 and said, "Hey baby."

"Hey Grandma, how you doing?" Jovan said, excitedly.

"Oh I'm doing ok, I would be better if you or your daddy was here." She said.

"Well Grandma, I don't know about my daddy but I'll be there soon."

"How soon baby?" Grandma asked.

"Sooner than you think Grandma, I just won my appeal!" Jovan said, jumping for joy.

"Jovan, stop playing boy, don't play like that!" Grandma said, screaming.

"Grandma, I ain't playing, I'm dead serious."

"Well, that's good baby. When you leaving?" She asked me.

"I think tomorrow morning. You gonna come pick me up from the Bus Station?"

"Yeah baby, I'm so glad you're coming home because now you can get that damn van from in front of my house, it's been sitting here for almost 2 years." We both laughed.

"I'll call you in the morning Grandma." Jovan said.

"Ok baby, love you."

"I love you too Grandma."

"Oh Jovan." Grandma said, before hanging up.

"Yeah Grandma."

"Did you read about your friend Bilal in the newspaper."

When Grandma said that, instantly Jovan thought Bilal had gotten killed.

"Naw Grandma, what happened and when was he in the paper?" Jovan asked her, afraid she was getting ready to tell me Bilal was dead.

"About two days ago baby, it said something about him being a drug kingpin and being arrested with a whole lot of money in his possession."

When she said he had gotten locked up, Jovan was relieved to find out he wasn't dead.

"Did they catch him with any drugs on him?"

"I dunno baby, it didn't say anything about drugs just money, and a whole lot of it too. I hope he'll be alright, Bilal's a good boy, he's just been through so much."

Jovan wondered if Bilal ever came by his Grandma's while he was away.

"Hey Grandma."

"Yes baby?"

"Did Bilal ever come over there while I was locked up?" Jovan asked her.

"Oh yeah baby, he came over a few times, I was supposed to give him your address, but every time he came over I couldn't find it." Grandma said.

Damn, my man was out there getting all that money and he was still loyal. I bet if Grandma had given him my address, my account would have been fat as shit. Now this nigga gets locked up and I'm on my way out the door.

CHAPTER 9

"A New Beginning"

On December 31, 1993, Jovan was home free. The first thing he did when he got home was call Peppa over to his Grandma's house. He fucked her all night long, he fucked her so hard that when she got up in the morning, she couldn't even walk straight.

"Damn Jovan, you act like you ain't never had no pussy before." Peppa said when she woke up the next morning.

"It ain't that Pepp, it's just that I ain't had none in two years."

"Shit, I know you was in there playing wit that thing."

"Yeah, I jerked off a few times, but it ain't nothin' like the real thang." Jovan said, laughing.

Jovan didn't have to make love to Peppa because she was a hood rat, so it didn't matter if he fucked her like a hoe or caressed her like a gentleman, she was gonna fuck with a nigga like him regardless, because she already knew his status and capabilities of getting money again, so giving him that pussy anyway he wanted it was more like an investment to her.

After Peppa left, Jovan went outside to check on his van. He popped the hydraulic stash and saw that he still had his P13/16 shot .45 automatic. He closed the stash back and took his van to the nearest detail shop and after his van was done, he went back home to spend sometime with his Grandma. She had cooked a nigga so much food that when Jovan got up from the table, he almost threw up. Jovan kicked it with his Grandma for a while talking about what he was going to do with his life.

The next morning, Jovan decided to get his tags renewed along with his license. He got together all his old clothes, well not old because most of the shit he had was still brand new, the tags were still on 'em. He still had a nice wardrobe, mostly Versace and Armani, and you know that shit ain't going outta style for a minute, plus most of the Versace shit he had he brought from California on Rodeo Drive, he had shit niggas hadn't seen yet.

Jovan was glad Keda went back to his townhouse and got his shit for him when he got locked up cause, if she hadn't, he'd really be fucked up. Jovan hadn't seen Keda yet, but when he did he was gonna let her know how much respect a nigga got for her, because the whole time he was down, outta all the bitches he had Keda was the only one that kept it real. She'd send him a few dollars, some cards and a couple of flicks of herself with thongs on. Although he wasn't too impressed with that at the time, he still recognized real when he saw it.

After Jovan left the Department of Motor Vehicles, his next plan for today was gonna be hard, he had to get a job. Yeah, Jovan C. Price, outta jail with a Paralegal Diploma trying to find a job at any law firm that would accept him.

The first place Jovan went to was the Law Offices of Rohon & Robinson. As he was parking his van in front of the office, Mark was just pulling up in his green 535I BMW. Good, perfect timing he thought as he grabbed is Diploma and hopped out the van. Just as Mark was getting outta his car with a flimsy brief case full of motions, Jovan greeted him.

"What's up Mark, how you doin'?" Jovan said.

"Hey, my main man Jovan, what's up? What brings you by the office, you caught a new case or something?" Mark asked.

"Naw Mark, the life of crime is over for me, I came to ask for a serious favor."

"Well Jovan, if you want me to represent one of your friends or something and they don't have any money, then I can't do that for you, but I'll work with you if you can pull a rabbit out your hat and drop me a few Franklins." Mark said, laughing.

Jovan laughed at Mark's slick way of telling me if your bank ain't right, you better get outta sight.

"Naw Mark, it ain't like that, it's a little more important."

"Tell you what Jovan, I've got a few minutes before I have to go back to court, come in my office so we can talk."

Mark's office had changed a little since the last time Jovan was there. He also had a new secretary that was phat as hell, she had booty like J-LO, her name was Cindy and she looked alright to be a white girl.

"I see you made a few changes huh Mark?" Jovan said.

"Yeah, Jovan, the more money I get the better the office looks. Now what's your problem and how can I help you?"

Jovan told Mark everything he needed to know, he told him how bad he wanted to be a lawyer and how bad he needed a job so he could pay for his next 2 years at Howard University, and to his surprise, Mark accepted his plea.

"Look Jovan, I'm going to hire you and teach you as much as I know, but for a thousand dollars a week, you're gonna have to bust your ass for this law firm. We don't lose many cases, and for the ones we do lose, we end up winning on appeal. Another reason I'm hiring you is because I know you know a lot of these fools that keep getting locked up and you may have a better approach to them than I do. So yeah, I'ma need you but you're gonna have to work hard Jovan." Mark said.

"Thanks Mark, I'll never forget this. When do I start?"

"Is there some place you gotta be right now?"

"No." Jovan said.

"Well, you can start as of this moment. Here's some cases, look them up and copy them for me."

Jovan picked up the cases and was about to go straight to work.

"Oh, Jovan." Mark said, as Jovan was about to leave his office.

"What's up Mark."

"I see that you're casual today, you think you could dress like that often?"

"Oh don't worry 'bout that Mark, all my clothes are casual, expensive but casual. I haven't owned a pair of Nikes since 1991."

Mark laughed at Jovan's remark but it was true, he doesn't wear sweat suits and tennis shoes anymore, only if he's working out. He's a fly nigga, always was and always will be.

CHAPTER 10

"6 Months Later"

Jovan was still at Mark's office learning as much as he could.
Today, Mark was in court representing his best friend, Bilal
Davis. Mark doesn't know that Bilal and him are best friends and
he intended for it to remain that way. Bilal got arrested on some
bullshit charge of a one count conspiracy with no co-defendants, no drugs involved and no murders. He was charged with
conspiracy because of the amount of money they found in his
stash house, they confiscated 3.5 million of Bilal's money.

The house wasn't in Bilal's name and he wasn't on the lease.
The only way they connected Bilal to the money was from a suit-
case full of expensive clothes and two plane tickets to Paris in his
name, along with his passport. Bilal was going away to take a
break from the streets and he was taking some broad he messed
with to Paris for a month.

Come to find out that one of Bilal's customers was caught
with a couple of bricks down Southwest, and in turn for his freedom, he agreed to be an informant for the 6th District Police.
The officers at this Precinct hated Bilal, they wanted him bad but
could never get anything on him until they got a hold to "Fat
Mike".

Fat Mike hustled down Southwest on Delaware Avenue and
Bilal used to look out for this nigga. Mike always brought only
two kilos but Bilal used to give him five and let him owe him the

rest later. Bilal always looked out for niggas that he thought had that hustle in 'em.

On the morning Bilal was going to Paris, he made one mistake by serving Fat Mike at one of his stash houses on Florida Avenue. The only reason why that much money was in that house was because Carlos was supposed to come over first thing in the morning and send it down to Mexico for shipment. After Bilal served Fat Mike, he went right around the corner and told the police that Bilal was in the house, never telling the police that Bilal had just sold him his last five bricks. Fat Mike was a bitch, he figured he'd pay for only 2 bricks and get Bilal locked up so he wouldn't have to pay for the other three.

The officers that were waiting called the Precinct for back up, they didn't even get a legitimate warrant, they just busted into Bilal's joint, locked him up and later he was sentenced to 30 years. After Bilal received 30 years, he hired Mark and Mark's motion for a new trial was so strong because of the newly discovered evidence indicating that the warrant in which the officers used was bogus and not signed by a Judge, the Judge immediately called Bilal's case back for a new hearing.

CHAPTER 11

"Long Time Coming"

On May 10, 1994, Jovan was granted a temporary pass as an attorney assistant. As Mark and Jovan went upstairs, Jovan chose the first conference room and Mark chose the one across from him. Jovan had to do that so Mark wouldn't look over and see Bilal and him smiling and talking like they knew each other, plus he wanted to see Bilal first and give him the eye so he wouldn't come out here all loud trying to hug a nigga, blowing Jovan's cover.

The first inmate they brought out was a little dude Mark was representing because he got caught up in a foolish carjacking with some friend while high off of PCP. His people had a little money so they hired Mark. As Mark started interviewing his client, the C.O. brought Bilal into the conference room.

Jovan hadn't seen Bilal in almost 9 years, he was big as shit, ripped up like Mike Tyson! He had on his blue DC Jail jumper, blue kuffi, a pair of Versace glasses and a pair of new blue and white Versace tennis shoes. Damn, even in jail Bilal was giving it to them. You could tell everyone in the prison respected him and that he was fucking the C.O., cause the C.O. that brought him in whispered something in his ear and felt his dick while patting him down. When Bilal turned around and saw Jovan sitting in the conference room, his eyes got big as shit! Jovan placed his fingers to his lips to let him know not to let the cat outta the bag and got up and reached out his right hand.

"Mr. Bilal Davis, I'm Jovan Price, paralegal assistant to your lawyer Mark Rohon. I'm here to talk to you about a few things."

Bilal had a slight grin on his face as he shook Jovan's hand. When the C.O. left and closed the door to the conference room, the first thing that came outta Bilal's mouth was, "Nigga, what the fuck you doin' here?"

"I come to pay my loyalty to my only friend." Jovan said, as he held back the tears with all his might.

Bilal sat back in his chair, looked at Jovan and shook his head as if in a state of shock.

"Man Jovan, we got a lot to talk about." Bilal said, as Jovan noticed he too was holding back years of unshed tears.

"Yeah, I know but first we gotta get this shit together cause I only got a hour with you." Jovan said.

"Man, don't tell me you're a real lawyer."

"Naw, I ain't no lawyer yet, I'm a paralegal."

"Get the fuck outta here." Bilal said, still shocked.

"Naw Slim, this is real."

"How the fuck did you become a paralegal?"

"Long story Lal, I'll fill you in later." Jovan smiled and said, "What's up Lal?"

"Ain't nothin', I'm just sitting here trippin' the fuck out because my fucking best friend who I ain't seen in 9 years becomes my lawyer."

"Nigga, I told you back in '85 that I'll never let no one do nothin' to you."

"And I told you visa versa." Bilal said, glad to see his friend.

"Bilal you already proved that, now it's my turn to show my loyalty. Now look and listen carefully." Jovan said, ready to get down to business.

Jovan filled Bilal in on everything, and I mean everything, from the time he got locked up in '85 all the way up until now. Bilal dropped a few tears then hurried up and wiped them away. We told each other that we loved one another and would forever remain loyal and from this point on we'd never lose contact again.

"Look Lal, you're gonna win your case next week, we only got an extension of time for one week." Jovan told Bilal.

Jovan told him everything about Fat Mike. Bilal never knew Fat Mike was the one who gave him up, he always thought that the police had came up into his spot and found the 3.5 mil. on a humble.

"Damn Bilal, them people took a lot of money from you Slim."

"Yeah Jay, they hit a nigga's head but I'm still cool though, I still got like 3.5 mil that Carlos is holdin' for me."

"How much you payin' Mark?" Jovan asked, inquisitively.

"He didn't tell you." Bilal said.

"Naw, I didn't ask him."

"I gave him two hundred thousand and told him if he could guarantee he'd win my case, I'd give him another fifty."

"You paying this ma'fucka all that money?" Jovan asked, shocked.

"Jovan, that ain't shit compared to my freedom, shit a nigga like me is worth two hundred fifty million."

"Yeah, I feel you on that one Lal."

"And nigga, when I get out, you're going to get a piece of the action too."

"Man, you know I can't hang with you when you get out, them people's gonna be watching you."

"No they ain't, not if I play it right. Jovan. This all I know, I don't know nothin' else, I'ma born hustler just like my Pops." Bilal said, sadly.

Jovan knew one day Bilal would think that he had turned into his Pops. He also knew what Bilal said was true, that this is all he knew. Personally Jovan thought, with 3.5 mil, he'd quit and do something else or at least try to wash that shit up.

"Look Bilal, your hearing is next week and if somehow Fat Mike doesn't walk up in that courtroom, you'll be walking out."

Bilal came closer, lowered his voice and said, "Jovan, look this is what I need you to do."

"What's that Lal?" Jovan asked.

"Ok, do you remember Lil G from around Orleans Pl.?"

"Yeah, I remember shorty, I hear he's out there killin' every-thing that moves."

"Yeah that's right, he's the lil youngin I fuck wit. Look, go around Orleans Pl. and tell Lil G I said to lay the demonstration down on Fat Mike ASAP and that I got fifty thousand for that move, and if it's done nicely, I got an extra 30 thousand as a bonus."

"Damn Bilal, giving up eighty thousand for Fat Mike's head, that's a nice start up bank." Jovan said. "Ok Lal, you got that, I'll get on top of that as soon as I leave here."

"Yeah Jay and next week when I get out, you and me are going somewhere and talk. I don't care what you're doin' nigga, you my family and some way you're gonna be a part of my team and play your position. You got that nigga, forever I remain loyal." Bilal said, seriously.

"Look Bilal, when we get up just shake my hand, don't try and hug me because we still wanna keep Mark in the dark."

"Ok Jay."

When Mark signaled to Jovan that it was time to go, Bilal and Jovan stood up and shook hands. This time when Jovan shook Bilal's hand, he saw the tattoo on his right forearm. It was a tombstone with flowers around it and it read, "In Loving Memory of Mal-Mal, My True Love". As Jovan looked at the tattoo he felt guilty, because for some reason, he always felt responsible for Mal-Mal's death.

As soon as Mark and Jovan left the jail and were about to depart because Jovan had something to do, he had to find Lil G, Mark asked him, "Hey Jovan, I'll see you in the office tomorrow or what?"

"Yeah, but first I gotta try and find this witness to see if he's gonna sign this affidavit." Jovan said.

"Ok, call me if you find out anything."

Jovan had been up all day without anything to eat, so before he went around the Northeast, he stopped somewhere and ate something. Normally, he didn't eat fast food because he tried to keep his figure tight, right now he was 178 lbs. of all muscle. But today he had to break one rule, he drove around the corner on Pennsylvania Avenue and pulled into the Kentucky Fried Chicken drive thru and ordered a bake chicken dinner. After pulling off, Jovan looked at his watch and saw that it was 6:00 p.m., damn he hoped this youngin was out here.

Jovan drove around Orleans Pl. and saw two dudes he didn't know. He didn't bother to ask them where Lil G was cause Lil G be killing so much they'd probably think Jovan was trying to do something to him. As he continued to drive down the street and before he got to the intersection of Orleans Pl. and 6th

Street, he saw Omar pull up in his Pathfinder. Jovan rolled down his window to signal for Omar to pull over and it looked like he was reaching for his gun until he saw Jovan's face.

Omar rolled down his window and said, "What's up Jovan? Damn nigga, where you been at, I ain't seen your ass in a long time."

"Yeah I know, I just been chillin'."

"You heard what they did to Bilal, them people smashed him with 30 years."

"Yeah Omar I know, but I'm looking for Lil G, I gotta holla at him about something." Jovan said.

"You a'ight Jovan, you ain't got no problems or nothin' do you?"

"Oh naw, I just need to holla at shorty about something important."

"Check around back, they're probably behind Wilson's playing craps." Omar said.

"Ok Slim, thanks."

"Sure Jovan, anytime. Slim, it's good to see you again man." Omar said. "Start coming around more often, for a minute I thought you was one of them niggas trying to get at me and I was 'bout to put this glock to your head."

"Yeah Omar? I'll see you later." Jovan said, laughing.

"A'ight."

As Jovan drove around back, he could see Short Dogg, Cat, Dre, Soup and one-eyed Sean shootin' craps. It was obvious these niggas was beefing hard as shit cause soon as Jovan pulled up, they all pulled their shit out.

Dogg had a Mac-11, Cat had a Glock 40, Dre had a Barretta

and Soup had the prettiest Smith & Wesson .45 Jovan had ever seen. He didn't see one-eyed Sean pull anything out, he guessed he felt safe knowing these niggas were strapped.

When Jovan got out his van, the first nigga who said something was Cat, "Whodat?"

"It's Jovan." Jovan said to him.

"Who?" Cat asked.

"Jovan, Bilal's man."

As Jovan walked up closer so Cat could see who he was, the first thing he said was, "Nigga, where the fuck you been hidin' at?"

"Slim, you know I don't do no hidin'."

"What's up?"

"Ain't shit happenin', I see you niggas still the same way, ain't letting a nigga just walk up on you."

"Oh, hell naw, you know we ain't going for it!"

Everybody put their straps back in their dips but Short Dog. For some reason this lil nigga was on point, he was Lil G's young protégé and if he didn't feel comfortable, he showed it.

"Man Jovan, what'cha doing around here, you back in action or what, cause we do need a connect. Ever since Bilal went in, we've been fucked up and you know that bitch ass nigga Carlos ain't trying to do nothin' with us. He's scared we ain't gonna pay him, that nigga's a hoe, I don't understand what Bilal see in that him."

Jovan wanted to say to Cat what Bilal sees in Carlos is millions of dollars that you can't get, but instead he asked the question that he came here for.

"Naw Cat, I ain't back in action, I'm looking for Lil G." Jovan said to Cat.

When Jovan said that, Short Dogg looked at him as if he said he wanted to kill Lil G. This lil young nigga was on point, he knew Jovan never did business with Lil G before, so he could understand why he had his antennas up.

"Jovan man, come here for a second and let me holla at you in private." Cat said.

"Yeah, what's up Cat?"

"Look man, whatever you looking for my man for I know it must be a good reason, but for real Slim, we don't even know where he's at. You know homicide been around here all week looking for shorty, they're trying to pin some shit on him, so when he got whiff of that, he jetted. Shit, that's my man and he ain't even tell me where he was going."

"Damn Cat, I needed to talk to him bad."

"Slim, ain't too much I can do but you can give me your number, and if he calls or comes around, I'll give it to him." Cat said.

Jovan gave Cat his pager number and a special code for Lil G.

"Look Cat, as soon as you talk to him, tell him I've got a hell of a proposition for him and it would be in his best interest to get back at me ASAP."

"Ok Jay, I'll do that."

"A'ight, I'll holla at ya later."

"Ok Jovan, take care."

As Jovan got back into my van, he looked through his rear view mirror and watched Short Dog stick his Mac-11 into his pants and just shook his head. Damn, these young niggas out here going hard as shit, but in all actuality, they didn't know that Jovan had killed at the age of 15, way younger then they were.

CHAPTER 12

"The Next Day"

Jovan woke up the next morning and checked his pager to see if Lil G had paged him, but he didn't see the special code that he had given his man. Damn, he had to find this youngin. Fat Mike had to be dealt with before the hearing, which is only 5 days away. When Jovan went back around to Orleans Pl., it was about 1:00 o'clock and he didn't see anybody but some crack heads looking for coke, trying to trick anybody for a hit. Jovan drove all through the neighborhood and there was still no sight of Lil G. Damn, this shit was fucked up, he had to get Bilal out of jail. He rode around a few more times until he saw Cat and Soup in front of the Liquor Store on 6th & K, he pulled up and got out.

"Hey Cat." Jovan said, pressed and determined to find this nigga Lil G.

"Hey Jovan, what's up?" Cat said.

"You hear from youngin yet?"

"Man Jovan, I've got some fucked up news for you, shorty got locked up last night as soon he came around here. He called me this morning and said they got him out in Maryland, the Upper Marlboro Jail. He said they're trying to charge him with three bodies out there."

"Damn, that's fucked up!" Jovan said, looking disturbed.

"Jovan, you a'ight Slim? You sound like you're more fucked up 'bout my man then I am what, he owe you some money or something?" Cat asked, curiously.

"Naw Cat, I just needed him. Does he have a bond?"

"Naw, you know them people ain't giving a nigga like Lil G no fuckin' bond, they're gonna try and fry his ass." Cat said.

"Ok Slim, damn."

When Jovan got back in the van, all he could do was think about his man, I've got to get Bilal out, I can't let my man stay in jail. This nigga done took a murder rap for me and in some way I still felt responsible for Mal-Mal's death. I owe Bilal, I owe him my life, he's my best friend, my truest comrade and my family. Even though I'm a paralegal now and trying to get my shit in order, somehow this game always knows how to pull a nigga back in. I done killed before, twice to be exact, but those ma'fuckas had violated me and deserved it. Bilal was my family and I made a vow to him nine years ago that if anyone violated him, they violated me and I would remain as loyal to him as he had remained to me. I had to put the demonstration down on a nigga who truly deserved it, I had to kill Fat Mike, but the main thing I had to do was, just like in Lewisburg, I had to get away with it.

CHAPTER 13

"The Plan"

Bilal's hearing was only two days away and Fat Mike was still breathing. Jovan had spent all day yesterday scooping out all of Fat Mike's moves, what he drove, what time he opened and closed shop, how many runners he had, and most of all, did he carry heat? He knew that Fat Mike carried a gun when he saw him stash it as the police drove by. Jovan parked his van on the opposite side of Delaware Avenue and watched Fat Mike's every step, and since his windows were tinted, he had all day without someone peeping him out.

Jovan saw that Fat Mike had about four runners, at least three friends and one young nigga holding the stash. He also saw that he opened up shop around 2:00 o'clock. Mike was kinda smart because this was the time that the Police Department changed shifts, so when he had that 2:00 o'clock rush, he'd be able to get as much sales as he could without worrying about the jump outs.

Jovan couldn't just run up on Fat Mike cause he'd be ready, he stayed strapped and the young dude with the stash stayed strapped also. So, even if he did run up on Mike and blast him, he'd have to get the other one also and most likely it would come out a big mess. He'd be either at the morgue or on the 5:00 o'clock news, and for sure he didn't want any of that.

As Jovan was sitting in his van trying to figure out a way to eliminate Mike and get away with it, he noticed a Pepco Meter. He could see from a distance that the meter was broken and he wondered if there was another meter. Most of the time there'd usually be another one close by, so he looked toward the side of the building and there it was, the other meter broken just like the one on the other side. Jovan immediately drove off and went to the nearest Sunny Surplus Supply Store.

CHAPTER 14

"Forever Loyal"

Jovan couldn't sleep all night, he stayed up pacing back and forth trying to figure out what he was going to do. Bilal's hearing was tomorrow at 2:45 p.m. and Fat Mike was still alive and breathing, willing to get on the stand and empty his brains on Jovan's best friend. To him snitching was the ultimate sin, he hated that more then he hated cruddy niggas and we know how much he hated cruddy niggas, so putting the demonstration down on Fat Mike would not only be doing a favor for a friend, it would also, in his eyes, be doing justice by giving it to a nigga who truly deserved it.

Jovan left the house around 8:00 o'clock that morning and went to the office to check on some cases and to see if Mark needed him for anything, but he knew his main purpose for coming to the office this early was to try and get Mark to get Bilal another extension of time. Jovan got to the office about 15 minutes before Mark did and Cindy was already there and Jovan wondered if she had ever been fucked by a black guy because she was phat as hell for a white girl. He contemplated whether he should try and fuck Cindy, but as soon as he built his courage up to approach her, Mark came running through the door.

"Hey Cindy." Mark said.

"Hello Mark." Cindy said.

"Hey Jovan." Mark said.

"Good morning Mark." Jovan said.

"Jovan, what are you doing here so early?"

"Nothin' really, I was just checking up on some cases for today's hearing."

"Good, did you ever find that witness?"

"Sure didn't Mark, I don't even think he lives in DC anymore."

"Well, let's hope not, cause if he does, Mr. Davis is in a lot of trouble."

Damn, Mark acted like he didn't even give a fuck about Jovan's man and he was getting paid two hundred fifty for his services. Man, Jovan felt like killing Mark instead of Fat Mike.

"Look here Mark, if the witness comes in what kinda argument do we have?"

"Jovan, we really don't have an argument, my job was to get Mr. Davis' charges dropped on the illegal search warrant and I've done that, well not officially, but at 2:45 p.m. today my services are done. Now if the Government brings Mr. Davis up on new charges of conspiracy, then that's a whole new different case and we'll have to talk figures with Mr. Davis about that." Mark said.

Damn, Mark's a cruddy ma'fucka but this is the game lawyers play and this is how they get paid, so Jovan had to respect Mark's position as a lawyer because, in all actuality, he was right.

"Hey Jovan." Mark said.

"Yeah Mark, what's up?"

"Look, I've got a hearing to go to this morning at eleven o'clock for this young kid in a carjacking case, I want you to come along with me and take some notes so you can see how I work my shit. Like I told you Jovan, I'ma teach you everything you need to know about being a lawyer, and besides, you have on the perfect outfit. Who knows, you may meet one of those freaky ass prosecutors who likes to fuck in the office." Mark said, smiling.

"Naw Mark, I'll leave that part up to you." But what Jovan really wanted to say was, He'd like to fuck Cindy right here in your office.

CHAPTER 15

"Perfect Timing"

Jovan went into the courtroom with Mark and watched him lie and manipulate the court into dropping the carjacking charge down to an unauthorized use of a vehicle charge. The youngster's family was happy, although he would still had to do six months, it was a whole lot better than doing 60 years.

To Jovan, Mark was one of the best lawyers in DC because there were other lawyers that were just as good. For instance, his partner who was a black woman by the name of Michelle Robinson, was real good and her specialty was homicide cases. She could get a nigga off even if he was caught with the smokin' gun in his hand. There was also Kenny Roberts, whose specialty was conspiracy cases. He was known for getting major drug dealers outta fucked up situations, but he had started falling off after he lost a case and some niggas went to his office and shot his ass. But to Jovan, Mark was the best, maybe because he was his protégé, he didn't know.

After the hearing was over, Mark told Jovan to go back to the office because he was going to lunch with the prosecutor in the youngster's case.

"Hey Mark, I see you made a deal with the devil." Jovan said, laughing.

"Yeah Jovan, now I gotta fuck this fat bitch in order to get the charges dropped." Mark said.

"Whatever happened to your sharp ass lawyer skills?"

"This is one of 'em, you'll learn Jovan, it's just gonna take sometime." Mark said.

As Jovan was leaving the courtroom and on his way out of the building, this was the moment he locked eyes on Sonya. Bilal's hearing wasn't for another couple of hours and besides, he really didn't want to go back to the office, so to buy himself sometime, he figured he'd make contact with this lovely woman and hopefully be able to take her out to lunch. He carried myself like a true playa disguised in a gentleman's quality, his approach was so smooth there was no way that she could refuse his offer.

Sonya
When I held Jovan's hands and felt his palms, they were warm and smooth just like his approach. I wanted to take his hands and kiss his fingers then gently rub them over my hard nipples, but it was way too early for that, and plus, Jovan would have to wait a minute before I would ever give myself up to him.

"Hey Jovan, you don't have to talk about your family anymore, we can move onto another subject." I said.

"No, it's ok Sonya." Jovan said, looking at his watch again and I began to wonder if he had someplace else to be.

"Well Sonya, to answer your question, yes I did have a big brother and his name was Derrick and when I was eleven years old he was killed. Derrick was a hustler who used to run Barry Farms back in the day. He had a lot of money and whenever I wanted something he'd get if for me. He brought me bicycles, go-carts, took me to the movies, King's Dominion Amusement Park, he did everything a big brother was supposed to do. I looked up to him and loved him very much, he used to always tell me he was gonna buy Momma a big house way out in Maryland in one of those nice neighborhoods and we'd have all kinds of toys and stuff. I looked forward to that day until somebody stole that joy from me. One day my brother was found duct taped in his Benz with one shot to the head. The police never found out who killed my brother but they said the motive most likely was robbery." Jovan said, with his voice filled with pain.

"Oh Jovan, I'm sorry to hear that, I'm so sorry."

Damn, I really felt for Jovan because as he was talking his eyes began to water, although he didn't let a tear drop I knew it was painful for him to talk about his brother.

Jovan looked at his watch again and said, "Sonya, I got a conference call to make to my boss because he has a hearing in about an hour and I need to brief him on a few things. Can you excuse me for about ten minutes?"

"Sure Jovan, take you time, I'll be right here."

I knew Jovan was hurting about his brother and he probably wanted to go somewhere for a couple minutes to let it all out, or maybe he really did have to call his boss. Damn, it felt good to finally meet a smooth brotha with a job, and a good job at that.

Jovan
As I was telling Sonya about my brother, the pain grew deep and thinking about him gave me that hate, the hate that I have for all cruddy niggas, the hate that I couldn't wait to express on a nigga who truly deserved it. I looked at my watch and saw that it was about 1:45 p.m., perfect timing.

As I got up and was on my way out the door, I saw the same white waitress looking at me, so what I did was fake like I was going to the bathroom and as I walked by her I said, "Excuse me miss, my watch seems to have stopped, do you have the exact time?"

"Yes, it's 1:46 p.m.." The white waitress said.

"Ok, thank you very much."

As she walked away to attend to other customers, I slipped past the bathroom and out the door. I jumped into my van and headed to Delaware Avenue, which wasn't even three minutes away from the restaurant. As I pulled up on the opposite side of the street, I could see that Fat Mike was just about to set up shot. I figured that he'd hurry up and make a quick ten thousand on the 2:00 o'clock rush, then head down to the courthouse and catch diarrhea of the mouth by crossing a nigga who had been good to him.

I drove my van around the corner and parked by the dumpster on the side of the building. I popped my hydraulic stash, got my 16 shot .45 automatic and the new blue zip up jumper with the Pepco Gas Company logo on it along with a blue hat with the same logo on it, which I had brought the day before at the Sunny Surplus Uniform Supply Store. Then I grabbed my black notebook, which was stuffed with about 150 sheets of blank paper. I pulled the hat down tight, looked in the mirror on my sun visor and checked out my disguise. I wasn't satisfied with what I saw, so I reached in the back seat of the van and grabbed a pillow that I had left in there the day before when I was scooping the scene. I undid my belt and tied the pillow around my stomach then zipped up my jumper and looked in the mirror again. I was now satisfied with my disguise, I looked like a little chubby Pepco gas meter inspector.

As I got out of the van, I looked around to make sure no one saw me then I proceeded around the corner to where Fat Mike was telling everybody what positions to play. There were three fiends and two other younger dudes with him, damn, the day before there were only three fiends and one youngin. Shit, I couldn't turn back now because Bilal's hearing was less than an hour from now, so I walked up to the first meter with my notebook and began to fake like I was jotting down some notes.

One of Fat Mike's youngins came over and said, "Slim, what'cha doing around here?"

"Oh, excuse me young man, I work for the Gas Company." I said, with an experienced look as if this had been my job for years.

Fat Mike then came over and said, "Who that Lump?"

"It ain't nobody but the Pepco man fucking with the meters."

"Hey Pepco man, I sure hope you can fix that shit cause my people's gas is fucked up, one day it's working, the next day it's not." Fat Mike said.

"Yeah, I know what you're saying, it's a little messed up but it ain't nothin' I can't fix. Hey, there's usually another meter around here and from looking at this one, I can tell this isn't the main meter. If I can find the other one and fix that first, then it won't be a problem getting this old raggedy thing back to normal. Do you know where it's at?"

Fat Mike fell right into my trap. "Yeah, it's right around the corner, c'mon I'll show you. Lump, watch that shit I'll be right back and tell everybody to get ready because it's almost 2:00 o'clock."

"Ok Mike."

"C'mon Pepco man, hurry up so I can show you this shit, I've got something to do within the next hour."

"Ok, thanks my man."

As Fat Mike led me around the corner, I looked around and peeped the surroundings to see if anyone was in sight and I saw no one. So far, my plan was working perfect, I wasn't anxious, nervous or scared, just calm, cool and collective. Just like with my last two victims, I felt like what I was doing was justified, I was about to give it to a nigga who truly deserved it.

As Fat Mike walked closer to the meter, I pulled out my .45 automatic and when he turned around my .45 was stuck right between his eyes and before he could say anything, let alone blink, I pulled the trigger two times, "boom, boom" and Fat Mike's body hit the ground with force. I then took out my handkerchief, wiped the gun off and threw it down next to his body.

As I was walking away, I looked around to make sure no one saw me. My van was parked along side the trash dumpster. I took off my disguise and threw it in the dumpster, got in my van, put the pillow in the back seat and fixed my clothes. I didn't stay to see if Fat Mike was dead because I already knew he was.

As I drove back to the restaurant, all I was thinking about was my man Bilal because his hearing was at 2:45, and if everything went well, he should be a free man today and from that point on nobody was gonna be able to stop us.

When I got back to the restaurant, I didn't go straight in, I peeked through the window to make sure Sonya was still there, yeah she was still there looking lovely as ever. I hope she wasn't mad cause I had taken so long, but I was only gone for fifteen minutes. When I walked back into the restaurant, I saw the same white waitress and again she was smiling at me.

She came over to me and said, "My God, you've been in the bathroom all that time, are you ok? Was there something wrong with the food?"

"Something got caught down my throat, I'll be fine thank you. Oh by the way, what's your name?" I said.

"Kathy and yours?"

"Jovan."

"Alright then Jovan, I hope the next time I see you you're by yourself and not with a nice looking lady friend."

"Who knows, I may come back tomorrow all by myself." Then I gave her a wink and left.

As I was walking up to Sonya on the patio, I pulled out my cellular phone and acted like I was talking to somebody. I said to the dial tone, "Ok then Mark, I pray everything goes well, you're the best lawyer I know." I then pretended to end my conversation and hung up my phone. I then turned to Sonya and said, "Sorry sweetie that I took so long."

"Jovan it's ok, you've only been gone 14 ? minutes." Sonya said, smiling.

"Damn sweetheart, were you timing me?"

"No baby, while you were gone I was sitting here thinking about how wonderful a person you are and that I have never met a man like yourself."

"Is there something wrong with me?"

"Oh no Jovan, not at all, you're just different from any other man I've met."

I started laughing, but inside I was shaking my head saying to myself, "baby, you just don't know that I just finished blowing a nigga's brains out 15 minutes ago".

Sonya
Finally Jovan came back, and as he was walking towards the table, I could see he was on his cellular phone still in conference with his boss. Jovan was one cool ass nigga and the whole time he was gone, I was thinking about him. A sista like me could use to having a brotha like Jovan in her life. For one, he wasn't thugged out but he was aggressive. Two, he was handsome as hell and three, from the way he walked, it looked like he was packing, and boy did a sista need that. He's also got a good legitimate job and trying to go back to school to further his education, what more could a woman ask for. I hope he doesn't have anybody else, because I'd be one mad bitch if he told me he's got a girlfriend.

"Well Jovan, the attorney..."

"C'mon Sonya, I told you I'm not an attorney yet." Jovan said, cutting me off.

"But you will be soon." I said.

"How you know that?"

"Cause I can the see ambition in you Jovan."

"So you're saying you can tell the future?"

"Maybe." I said, smiling and Jovan smiled also.

"So, tell me this Ms. Psychic."

"Tell you what Jovan?"

"Where is this little lunch date gonna take us?"

I gave him a smile and a sneaky grin and said, "That's for me to know and you to find out."

"How am I supposed to find out?"

I took out a piece of paper and scribbled my home and work number on it and passed it to Jovan.

"Here's my numbers Jovan, it's up to you to use them because that's the only way you'll find out." I said, handing him the piece of paper.

"Don't be so mean sweetheart." Jovan said, jokingly.

"I'm not being mean Jovan, I'm just being a strong black woman. By the way, I hope you don't have a girlfriend or anything else that may get in the way of us getting to know each other better." I said, seriously.

Jovan laughed and said, "If that's your way of asking if I've got a girlfriend or any kinda baby momma drama, then my answer is no sweetheart but it would be nice to have someone compatible to my wants and needs."

I liked the way Jovan put that, he had a smooth way of getting his point across.

"So Jovan, it's almost 2:45 and we've been here all day talking."

"So you're just gonna leave me here?" He asked, with a devilish grin.

"No, not at all baby." I said.

"I was just playing Sonya, I know you probably have something to do and I have to be at the courthouse by 3:00 o'clock to meet my boss. So what time should I call you?"

"Call me whenever you think about me."

"Ok, then by the time you get home you should have about 50 messages from me." We both laughed.

"Jovan, you have such a good sense of humor, it was so nice meeting you." I said, sincerely.

"It was nice meeting you too Sonya, you just don't know how much you made my day." Jovan said, meaning every word of it. "C'mon let me walk you to your car."

CHAPTER 16

"Untouchable"

When Jovan got to the courthouse, it was 3:00 o'clock on the dot. He rushed into the building, got on the elevator and was headed to the 2nd floor where Bilal's hearing was being held. As he was getting off the elevator, he assumed that the hearing was already over and that his plan must have worked because Mark, Bilal and a female, that looked like she came straight out of a magazine, were walking out of the courtroom headed his way and they all had big ass smiles on their faces. The female looked like a Hawaiian or something, and she and Bilal were hugging so hard that it was obvious that this was his girlfriend. Damn, Bilal had a nice bankroll and a fine ass bitch to go along with it.

"Hey, there's my assistant. Bilal, you remember Mr. Price don't you?" Mark asked Bilal, once they reached me.

"Yeah Mark I remember him, he's the one who worked so hard on this case. How you doing Mr. Price?" Bilal asked, pretending like he didn't know me.

"Fine Mr. Davis, glad to see that everything worked out for you." Jovan said.

"Yeah, the Government was trying to put shit in the game, but Mark batted that shit down."

"So Mark, what did you do this time?" Jovan said, acting as if he didn't know what was goin' on.

"Well Jovan, I just went in there and showed my ass. I think the Judge is pissed at me."

"Why's that?"

"Cause the Government kept talking about they had a witness, but he never showed up so I got up and asked, 'Where's the ghost?'."

"He got mad at that?"

"No, I think he got pissed because the whole courtroom was laughing." Mark said, laughing himself.

Bilal said, "Yeah Mark, you did your thing like a real pro."

Little did Bilal know Mark didn't do a fucking thing, the reason why he was standing here was because of Jovan's work and he planned to tell him that later on.

"Mr. Price, let me introduce you to my fiancé Meeka."

"Hello Meeka, nice to meet you." Damn, she was a pretty ass bitch Jovan said to myself.

"You too Mr. Price." Meeka said, with a slight grin.

Meeka looked at Jovan as if she already knew him or heard about him from Bilal. Jovan hoped Bilal wasn't putting this broad down about him, cause he didn't want nobody to know Bilal and his business but Bilal and him.

As they continued to walk down the hallway, a little white man with some tight jeans and a Penn State sweatshirt came over to us.

"Bilal Davis, you think you got away but let me tell you something man, I'ma be on your ass day in and day out and the next time I get your ass, I'ma make sure I catch you good." The man said.

"Yeah, well thank you Detective, but let me inform you

about something, investigating me won't do nothin' but waste your time."

"We'll see." The Detective said, walking away.

Damn, he sounded pissed.

"Who was that Mark?" Jovan said, with an inquisitive look.

"Oh, he was the Detective who wrote up the bogus warrant to go into Mr. Davis' house." Mark said.

"Well Mr. Davis, it looks like you gotta keep your nose clean." Jovan said.

"Huh? My nose is clean Mr. Price, always was and always will be." Bilal said.

"Jovan, you coming by the office or what?" Mark asked.

"No Mark, I think I'ma head on home and get me some sleep."

"Ok, see you later."

"A'ight Mark, you too Mr. Davis and congratulations on your freedom."

"Thank you Mark, thanks for everything. I'll have somebody drop the rest of that off to you tomorrow." Bilal said, as he eagerly wanted Mark to hurry up and leave.

"Sounds good to me Mr. Davis."

With that, they all got on the elevator and headed out front of the courthouse to where their cars were parked.

"Bye, see ya'll later." Mark said, as he headed off to his car first.

As soon as Mark got in his car and left, Bilal jumped out of nowhere and said, "What's up my nigga!" He then gave Jovan such a tight bear hug that he almost lost his breath. "Meeka, this here is my best friend Jovan I've been telling you about."

"I kinda figured that Boo. So Jovan, I heard a lot about you. You know Bilal loves you like a brother, I can never get him to stop talking about you." Said Meeka, while she looked at Jovan as if she knew things about him that she shouldn't.

"Yeah, well I hope it was all good stuff."

"Believe me Jovan it was."

Damn, Jovan wondered if Bilal had told this broad everything. Naw, Bilal's too sharp for that, he's a real nigga, Jovan knew that he kept his females out of his business, he probably just talked about some childhood shit to her, that's about it.

"Look, come on with me, we got a lot to talk about." Bilal said.

"Bilal, I thought you and me were gonna be alone tonight." Meeka said, whining.

"Meeka, this is my family, my only family and he's coming with me whether you like it or not."

Meeka was so mad Jovan could sense the jealously as she stormed off to get into Bilal's silver 850 BMW.

"Look Lal, go head home with your woman, we can talk tomorrow. Go get some pussy nigga." Jovan told Bilal.

"Man fuck that, I got all year to fuck, plus I'm getting tired of her ass anyway."

"Bilal, that's a bad piece you got, you'd be a fool to let her go."

"She's a'ight but I've had bitches who looked way better than her. The only thing about it is she's real and she's the only one who pulled through and stayed down with the ole boy when I got that 30 years, so I owe her."

"I can respect that, a nigga always need a soldier in his corner."

"What you driving Jovan?"

"I still got the MPV I had back in '91."

"Damn, you still pushing that bullshit?" Bilal asked, amazed.

"Yeah, but the real reason I've still got it is because it has a hydraulic stash that can hold 8 bricks." Jovan told Bilal.

"Yeah, you better keep that joint it might come in handy. Look, go get your van and follow me out to my house so we can talk. Oh Jovan, how's my baby Grandma Price doing?" Bilal asked.

"She's a'ight but her legs fucking with her though. You know she got arthritis." Jovan said, sadly.

"We're gonna have to get her to one of those expensive hospitals so she can get rid of that." Bilal said, as if it would make me feel better.

"Yeah Lal, I feel you."

Jovan followed Bilal and Meeka to their house, which was about a 45-minute drive out to Potomac, Maryland. This spot doesn't have nothin' for under 600 thousand, all types of celebrities live out here; Sugar Ray Leonard, Chris Webber, Jawauhn Howard, Pebo Bryson, Johnny Gill and a few other no names with a rack of bread.

As Bilal and Meeka pulled up into their driveway, Jovan couldn't believe that this was their house. The last time Jovan saw a house this big is when they interviewed "Puffy", the owner of Bad Boy Records, in his home on MTV. Now he was witnessing all the lavish jailhouse stories he had heard about his best friend while in Lewisburg.

In the front driveway, there was a black range rover, a green

Lexus Coupe, a white 600SL and in his garage there was a blue Mercedes V12 600S Coupe, the new joint, plus the silver 850 BMW they were in. Here Jovan was stuck with this fucking 2? year old van, but from what he did earlier, this van comes in handy. When Bilal and Meeka got out the 850, he told her to go in the house.

The first thing Jovan said was, "Nigga, I see why you got locked up, what the fuck you doing with all this shit layin' on your lawn?"

"Oh Jay, this ain't nothin', the Lex and SL is Meeka's, the rest of that shit is my toys."

"Your toys?" Jovan said.

"Yeah nigga, my toys. In case you haven't heard Jay, I got the city locked, 1994 is my year, better yet, our year cause whatever I got you got." Bilal said, as he looked at me with all sincerity. This was the same look he gave Jovan nine years ago when he first talked about makin' this dream come true.

"Damn, it feels good to be a part of some real cash. But for real, whatever position I play it's got to be low key cause I ain't going back to jail." Jovan said, as he admired his best friend's lavish lifestyle.

Bilal showed Jovan around the house, he started with the living room, then he took him see to all seven bedrooms, the kitchen and then downstairs where he had a miniature movie theater, pool tables and all. This nigga had Versace curtains, bedspreads and paintings he even had Versace dishes lying in the china closet.

"Damn Lal, I see you went Versace crazy, I thought I loved the shit, but after seeing all this you must own the store." Jovan said, laughing.

"Naw Jay, Meeka did all this crazy ass shit. When we moved in I gave her a mil to play with and the bitch went crazy." Bilal said, laughing also.

"How long you've been fucking with her Lal?"

"Shit, ever since I came home off the juvenile life bit."

When Bilal mentioned the juvenile life, Jovan felt a little fucked up. He had never thanked Bilal personally, but he knew where his heart was at and he must have sensed it also.

"Hey Jovan, c'mon out back on the court, we need to sit down and talk. Meeka." Bilal called.

"Yes sir master?" Meeka said, sarcastically.

"Cut that shit out girl."

"Ok, what's up baby?"

"Get us a bottle of Crista, will you baby?"

"Like I said at first, yes sir master." She said, as she stomped off.

"Damn Bilal, why she acting like that?" Jovan asked him.

"You know how they get, shit Jay the bitch ain't had no dick in almost eight months."

"Well, from the way she's acting, I think you need to hurry up and give her some."

"I'll deal with her later slim, right now I'm wit my man."

When Bilal and Jovan went outside to talk, Jovan saw that he had a full court basketball out back, weights and a pool with a Jacuzzi.

"Hey Lal, how much you pay for this house?" Jovan asked him.

"With all the accessories, about a cool 4 mil."

At that, Jovan started counting Bilal's bank in his head. He had lost 3.5 mil in the raid and he told him he still had 3.5 mil plus 4 mil for the house, and at least 1 mil for the cars, and Jovan hadn't seen his jewelry but he guessed that may be worth about a mil or half at least, Bilal had to have had at least 13 million at one time. Damn, this nigga really was the king of DC.

"Damn Bilal, I see you spend a lot of money."

"What's the use of having it Jay if you can't spend it?"

"You got that right slim, but you know you gotta find a way to wash that shit."

"We'll worry 'bout that when we get there, right now I'm broke."

"Broke! How the fuck you broke and you still got 3.5 mil?"

"Jay, half that shit isn't mine, half of it belongs to Carlos."

"Yeah, I heard about Carlos, give me the reading on him." Jovan said, wondering what Carlos was really like and how did Bilal get hooked up with him.

"Well, Carlos and me were down Oak Hill Youth Center together. Carlos ain't no sucker but you know he's Spanish and niggas used to try him all the time, so I taught Carlos how to box and after that we became cool."

"Yeah, I heard you were down there on the boxing team knocking niggas out."

"Yeah, I was like that at one time but a nigga a lil rusty right now, but believe me I still know where my ass at."

"Finish telling me 'bout Carlos."

"Well, Los and me became real close."

"Like you and me?" Jovan said, knowing deep down inside that no one could ever take his place, but he just wanted to hear it come outta Bilal's mouth though.

"Naw Jay, there will never be another you. Anyway, some

uptown niggas put a vicious press game on Los cause they knew he was getting some money and Los wasn't going for it but he was outnumbered. One day they came in his room, about six of 'em, pulled knives on him and they had him too, they were 'bout to burn his ass up. I peeped the move and busted in the room before they could do anything and knocked three of 'em the fuck out. When I did that, the other three flunky ass niggas ran. I hear these same niggas down Lorton right now getting fucked."

"For real Lal?" Jovan asked him.

"Well not all of 'em, just two of 'em. Two are behind the wall going hard and the other two got killed when they came home."

"Damn." Jovan said, as he thought about Bilal and how hard it was for him growing up in the system.

"Well ever since that day, Carlos vowed to me that he'd never forget that and that whenever I came home he had a spot for me on his team. So when I came home, he gave me two bricks for twenty-five thousand and I have never looked back. Jay, Carlos is a good dude, I want you to meet him." Bilal said, as he looked Jovan in the eyes.

"Naw, that's a'ight Lal, I ain't really trying to meet too many new niggas." Jovan said.

"He ain't just no new nigga Jay, he's my partner, our partner." Bilal said.

Jovan could tell that from the way Bilal was looking, he was beyond serious.

"In that case, I guess I do have to meet him. Look Bilal, I gotta tell you something. I never could find the dude Lil G, I searched everywhere for him, come to find out he got locked up out in Maryland for three bodies." Jovan told Bilal.

"Yeah, so who you get to lay the demonstration down?" Bilal said, curious as to why Fat Mike never made it to court.

At that moment Jovan looked Bilal straight in the eyes and said, "I did it."

Bilal laughed and said, "Get the fuck outta here!"

"Yeah Slim, I gave it to him good like the bitch nigga he is, or better yet, was."

"How you do it Jay?"

"Man, I had the perfect plan. I laid on this nigga, peeped his every move, then went to Sunny Surplus and brought a gas uniform."

"What!" Bilal said, looking surprised.

"Yeah nigga, I was disguised as a gas meter inspector." Jovan said, smiling.

"Get the fuck outta here Jay!"

"Man listen Lal, I laid this shit out so tight, covered all my tracks and then went about my daily routine."

Bilal was shocked at how Jovan put his murder game down.

"Jovan, how the fuck you think about being a gas meter inspector?"

"Lal, I'm a paralegal and if I'ma commit a crime, I've got to know how to get away with it, and guess what Bilal, you ain't gonna believe this shit."

"What Jay?" Bilal said, looking at Jovan as if he wasn't telling the truth.

"It's hard for me to believe this, but I did all this while taking a broad to lunch at Phillips Restaurant." Jovan said, smiling as he thought back to his lunch date with Sonya.

"Hell nigga, you ain't that tight, you've been in jail reading too many Donald Goines books!" Bilal said, laughing.

"C'mon Bilal, how the fuck a Donald Goines book gonna teach a nigga how to contemplate a murder like that?" Jovan asked Bilal.

"Yeah you right, but damn Jay, this shit is unbelievable. What broad did you take down to Phillips today?" Bilal asked, amazed.

"I met this bad ass broad in the courthouse this morning. We went to lunch and I kicked it with her for a while. She's got a good head on her shoulders, she's an Assistant Producer at BET and bad as fuck Slim. Man, this the baddest broad I've seen in years."

"How you get away from her to go lay your demonstration down?" Bilal asked, still finding Jovan's story hard to believe.

"I faked like I had a conference call from Mark."

"Damn nigga, I ain't never heard no story like that, you tight as shit Jay. Outta all the killers I know in the city, I ain't never heard a nigga put it down like that, that's some professional Mafia type shit. Damn, now you've got two bodies under your belt."

"Naw Lal, now it's three bodies." Jovan said.

"What!" Lal yelled, as his eyes opened wider.

"Yeah, I had to punish a New York nigga while I was up Lewisburg." Jovan said.

"You killed a nigga in jail and got away with it?" Bilal asked, totally shocked by this new admission.

"Yeah Lal, I had to."

"Ok Jay, let me hear it, I'm dying for this one." He said, with a smirk on his face.

Jovan told Bilal every detail of how he killed Shorty and Bilal was in such a state of shock that he didn't believe Jovan.

"So you on some old James Bond shit huh?"

"Naw Slim, I just learned my lesson nine years ago, if you gonna kill a nigga make sure you do it right so no one but the nigga you kill suffers."

Bilal put his head down and said, "Jay, what you did nine years ago was outta love nigga."

"What I did a couple of hours ago was still outta love and there's one thing I wanna say to you that I wasn't able to say in nine years." Jovan said, as he held his head down not wanting Bilal to see his eyes water.

"What's that?" Bilal asked.

"I'm sorry for not telling you I was strapped and I thank you from the bottom of my heart for taking the beef."

"Jay, you ain't gotta thank me for that shit, back then was outta love and until the day my casket drops, everything I do for you is outta love."

Bilal and Jovan gave each other a strong hug just like they did nine years ago.

"Look Jay, what'cha gonna do, you gonna get this money with me or what?"

"Man for real, you know I ain't too good at hustling, every time I hustle and get a few dollars, something always go wrong." Jovan said, thinking back.

Jovan told Bilal 'bout his fifty thousand getting stolen back in '88 and he told him about his New York connect and how shit went wrong.

"Face it Jay, the hustling thing ain't me, plus I'm tryin' to go to Law School and get my License so I can represent niggas like you and get a free two hundred fifty thousand for doing nothin'." Jovan said, laughing.

"Yeah right, I forgot you're supposed to be some lawyer. Damn, picture that a "Lawyer-Killer". Jay, you a ma'fucka, you're the tightest nigga I know."

"Go head with that shit Lal."

"Naw Jay, I'm serious, this is the move and you've got to be a part of this team. I do all the hustling and you do the killing, the same position we played nine years ago. You can still do the lawyer thing, I like that shit, but when it's time to lay a demonstration down, I'ma need you." Bilal said, seriously. "Jay, you know I ain't never killed nobody, I ain't saying I won't but from hearing your stories, I don't think I'm that smart to be pulling moves like that. Plus, Lil G is locked up and even if he was still home, I wouldn't fuck with him on that tip no more cause he ain't shit compared to you."

"Yeah Lal, I'm flattered, haha, but for real I ain't trying to be no killer for hire. You ain't gotta pay me to put in no work, if a nigga fuckin' with you and I see that I can help then I'm there Slim. I owe you, you're my best friend but one thing Lal."

"What's that Jay?"

"Man, you know we can't be hangin' together in the streets, the Feds is gonna be watching you now especially the one that was in the courthouse today."

"Yeah, he's a piece of shit, Detective Tony Bridges, that white ma'fucka wants me bad."

"You've got to do your thing on the low Lal."

"Yeah, I understand Jay. Hey c'mon in the house, I've got something for you."

Bilal went downstairs for a minute and came back with a gym bag.

"Here nigga." He said, as he threw the bag at Jovan.

"What's this?" Jovan asked Bilal.

"Open it." He said.

When Jovan opened the bag all he saw was stacks of money.

"How much money is this Lal?" Jovan said, his eyes damn near popping outta his head at the sight of all this money.

"That's only two hundred and fifty thousand. I really can't hit you off like I want to yet, you know Los and me only got 3.5 mil and our connect won't sell us nothing under 200 bricks."

"Damn Slim, what the fuck was Los doing while you were in?"

"He held shit down, got rid of the remaining shit and laid low for a minute. The fact that I was locked up had niggas trying him and we got one nigga now I'ma have to go see tomorrow. I gave this nigga 30 bricks before I got locked up, and when Carlos went to holla at him about the money, he started acting shady talking 'bout he only dealt with me."

"Yeah, you've got to get that up off him, 30 bricks is a lot of money." Jovan said, instantly calculating the price in his head.

"Yeah, I'ma see Slim first thing in the morning. Jay, where you staying at?" Bilal asked Jovan.

"I'm chilling with Grandma for a minute."

"Man, I wanted to get Grandma Price a house so bad but I didn't know how to ask."

"I'm glad you didn't ask because she probably woulda cursed you out, you know she's been living there ever since my Pops was born and she ain't going nowhere." Jovan said, laughing.

"Yeah Jay, what's up with your Pops anyway?" Bilal asked.

"I dunno, I ain't seen him and I'm not trying to either."

CHAPTER 17

"Sky's The Limit"

Jovan went back home to his Grandma's house and kicked it with her for a while. He wondered what Grandma would say if he asked her if she wanted a new house. Since she was in a good mood he figured now would be the proper time.

"Hey Grandma." Jovan said.

"Yes baby?" She said.

"What would you say if I told you I wanted to buy you a new house?"

"Well baby, first thing I'd tell you is that you must be crazy and that I've been living in this house for almost 45 years, this house is sentimental and it is the landmark for our family. This is home Jovan, always was and always will be. Second, I'd tell you to keep your money and put it to good use to buy some business or something and after that, if you have some money left over, then you could give me some so I can fix up this raggedy ass house that we call home." Grandma said.

At that, Grandma and Jovan both laughed so hard. It was cool chilling with his Grandma because after all the shit he'd been through today, she sure knew how to make a nigga feel good.

"Hey Grandma, it's getting late and I'm a little tired plus I gotta go to work tomorrow, I'm going up to bed now."

"Ok baby, you want me to wake you up in the morning."

"Naw Grandma, my alarm is already set."

"Ok. Oh Jovan, your daddy called today, he asked about you and told me to tell you he loves you."

"Ok Grandma, next time he calls tell him I said what's up."

"Ok baby."

"Oh Grandma." Jovan said, before going upstairs to bed.

"Yes baby."

"I love you baby girl, you know you my world!" Jovan said, kissing her on the cheek.

"Boy, take your silly butt upstairs and go to bed." Grandma said, hugging Jovan.

Grandma loved whenever Jovan expressed his love for her because it always made her day. He went upstairs to his bedroom, sat and thought for a moment about his life and what he just committed himself to do. Damn, Bilal had pulled him right back into the streets, right back into the game. Well not really Bilal, but standing on his principles of his loyalty to Bilal had pulled him back. Plus he still felt responsible for Mal-Mal's death, which in turn made him feel obligated to his best friend, and besides, there's a whole lotta bank involved.

Jovan opened up the gym bag full of the money Bilal had given him, this was the most money he'd ever had at one time, two hundred fifty thousand. The sight of it made his dick hard, but this ain't shit compared to what Bilal's got, even in his broke stage this nigga was still rich. Before Jovan went to bed, he checked all his pants pockets to make sure he didn't have anything in them before he sending them to the cleaners tomorrow.

He reached in his right pocket and pulled out a piece of paper with Sonya's work and home number on it, placed it on his dresser and laid back on his bed and began to think about her. Damn, she was pretty, he wondered if their friendship would blossom into something special. He wondered if she liked him or not, he looked good and dressed well, he had a job and now he was two hundred and fifty thousand dollars richer. What the fuck did he have to do to get this broad? He fell asleep thinking about Sonya.

Sonya

Damn it was 10:00 pm and I still hadn't gotten a call from Jovan. I wondered if he liked me because most niggas I met and gave my number to called me at least an hour later. I hope I wasn't too much for him today at lunch. I had told him about my past, well not everything, but I'm sure our conversation went well. I wonder if I had said anything wrong or maybe he didn't like the way I looked. Why hasn't this man called me yet I thought as I laid back on my bed thinking about Jovan. How was I going to get to this man? Face it, he must not want me cause if he did, then he would have given me his number.

Ring, Ring, Ring. Damn that must be him. "Hello!" I said into the phone, praying it was Jovan.

"Damn girl, you answered the phone like you just won the lottery."

"Oh hi Germain, I thought you was somebody else." I said, disappointed that it wasn't him.

"Somebody else, girl whose gonna be calling you at 10:00 o'clock at night, ain't like you gotta man or nothing." Germain said, laughing.

"Fuck you Germain and why are you calling me this time of night anyway, you couldn't wait to see me at work tomorrow?" I asked her.

"Girl, my husband and I had an argument tonight and his stupid ass stormed outta the house like a fucking kid."

"So what am I supposed to be some marriage counselor or something?" I asked Germain.

"Shut up silly, just talk to me until he gets back."

"Look Germain, I'm not gonna be on this phone all night long but I'll talk to you for awhile, you know you my girl.'

"Good, so what's up and why weren't you at work today?" Germain said, prying.

"Now you wanna be my mama. Well if you must know, I had an appointment at the courthouse today."

"What did you have an appointment at the courthouse for?"

"None of your business nosy."

"Ok, go ahead with you lil secretive self."

"Anyway, while I was at the courthouse, I meet this fine ass brotha."

"What, you finally gave somebody the time of the day."

"Yeah girl and we went to lunch together and had a nice time." I said, smiling remembering our lunch date.

"What's his name? Who the hell is this mystery man?"

"His name is Jovan."

"Jovan?"

"Yeah girl, he's tall, light brown, with dark wavy hair, physically fit, he dresses nice and guess what girl?"

"What?"

"He's got a job."

"Stop lying!" Germain yelled.

"Yeah and he's got a good job too."

"What does he do?"

"He's a paralegal and he works at this big law firm. He's gonna go back to Law School and finish up so he can become a lawyer and get his own office." I said, proudly.

"Damn girl, how old is he?"

"He's 24 and will soon be 25."

"So you got yourself a youngin?" Germain said, laughing.

"No girl, I only got him by less than 2 years."

"Damn Sonya, 24 with a job like that, that's wonderful. So did he call you yet?" Germain asked.

"No, actually when you called I thought it was him."

"Hold on Sonya, my stupid ass husband just walked in the door. Where the hell you been?" Germain asked her husband.

"None of your fuckin' business!" Kevin, Germain's husband, said.

"What? Sonya, let me get off this phone before we get to fighting up in here, I'll see you tomorrow at work."

"Germain, you need to stop acting like you a nun and give that man some pussy." I said, laughing.

"Mind your business, this is a married life and when you get married then you can say something, until then keep your damn mouth shut." Germain said.

"Girl you so silly, I'll see you at work tomorrow."

"Ok, bye bye Sonya."

"Bye Germain."

Jovan

When I woke up Grandma was already downstairs cooking breakfast. She had made egg and cheese omelets, toast, grits and hash browns.

"Jovan." Grandma called from downstairs.

"Yeah Grandma." I answered, sitting on the side of my bed.

"You up boy."

"Yeah Grandma I'm up."

"Come on down here and get this breakfast."

I went in the bathroom, got myself together and went downstairs.

"Good morning baby girl, what'cha cook for the ole boy." I said, giving Grandma a kiss on the cheek.

"Sit down and eat your food with your silly self, you act just like your damn daddy."

Grandma loved it when I joked with her. I just wished she would stop throwing my Pops all up in my face but I know why she does it, Grandma misses him and the fact that I resemble him so much makes her happy and sad at the same time.

"Grandma." I said.

"Yeah baby."

"Remember last night when we talked about a new house."

"Yeah and I told you no."

"Well look, I've got a few dollars tucked away so you can go ahead and fix up the house." I told her.

"Oh no baby, keep your money, you need it for Law School."

"Grandma believe me, I've got enough money for school."

"Well then, why aren't you in school yet?" Grandma asked me.

"Cause."

"Cause what?"

"Cause right now I like my job and I'm learning more working with Mark then I would if I was in school, and when I get it all down pack I'ma go to school and come out two steps ahead of everybody in my class."

"Well it sounds good but keep your money baby."

"Grandma, you must not have heard me, I've already got enough money for both of us."

"Ok baby, but it may cost a lot to get the basement redone and my ceiling fixed." Grandma said, still not sure I would be able to afford to pay for school and get her house fixed.

"Whatever it cost you got it, just call the people today and get an estimate and let me know." It felt good to be able to give Grandma some money.

"Ok baby."

I went back upstairs to get myself ready for work. Today was nice, not too hot or too breezy, it felt good. I went into the closet, pulled out some cream Armani slacks I had never worn. I then grabbed a cream Armani mock neck t-shirt, I had brought it one size bigger so it wouldn't be fitting all tight like them gay ma'fuckas be wearing their shit. I also grabbed a pair of light tan soft bottom Ceasar Picotti slip-ons with a matching belt.

I took myself a good long shower, brushed my hair to let the waves pop out, put on some Giorgio Armani cologne and got dressed. I reached on my dresser to put on one of my watches, I had three, a Movado, an 18k white gold Cartier and a Rolex. I chose the Cartier and I also put on my 18k white gold bracelet. As I was reaching for the bracelet I saw Sonya's number, I put it in my pocket, went downstairs and kissed Grandma then headed for the office.

I got to the office at least 10 minutes early. As soon as I came through the door, I saw Cindy in a tight ass plaid skirt looking phat as hell.

"Hey Cindy." I said.

"Morning Jovan, you look nice today."

"Thank you Cindy, you look nice yourself."

Lately Cindy had been complimenting me on my style, I think she wanted a nigga to put some dick in her. I didn't fuck with white girls but if she offered me the pussy, I wouldn't turn it down.

"Hey Cindy, is Mark here yet?"

"No he hasn't gotten here yet. You know he might be late being as though he doesn't have to go to court today. Hold on Jovan, speak of the devil here he comes now." Cindy said, as Mark came through the door. "Morning Mark." She said to him.

"Morning Cindy. Look Jovan, we don't have much to do today but knock off a few briefs, most likely we'll be done around 11:30 or 12:00, after that you can take the day off." Mark told me.

Yes, I loved my job, work for half a day and still get paid for a full day.

"Cool Mark, just tell me what you need."

"Well, I need two motions drawn up, one for faulty and deficient indictment. This kid got convicted for a gun that wasn't even in his indictment."

"Ok, that should be easy."

"The other is for a Brady material violation. The Government didn't give the defense the fingerprint lab's report on the gun before trial started."

"All this is on the same case?" I asked Mark.

"Yeah."

"Oh that's light, I should be finished in about an hour or so."

"I already know that, that's why I told you you could take a half a day." Mark said, sarcastically.

"So you're telling me you know my work like that."

"Don't flatter yourself Jovan, you're good but you're not a lawyer yet."

Mark was always letting me know when I was advancing and you could tell he was proud of me. Almost every motion that's filed and come out of this office has my name on it right under Mark's, it reads: On the brief for Appellate, Attorney Mark Rohon and Paralegal Specialist Jovan Price of Rohon's & Robinson Law Firm. Mark's partner, Michelle, already told me how Mark be down at the courthouse braggin' on me, telling other lawyers that I'll be taking their business soon.

After I finished the briefs, which took me way more than an hour, more like two and a half hours, I took them straight to Mark for him to go over them.

"Here you go Mark." I said, handing him the motions.

"So you finally finished huh?"

"Yeah, it took me a minute to put up a good argument for the Brady violation."

"Sit down Jovan, let's go over them right now."

Mark read my motions then placed them on the desk, leaned back in his chair and crossed his legs. He was silent for a moment.

"What's wrong Mark, you don't like the briefs?"

Mark then pulled his chair to his desk and looked me straight in the eyes and said, "No, I don't like the briefs Jovan I love 'em. Look I'ma give it to you raw, most of the work you do for me is better than some lawyers who've been practicing 20 years. Jovan, you gotta get into Law School and finish up so you can take your bar exam, there's a lot of money out here waitin' for you. You'll be the perfect lawyer, you're young, smooth and plus you know some of these fools who keep going to jail. Face it, you'd be the perfect attorney, shit if I got into some trouble I'd hire you."

"Why thank you Mark. So if I pass the bar exam does that mean I can get a partnership in the firm."

"Don't flatter yourself buddy, a partnership is out of the question, but you better bet there will be an office here waiting for you."

Damn, Mark sure knew how to make a nigga feel good. I wondered what Bilal was doing. I went into Michelle's office to use her phone to call him while she was in court.

Ring, Ring, Ring. "Hello." Bilal said, as he picked up the phone like he was anxiously waiting for a call.

"Damn nigga, you answering the phone on the first ring like you were waiting for my call." I said.

"What's up Jay, I thought you was this nigga that owes me that bank. I've been paging his ass all fucking morning." Bilal said.

"He ain't called back yet?"

"Fuck no, I hope this nigga ain't playin no games. Where you at anyway Jay?"

"I'm at work."

Bilal instantly burst into laughter at the thought of his best friend really taking this lawyer shit seriously.

"What you laughing for Lal?" I asked, knowing he was indirectly teasing me.

"Cause man, I can't believe this shit." Bilal said, still laughing.

"Believe what shit."

"You being a lawyer man. For real Jay, I'm just fuckin' with you. Look I gotta go meet Carlos up on Kennedy Street. Call me back later on so we can go out or something."

"Look Lal, I told you we can't be doin' it like that."

"I know Jay, but I'ma bring Carlos so you can meet him."

"Ok then Lal."

I hung up the phone, sat back and imagined what this nigga Los was like. I wondered if Bilal would tell him about all the work I put in. Even though he and Bilal were cool and shit, I still didn't want no one but Bilal to know my work. You gotta keep that shit quiet to the fullest degree cause that's how niggas be getting locked up, braggin' about the shit they did and I refused to go back to jail.

It was almost 11:30 a.m. and I had the rest of the day off. As I was wondering what I should do, I reached in my pocket and looked at Sonya's number, I hesitated for a second then said what the fuck and I dialed Sonya's work number.

Ring, Ring, Ring. "BET Studios, may I help you." A female voice said.

Damn, I had forgotten Sonya's last name.

"Uh excuse me." I said, stuttering.

"Hello." The female voice on the other end said again.

"Yes, may I speak with Sonya?"

"Sonya who sir?"

"Sorry I don't know her last name, but I..." I started to say, but the voice on the other end cut me off.

"Jovan, is that you." Sonya said.

"Yeah who's this, Sonya?" I said.

"Yeah crazy, it's me. You call my job and you don't remember my last name." Sonya said, laughing.

"I'm sorry Sonya, but I don't think you ever told me your last name."

"Well, if I didn't it's Dunkin and soon to be changed cause these people here are getting on my last nerve."

"Oh yeah."

"Yeah and why didn't you call me last night? Sonya said, with a slight attitude.

"Hold up sweetheart, we just met yesterday and you demanding calls already, you're real persistent aren't you." I said, jokingly.

"Yes I am and if I had your number, I woulda called and cussed your ass out."

"You wouldn't do that to a brotha like me would you."

"Try me Mister."

We both laughed. I liked Sonya's little act of aggressiveness, it only showed me that she was really diggin' me.

While I was on the phone talking to Sonya, Bilal and Carlos were meeting uptown on Kennedy Street. Los was a short, chubby light skinned Puerto Rican and he drove a blue 4-door 600S Mercedes Benz. As Lal pulled up in his 600S coupe, Carlos got in and immediately they began talking business.

"Los, what's up with this nigga Petey, he's owed us three

hundred fifty thousand for like eight months now, why you ain't get it from him yet?" Bilal said, angrily.

"Cause every time I went around Trinidad the nigga was kinda acting funny." Carlos said.

"Funny how?" Bilal said, his anger building up even more.

"I asked the nigga 'bout the bank and he was like, 'Los, I do business with Bilal and Bilal only, so when Bilal come around then he'll get his money'."

"Yeah, this nigga knew I had 30 years didn't he?"

"Yeah that nigga knew, he just wasn't tryna pay me. He thought you had 30 years and you was washed up."

"Why you ain't get somebody to punish his ass? You know the nigga Lil G locked up in Maryland on three bodies and I don't fuck with the rest of his crew, them niggas cruddy."

"Yeah I know and I couldn't do it myself cause every time I came around, he had the dude Chicken Wing wit him and them niggas kept touching their shit just to let me know they were strapped." Carlos said.

"Man, I don't believe this nigga Petey. As much as I looked out for this dude and it ain't like he don't got the money, this nigga pumpin' like shit. Did he ever put something down on that thirty?" Bilal said.

"Yeah three hundred thou, so he owe three fifty, he gotta have that by now."

"Yeah his ass got it he just thought he got away with some free money when I got locked up. I've been paging this nigga all morning too. C'mon, we're going round Trinidad to see if this nigga out there." Bilal said.

"Oh yeah Lal." Carlos said.

"What's up Los?"

"You know that nigga Fat Mike got his head hit."

"Yeah I heard, who did it?" Bilal said, as if he didn't know already.

"Word on the street is that the dude Lil Dog from Southwest put it to him."

"Lil Dog, yeah I know youngin, that's one of Big Silk's protégés. Good lil dude but he's got a vicious gambling problem."

Damn, Jovan really is tight, he killed Fat Mike and Los thinking somebody else did it. As Los and Bilal pulled up on 16th Street around Trinidad, Petey and Chicken Wing were sitting on their cars in front of Petey's stash house where he kept all his bricks. Petey had a green convertible Mercedes and Chicken Wing had a black 928S4 scarface Porsche with chrome BBS wheels.

When Los and Bilal pulled up, Petey and Chicken Wing both pulled their straps out.

Lal rolled down the window and said, "Nigga it's me, put that shit up."

First thing Petey said was, "Man, what you do to escape?"

"Naw, I ain't escape nigga." Bilal said, as he grilled his face at Petey.

"Then how you get out?" Petey said, looking nervous.

"I won my appeal. Look Petey, all that shit is neither here nor there, I need to holla at you in private."

Bilal got out of his car and Petey and he walked a couple of steps away.

"Look Petey, I need my money." Bilal said, getting right to the point.

"Bilal, hold up." Petey said, as he tried to stall the conversation.

"Petey, I ain't tryna hear no bullshit, you owe me three hundred fifty thou and I need it like now."

"Man Bilal, shit's a little fucked up for me right now."

"Fucked Up? How nigga, you got a brand new convertible Benz that cost like seventy-five thousand and your man got a Porsche worth 'bout sixty-five, I know you ain't get that shit with your last."

Carlos got out of the car and walked over to Bilal and Petey.

"What's up with you not paying my man here? He said he came round here like three different times." Bilal said, pointing to Carlos.

"Man Lal, this nigga came round here on some different shit like he was pressin' me or something."

"How he pressin' you for something that's his Petey."

"Man Petey, you knew Bilal had 30 years, you just wasn't tryna pay me." Carlos said, as he looked at Petey with eight months of built up hatred.

"Like I said before Carlos, I dealt with Bilal when I got them thirty bricks, I put three hundred thousand in Bilal's hands not yours nigga." Petey said, attempting to break bad with Carlos.

"Petey, who the fuck you think you talking to like that?" Carlos said.

"I'm talking to you Carlos, you don't even know me like that to be coming at me."

"Nigga, you owe me three hundred fifty thousand and you sayin' I don't know you like that, fuck that where my money at!" Carlos yelled.

"You bitch ass nigga, you wait for Bilal to come home and try to get some heart."

At that time, Chicken Wing got up and started walking towards Petey.

"Hold up. Look Los and Petey, ya'll cut all that bullshit out, it's obvious you two niggas can't get along. Like you said, you dealt with me, well I'm here now so where my doe at?" Bilal said, as he peeped Chicken Wing about to pull out his strap.

"Look Lal, come around here tomorrow, I'll have your money then." Petey said.

"Oh Yeah? You know I've been paging you all morning, why you ain't call me back?" Bilal said.

"Man, I left my pager over my baby mother's house last night."

"Petey, I suggest you have it on you at all times from now on."

"Yeah ok, Lal."

"A'ight then." Bilal said, before going back to his car with Carlos and driving off.

"Man Lal, that nigga lying like shit, he was just looking at his pager when we pulled up." Carlos said.

"Yeah I know, I just wanted to see how he looked when he lies. Los, how much money we got?"

"3.5 mil still, plus about 1.5 mil still in the streets."

"Damn, what was you doing while I was gone?"

"I wasn't fuckin' with the connect cause I was a little skeptical about coping with our last, you know we can't buy no less than 200 bricks."

"Who where were you getting shit from then?"

"I was fuckin' with the dudes from cross town and they'd give me like 25 bricks here and there."

"Was the number high?"

"Fuck yeah, them niggas want all of theirs."

"Ok, when you come by the house tonight bring that money with you."

"Ok Lal."

Jovan
Sonya and me talked for a little while, laughing and having a good time. It was around 11:45 a.m. and I didn't have anything to do, my day at work was practically finished so I popped the magic question.

"Hey Sonya." I said.

"Yeah Jovan?"

"What you doing for lunch?"

"I dunno my friend Germain and me might go down to Houston's in G-Town or something, why?"

"Whose Germain?" I said, curiously.

"Germain is a female." Sonya said, chuckling.

"Oh ok, cause for a minute. . ." I started to say, cause for a minute I thought it was a man, but decided not to.

"What was you gonna say Jovan?"

"I wasn't gonna say anything, I just wasn't gonna call anymore."

"Damn Jovan, you wouldn't have given me a chance to explain? Shit, I coulda had a uncle or cousin named Germain." Sonya said.

"Well you don't." I said.

"And how do you know that?"

"Cause you woulda told me."

"Jovan, you're crazy." Sonya said, laughing.

"Yeah, crazy 'bout you Sonya." I said, smiling.

"Yeah whatever and why did you ask me what I was doing for lunch anyway?"

"Obviously I was gonna ask to take you out to lunch."

"Well, Mr. Jovan Price the "Lawyer", it's still not too late to ask me."

"So you're not going to lunch with your friend?" I said, glad that she was willingly to change her plans to have lunch with me.

"No, not if you're still considering taking me to lunch." Sonya said, as she smiled at the thought of having another lovely afternoon with him.

"So when will you be ready to take your lunch break?" I asked.

"In like 20 minutes." Sonya said.

"Perfect, I'll be out front waiting." I said.

"No Jovan, just come on in to the front desk."

"Ok."

When I got off the phone I began to think about where I should take Sonya for lunch. The weather was nice, my bank was right and I was dressed for the occasion, wherever we went it had to be outside. Maybe I should take her down to Tony & Joe's and eat out on the deck or Saquoias, or the Cheese Cake Factory on Wisconsin Avenue. I didn't know where, but I would think of something.

Mark came into Michelle's office, saw me sitting there and said, "Hey Jovan, you'd better get your ass outta Michelle's office, she'll be back in a few minutes."

"That's alright, I'm 'bout to leave anyway."

"You going home?"

"Naw, I'm gonna take this nice female I met yesterday out to lunch."

"Oh, you met a new bun." Mark said, jokingly.

"Bun? Mark, you're silly. Yeah man, I met this girl yesterday and it already seems like I've known her for years."

"Damn, that's the sign."

"The sign, what you talking 'bout Mark?"

"The sign of love."

"Man, ain't nobody say nothin' 'bout love."

"No Jovan, that's just how it was when I met my wife."

"Yeah, which one?" I said, with a sarcastic grin.

"You know you can be a pain in the ass sometimes Jovan." Mark said, grinning at my comment.

"Go 'head Mark." We both laughed. "Look, I'll see you tomorrow, tell me how it goes with those briefs."

"Ok Jovan. Oh, hey Jovan."

"Yeah Mark?"

"You taking that girl out in your van?" Mark asked.

"What else I'ma drive?" I said.

"Here, take my car just bring it back unscratched." Mark said, throwing the keys to his car to me.

157

Mark had given me the keys to his brand new BMW. I had one before back in '91 but this one was a new joint, fresh off the lot. I went into my truck and got a few things and headed for the nearest deli. When I got to the deli I brought a turkey and cheese sandwich on rye, a tuna fish on wheat, some potato chips, a freshly made fruit salad, two Evian waters and a freshly squeezed grapefruit juice.

I pulled up in front of Sonya's job, looked in the mirror to make sure my appearance was cool and got out my car, well Mark's car, and headed inside to the front desk. There was a little chubby young girl at the desk. She was cute but she was too much on the heavy side.

"Excuse me, may I help?" She asked me.

"Yes, I'm looking for a Sonya Dunkin." I said.

"Hold on a second."

When she got on the phone to page Sonya, I got the feeling they must of known each other because I was ear hustling and I heard the girl say, "Sonya girl, it's this fine ass man down here asking for you. Yeah girl, he looks too good in his cream outfit and jazzy shoes. Ok, I'll tell him you'll be right down." She then hung up the phone.

She turned to me and said, "Excuse me sir, she'll be right down."

"Ok, thank you."

"Anytime." She said, while she looked me up and down with a devilish grin as if to say, you can fuck me too.

When Sonya came downstairs there was another woman with her, she looked like she was whispering in Sonya's ear.

"Hey Jovan." Sonya said.

"Hey sweetheart."

"This here is my co-worker and friend Germain."

"How you doing Germain?" I said to her friend.

"Hello Jovan, I've heard a lot about you." Germain said, smiling.

"Oh yeah?"

From what Germain just said, it made me wonder what Sonya was saying about me, shit after all I had just met her only two days ago.

"Alright Germain, you've met Jovan, time to go now bye." Sonya said, grabbing my hand to leave.

"God Sonya, you ain't even let me say nothin'." Germain said, looking mad.

"You said enough bye, we gotta go, see you later."

"Ok Germain, have a good day." I said to her.

"I will if you keep her with you and don't bring her back." Germain said, laughing.

"I just might do that." I said, as I looked at Sonya out of the corner of my eye, waiting to see her expression.

Sonya stuck her tongue out at Germain and Germain gave her the finger. When we got in the car Sonya started talking first.

"Jovan, you look very nice today, you're dressed real jazzy to be a paralegal."

"Thank you, you look nice yourself Sonya, more like a model then a assistant producer." I said, as my eyes pierced her whole body.

"Jovan, where are you taking me?"

"I figured since the day was nice we'd go somewhere outside and chill."

As we were driving, I put on a Sade CD and went straight to the song "Cherish The Day". Sonya laid back in her seat looking good as shit. You could tell she was into the music cause her feet were moving and her head was bobbing as she closed her eyes.

When we pulled up to this secluded area at Rock Creek Park, Sonya opened her eyes and said, "Oh Jovan, I haven't been here since I was a little girl. What are we doing here?"

"Well sweetheart, I thought it would be nice if we just had a little picnic, just you and me chilling. Is something wrong with that, you wanna go someplace else?" I asked, afraid she was not pleased with my choice.

"No Jovan, a picnic is perfect, it's just that I've never been on a picnic with a man before."

"Well boo, you're going on one today."

I took the blanket and pillow outta my van, along with the food from the deli, which I had put in a basket and found us a nice spot under a tree. I laid out everything then went back to the car to get Sonya.

"Jovan, I have on heels, how am I gonna walk on that grass?" Sonya asked me.

"Tell you what, just get out of the car."

Sonya got out then she asked Jovan, "What are you gonna do?"

At that moment I lifted Sonya up in my arms and carried her across the grass. She held onto me tight as if she didn't want to let go as I placed her down on the blanket.

"Jovan, that was fun but I must say I was a little surprised by your actions. I do not know of any man who would have done what you just did. If only there were more men like you these day. Was I heavy?" Sonya said, still in shock by Jovan's quick thinking.

"No sweetheart, you wasn't heavy I could carry you forever."

I sat down beside Sonya and she began to take her shoes off.

"Here, let me do that for you." I took off each shoe slowly and began messaging her feet.

"Oh Jovan, that feels so good, you sure know how to treat a woman."

"Sonya, you've got the prettiest feet I have ever seen." I said, as I admired her perfectly manicured feet.

"Thank you Jovan and you are the most romantic person I have ever dated." Sonya said, looking deep into my eyes.

"Now, how you gonna say that when this is only our second time with each other?" I said, grinning slyly at her.

"Yeah, you're right, I may be speaking too fast." Sonya said.

We both laughed. I then got our food out of the basket and placed it on the blanket.

"Well Sonya, I wasn't sure what you liked so I got a turkey on rye and a tuna fish on wheat." I said, placing both sandwiches in front of her for her to choose which one she wanted.

"I'll take the tuna and what's that over there?" Sonya asked, pointing to the container of fruit.

"Oh, this is a freshly made fruit salad."

"Umm, it looks good."

Sonya and me ate and talked about almost everything, she had this way about her that put your soul at ease. I had just met her and I was digging her style already, this shit never happened to me before, I mean I've had a lot of women before but not one like her.

"Jovan." Sonya said, bringing my attention back to her.

"Yeah Sonya?"

"Come over here closer to me."

As I moved closer, Sonya began to message my back and neck.

"Jovan, do you work out?" She asked, as she continued massaging my neck.

"Yeah baby I do, I go to the gym three times a week." I said, enjoying her soft hands as they massaged my neck.

"I can tell."

Sonya was rubbing my back and neck so good that my dick started getting hard. After she had massaged me I returned the favor as we continued talking.

"Jovan." Sonya said.

"Yeah?"

"I wanna taste that fruit salad."

"Well Sonya, the only way you can taste it is if you let me feed it to you." I said, opening the container of fruit.

"I'm cool with that."

I fed Sonya strawberries, watermelon, cantaloupe and all the other fruit that was in the salad. The way she closed her eyes and held her tongue out made my dick even harder, I started imagining how she'd look while we were making love. After I fed her the fruit salad she fed me a few strawberries and I did the same thing she did, closed my eyes and held out my tongue. Suddenly something sweet, soft and warm touched my tongue but I didn't bother to open my eyes because I realized that Sonya was kissing me and I kissed her back. The kiss itself was explosive and I could have kissed her all afternoon.

"What was that for?" I asked, after she had stopped.

"Just a little something to let you know how much I appreciate you doing all this for me. Jovan, you've made me feel special today, I've never had no one take the time out to do something like this." Sonya said, seriously.

"And I've never had no one to take out like this until I met you."

"Yeah right Jovan, you've probably got women crawling on their knees trying to be with you."

"I was just thinking the same thing about you Sonya."

"No baby, you don't have to worry about that."

"Visa versa. So are you sayin' we can see each other again?" I asked, hopefully.

"You damn right, every chance we get Jovan."

"So I take it you're feeling me right about now huh?"

"Jovan, men like you don't just fall out the sky, so when I find one I gotta grab hold to him."

"Sonya, I'm thinking the same thing about you."

"C'mon baby, I gotta get back to work." Sonya said, getting up off the blanket.

I got up and carried Sonya back to my car, packed everything and drove her back to work. When we pulled up to Sonya's job, I gave her my number and a light kiss on the lips.

Before she got out the car Sonya said, "Jovan, again thank you for today, I had a wonderful time and by the way, your ass better call me tonight or else."

"Or else what?"

"Don't call and see what happens."

"So you're threatening me now?"

"No, that's not a threat baby, it's a promise."

As Sonya was getting out of the car, Germain and another female were standing out front waiting for her. Germain and me waved at each other and as Sonya closed the door, I could hear her say to Germain, "Damn ya'll so nosy!"

Sonya
Jovan and me had a nice time at the park and to tell you the truth, he romanced the hell outta me. Most niggas don't even think about doing shit like that, they think they gotta show their money off to get somebody to like them. It was wonderful being with Jovan just looking at the sky, trees and all of nature. I was on a natural high with him, he gave me inspiration and he wasn't like other guys I've dated. He had an aura about him that made you smile and made your pussy get wet all at the same time, I guess that's why I kissed him like that, I couldn't hold it back. Jovan made my day and I know if I continue seeing him eventually he'd make my world.

Jovan
After I dropped Sonya off, I went back to the office and gave Mark his keys.

"Hey Jovan, how did it go?" Mark asked me.

"It went real cool Mark, I laid it down like a true playa suppose to." I said, and told Mark how my day went and what happened.

"Man Jovan, you're smooth, I might have to try that one."

"Naw Mark, you couldn't do that, your shit would be in the newspaper on the front page, 'Lawyer Fucks Prosecutor in Public Park'." We laughed.

"Jovan, you're crazy man. Look, I'll see you tomorrow." Mark said.

"Ok." I said to Mark.

It was about 2:00 o'clock and I had a lot of time before I had to go to Bilal's house. I had about two thousand in big bills on me, so I decided to go down to Georgetown to Solbiato's and get a few shirts and some shoes. I got down to Georgetown and parked on the opposite side of the store. I looked at all the cars in front of Solbiato's, it looked like a car show. There was a Lexus LS400, Benz Coupe VI2600, Benz 500SL, Infiniti Q45 and a Range Rover, this is where all the players in the city shopped at and believe me, the joint be flooded with bitches.

When I came in the store, I saw two dudes I knew from the southeast side, D & Ant. I shoulda known all that big shit outside was theirs and their crew. These niggas were getting it, they were the only niggas in the city that wasn't coping from Bilal. When I came through, the first person that made contact with me was D. D and me were cool back in '91 when I had a few niggas on the Southside movin' ounces like welfare cheese. We never did business together but we always respected and acknowledged each other. I guess mainly because our styles were similar, the nigga was smooth just like me and he wore top flight shit and kept a bad bitch with him.

When I was locked up in Lewisburg, I used to hear good things about him, about how he stayed loyal to his man Ant when he was down Lorton and how he broke him off something real nice when he came home, sorta like Bilal and me but the only thing different was that Bilal and me didn't hang out together or hustle together.

"Hey, what's up Jovan?" D said, coming over to me.

"What's up D?"

"Ain't shit going on. Damn Jovan, I ain't seen you in a while, where you been at?"

"I was in the Feds for a minute." I said.

"How long you've been home?" D asked.

"About eight months now."

"Yeah, so what you doing?" D said, as he checked me out to see if he could notice any signs of me getting back into the hustling game.

"I'm a paralegal now, I work for Mark."

"Who, Mark Rohon?" D asked, surprised.

"Yeah, I've been working for Mark for the past six months now."

"Damn Jay, I was 'bout to ask you was you tryin' to get down. I know we ain't never did business before but I do know your hustling skills and I'd loved to have a nigga like you on my team." He said, eagerly wanting me to accept his proposition.

"Naw man, I ain't fucking around no more, I'ma do this paralegal thang."

"If that don't work out for you, you know you can always holla at me." D said. "So what, you getting ready for that party tomorrow?"

"Naw, what party?" I said, thinking about all the lavish parties I went to back when I was hustlin' real good. Damn, that shit was fun.

"The Madness Connection is giving a hair show and an after party downtown at the Spinx Center." D said.

"The Spinx Center, that's off of 14th Street ain't it?"

"Yeah, you going?" He asked, as he watched me fumble through the shirt racks.

"Naw, I doubt it I'm just here tryna find a couple shirts or something." I said, continuing to look through the shirt racks.

"They got some a'ight shit in here, but I already got most of this shit. Jovan, you know me, I gotta go up to Wisconsin Avenue to the "V" shop and get that Signature Versace shit. I'ma holla at you slim, take care." D said.

"A'ight D, keep your head up."

Damn, if I ever wanted to ever hustle again I had the biggest opportunity in the world. I checked out a few shirts, I didn't see anything I liked but I did see some shoes I liked. I brought a pair of Versace soft bottom shoe boots, some Ceasar & Picotti slip-ons, and a pair of nice ass Salvatore Farrangomo lace ups, all together it came up to eleven hundred dollars. As I was leaving out, I saw this gray Hugo Boss sweat suit. Now, I don't wear sweat suits but this joint was hitting, I had to get it. The sweat suit was six hundred dollars.

I left and went to Grandma's to see if she had gotten those estimates to get the house fixed. As soon as I came through the door, I heard Grandma hanging up the phone.

"Hey Grandma, what's up baby girl?" I asked her.

"Hey Jovan, I wish you would have came in a little earlier you would of caught your daddy. That was him on the phone and he asked about you, he wanted to talk to you."

"Oh yeah. Grandma, did you call and get the estimates on how much everything will cost?" I said, quickly changing the subject off my Pops.

"Yeah baby but I dunno if you got that kinda money."

"C'mon Grandma, how much is it?"

"They want seven thousand for the basement and three thousand for the ceiling."

"I got that for you baby girl."

"Jovan, where you get that kind of money boy?"

"It fell out of the sky Grandma."

"Fell out the sky my foot, you better not be out there doing nothing illegal." Grandma said, seriously.

"C'mon Grandma, I'm a lawyer's assistant, what I look like breaking the law."

"Yeah, you better not cause if you do, I'ma be breakin' my foot off in your ass."

"Go head with that baby girl." I said to her, laughing.

"You so damn silly, did you eat yet?"

"Naw Grandma, I ain't hungry."

I went upstairs to get ten G's out for Grandma and gave it to her. It was about 6:30 p.m., so I decided to call Sonya, she had been on my mind all day since our picnic.

Ring, Ring, Ring. "Hello." Sonya said.

"May I speak to my wife?" I said, happy to hear her voice.

"Your who?" Sonya asked, thinking the person had the wrong number.

"My wife." I said, smiling.

"Who is this?"

"Who do you want it to be?" I asked her.

"Jovan, is that you?" Sonya said, after realizing it was him.

"Yeah baby, what's up?"

"Boy you crazy." Sonya said.

"Crazy 'bout you that is."

"Yeah right, I see you finally called."

"Yeah, I was getting scared, I didn't want you to call me and cuss me out."

"Whatever Jovan." Sonya said, glad that he had called her.

We both laughed. Man, it seemed like I already knew Sonya. Outta all the broads I've been with ain't none of 'em made me feel like she did.

"So Jovan, what did you do the rest of the day?"

I told Sonya everything I did and she told me how her day went and how she bragged to her friends at work about our lunch date. She asked about my Grandmother and when she would meet her. We talked for about two hours like teenagers in high school.

CHAPTER 18

"A Way Out"

It was about 8:30 p.m. when Bilal called.

Ring, Ring, Ring, "Hello." Jovan said, answering the phone.

"Jovan, you're supposed to be at my house." Bilal said.

"Nigga, you never gave me a time."

"Ok, well I'm on my way home so hurry up and come over." Bilal said.

"I'm on my way." Jovan said, about to hang up the phone.

"You eat yet Jay?"

"Naw, Grandma cooked but I wasn't hungry."

"Cool, I'ma have Meeka cook something for us."

"A'ight then."

After Jovan got off the phone with Bilal he put on his tan Armani summer jacket and headed for the door. As he was leaving, he called out, "Grandma, I'm going out."

"Ok baby, what time you coming back?"

"C'mon Grandma, I'm a grown man now, you can't be putting your press game down on me like that."

"Boy, shut up wit your crazy self, I wanted to know if I should wait up for you so we could talk."

"Naw, you ain't gotta wait up I might be out for a while." Jovan said, giving her a hug.

"Ok baby, you be careful out there." She said, kissing me on my cheek.

"Always, baby girl." Damn, Grandma always be putting me on a serious guilt trip, I wanna get out and get my own place but it would probably break her heart. I guess I'll give it a little time before I roll out.

On Jovan's way to Bilal's, he listened to the whole Scarface CD, "The Diary", his favorite song was "Never Seen a Man Cry". For some reason, that joint and the other joint "Jesse James" fit his lifestyle, both of them joints used to put him in a zone mainly because there was so much truth in 'em.

When Jovan arrived at Bilal's house, as usual all that big shit was sittin' on his lawn, you woulda sworn Mike Tyson lived at this joint. There was an extra car that wasn't there the last time he was there, a 600s 4-door Benz and he figured it was Carlos joint. As Jovan came to the door, Meeka was right there with much more attitude then the last time.

"Hi Jovan c'mon in, the fellas are downstairs in the game room. Jovan, I'm cooking you don't eat beef do you?"

"Naw Meeka, I don't red meat."

"Good then, tell them the food will be ready in a minute."

"Ok Meeka." Jovan said, heading downstairs.

When he got downstairs, Bilal and Carlos were playing pool.

"Hey, my ma'fuckin' nigga Jay, what's up slim!" Bilal said, coming over to give him love.

"What's up Lal?" Jovan said, returning the love.

"Los c'mon here, Jay this Los, Los this Jay." Bilal said, making the introductions.

"What's up Jay, as you already know Bilal speaks very highly of you. I've been hearing your name come out of this nigga's mouth since Oak Hill." Los said.

"Yeah, I heard a few things 'bout you also Los and finally we meet." Jovan said, shaking his hand.

"And from here on you niggas is family." Bilal said, butting in.

"That's already understood Lal." Jovan said, giving him a stern look.

When Jovan looked over to his right, he laid his eyes on the most money he had ever seen in his life, stacks and stacks of doe, along with four money counting machines.

"Damn, ya'll niggas got a lot money layin' around!" Jovan said, amazed at all the money.

"We just finished countin' that shit Jay, well I just finish countin' it cause this nigga was upstairs playin' house with Meeka." Los said, as he looked over at Bilal and laughed.

"Go head with that shit Los. How much money is that?" Bilal said.

"A little more than 5 million, about 5.3." Los said.

"Man Lal, that's a lot doe." Jovan said, not taking his eyes off the money that looked like stacks of cinder blocks.

"Nigga, a percentage of this shit is yours so go ahead and kiss it." Bilal said.

"Naw, I'm a'ight. What's up, give me the run down on what you plan to do with all this money." Jovan said, curiously.

"Look Jay, this is the plan. We got 5.3 mil, we're gonna cop with 3.5 mil. After we get finish pumpin' all this shit, I'ma sell the house and most of these cars, head down to Atlanta and turn all this shit legit, get some kind of business, maybe a few car lots. After we cop and move everything, we're gonna come out ten million strong and after I sell the house and cars, we're gonna have like seventeen million all together.

Los is going back to Puerto Rico and I'm going to Atlanta, and Jay you're going to Law School to get that license cause we're gonna need a way on how to legitimize this shit. Jay, I want you to go to Atlanta with me, get yourself a law firm and we can enjoy this money together cause like I said, a percentage of this shit yours."

"Yeah Jay, Bilal talking some serious shit. You know the Feds gonna be closing down on us soon so we wanna be legit when they come and from what I'm hearing from Bilal, you're the lawyer that can make that shit happen." Carlos said, smiling.

"I ain't no lawyer yet Los." Jovan said to Carlos.

"Well in 2 years you'll be and by this time next year, we'll be finished with seventeen to twenty million strong divided three ways. So what's up Jovan, you wit it or what?" Los asked.

"I'd be a fool not to be nigga."

"You were wit it ever since we were 15 years old, you just ain't believe me when I told you we were gonna be rich." Bilal said, with a big smile on his face.

"Yeah Lal, this here is surely a dream come true."

"Los, how much money we got left in the streets?" Bilal said.

"Not that much, Petey still owe that three hundred fifty thousand, Lil Manny owe me like 200 thousand. He just called me a minute ago and told me come get it." Carlos said,

"Yeah and I'll go get that from Petey tomorrow at 1:00 p.m."

"Ya'll know the Madness Connection is giving a party tomorrow and since I ain't been nowhere in eight months, I'm tryna go. What's up Los you wit it?" Bilal asked.

"Yeah, I'll go Lal."

"Jay what's up, you gonna roll or what?"

"Man Lal, I told you we can't be hangin' out together, I don't want the Feds seeing your face next to mine, nor do I want any of these bitch ass niggas out here knowing that you and me are best friends, that's the only way we're gonna come out this game on top." Jovan said to Bilal.

"Yeah, you right Jay, you're the lawyer and you know the law and how funky they play."

"Damn, this shit reminds me of some old Godfather movie." Carlos said, happy to see Jovan join the team.

"Shut up Los, you a fool man. C'mon let's play some pool." Bilal said, going over to the pool table.

"Jay, you know how to shoot pool?" Carlos asked.

"Yeah, I know how to play a lil bit."

"How much money you got?"

"Something light, 'bout five hundred."

"Put it up then nigga, money on the wood make the game go good." Carlos said, laughing.

"If that's so Los, then where your bank at?"

"I got something special for you if I lose."

"Ok rack 'em then."

"Los, go easy on him, he ain't got but five hundred dollars." Bilal said.

"Damn Los, you must be good like that huh?" Jovan said.

"Yeah and I'm 'bout to punish you!" Carlos said, racking the balls on the table.

"Damn, since you 'bout to punish me, you might as well let me bust 'em and get the first shot."

"Ok, go ahead Jay I really ain't tryna embarrass you in front of Lal."

"Whatever nigga."

They all laughed. Jovan grabbed the heaviest pool stick, chalked it up and bust the balls. His first shot he hit in two balls then he put in two more, then two more, he didn't even give Los a chance to get on the table. Bilal and he were looking at Jovan in shock.

"What's wrong Los, I thought you were gonna punish me." Jovan said, laughing at the look of shock they both had on their faces.

Lal was laughing hard as shit as he said to Carlos, "Nigga, you always jumpin' out there losing on that pool table!"

"Fuck you Lal and fuck your funky ass pool table!" Carlos said.

Jovan shot the last shot and the eight ball went into the corner pocket, "bing" straight down the pipe. As soon as the eight ball went into the corner pocket, Los threw a set of keys onto the table.

"What the fuck is this Los?" Jovan asked him, looking at the keys lying on the pool table.

"You won the game, their yours." He said.

"Fuck you talking 'bout?"

"The silver 850 BMW sitting out front, that's yours nigga. Ain't nobody ever drove it but Meeka and that was the other day when she picked Lal up from the courthouse."

"Yeah Jay, Los was gonna give that to you as a present but I guess he wanted to get a good game of pool outta you first, or better yet, a bad game of pool." Bilal said, still laughing.

Carlos did not find Bilal's statement funny, he said, "Fuck you Lal! Look Jay, the joint got a hydraulic stash spot too, it's small though it hold like two guns, I'll show you how to work it later."

"A'ight and thanks Los." Jovan said, picking up the car keys.

Meeka came downstairs and said, "Ya'll food is ready."

"Ok Meeka, we'll be right up."

Carlos then said something to Meeka in Spanish. Jovan looked at Lal as if to say, what the fuck is going on, Lal just laughed and said, "Oh Jay, Meeka is Los cousin, he introduced us back in Oak Hill and we've been together ever since."

"Now I understand why she gets a million dollars to play with, she helped build this shit and was with you when you had shitty underwear."

"I dunno about shitty underwear Jay, but she been with a nigga from rock bottom and we're getting married after all this shit is over. We're gonna do it in Atlanta and I want you to be my best man Jay."

"Always was and always will be Lal, forever I remain loyal."

"Visa versa nigga."

We then went upstairs to eat and afterwards we went outside to talk.

"Damn Lal, Meeka can cook her ass off." Jovan said, still savoring the taste on my tongue.

"That comes from our family Jay, all of us can cook." Carlos said.

"Los stop lying, only thing you know how to cook is crack."

"Fuck you Lal!" Carlos and Bilal started play wrestling and could tell they loved each other. Jovan thought Bilal looked at Carlos as his little brother, like he could fill the void of Mal-Mal's place in his life.

Los taught Jovan how to work the hydraulic stash in his new BMW 850I, that joint was brand new and silver with light gray leather interior.

"Lal, I'ma keep this over here til I find somewhere to park it." Jovan said to Bilal.

"A'ight Jay."

"Look, I'll see ya'll tomorrow."

"Jay be over here at 8 o'clock tomorrow, we got something for you."

"Ok fellows."

Jovan gave both of them hugs and went back to Grandma's house. It was about eleven o'clock when he got in and he went upstairs to get himself ready for bed and the phone rang.

Ring, Ring, Ring. "Hello."

"Hello, may I speak to Jovan?"

"Yeah, this me." Jovan said, realizing it was Sonya on the other end.

"Why didn't you call me?" Sonya asked.

"What's up baby, you miss me already."

"Don't baby me and yes I do miss you but like I said before why didn't you call?" Sonya said again, this time with a serious attitude.

"What, you beefin' Sonya?" I asked her, not sure where the attitude was coming from.

"Yeah I'm beefin' Jovan, I've been thinking about you all day." Sonya said, this time with less attitude.

"Me too baby, you've been on a nigga's mind like shit. It seems like we've known each other for years."

"Yeah I know, you sure we haven't met in another lifetime before."

"I dunno we might have."

"Jovan, am I gonna see you tomorrow or what?"

"You better say ain't a day gonna pass that I don't see you."

"Don't make promises you can't keep Jovan."

"Baby all I got in this world is my..." I started to say, but Sonya cut me off.

"Hey, you better not say that, I saw Scarface before!" She said, laughing.

We laughed and talked for about an hour then I went to bed.

Triple Crown Publications presents

CHAPTER 19

"No Way Out"

Jovan woke up this morning feeling good, last night after Sonya and him talked, Jovan laid back and thought about what Bilal was saying last night. Atlanta is cool and a new identity, legit money and plus you can get a million dollar home down in Atlanta for like three hundred thousand, sounded real good. Yeah, Jovan thought Bilal's suggestion was a smart move for everybody. Seventeen to twenty million strong divided three ways, you can't go wrong.

Jovan arrived at the office kinda late and ran right into Mark.

"Hey Jovan, you're late." He said.

"I know Mark, I had a long night."

"With who, your new girl? You mean to tell me you got some already." Mark said, smiling.

"Naw Mark, I had a few things to take care of."

"Ok Jovan, but now that you're here we've got a lot of work to do today."

"Break it down to me Mark."

Mark had Jovan doing more work today than he ever did since he first started working for him. That's just how this legal shit is, one day you're busy, the next day ain't nothing happening.

Carlos called Bilal about 12:00 o'clock.

"Lal." Carlos said.

"Yeah Los."

"Look, I'm on my way round Georgia Avenue to go pick that money up from Lil Manny."

"I thought you did that last night."

"Naw, when I left your house I picked this lil freak up and went to the hotel out in Crystal City."

"Where you at now?"

"I'm on 7th Street getting ready to cross Florida Avenue."

"Ok slim, call me after you pick that up. I'm on my way round Trinidad to go see Petey."

"Did you page him again Lal?"

"Yeah, I paged that nigga like three times."

"Man, I think we may have some problems outta Petey plus I don't trust them niggas, you know how they got on in the first place."

"Yeah, they were supposed to rob the dude Chink for like three hundred thousand."

"Yeah, after this I ain't fuckin' wit 'em no more."

"Ok slim, meet me around Orleans Pl. after you get that from Lil Manny."

Carlos met Lil Manny at the McDonalds on Georgia Avenue and he gave Carlos the 200 thousand and wanted to know the next time he would be able to get down.

"Sometime next week Manny and I'ma do something real nice for you cause after that I'm finished." Carlos said.

"Ok Los." Lil Manny said.

Manny got back in his Corvette and rolled out. As Carlos was putting the money in the trunk of his car two dudes walked up on him with .45s pointed at his dome.

"Get back in the car Los." One of the dudes said to him.

Carlos turned to see who it was and when he saw Petey and Chicken Wing he said, "Petey man, you ain't even gotta do this."

"Shut your bitch ass up and get in the car!" Petey yelled to him.

Carlos got back in his car with Chicken Wing in the back seat and Petey on the passenger side, they both had their guns on Carlos.

"Look Petey, I've got two hundred thousand in the trunk, this Rolex and about four thousand in my glove compartment, man just go 'head take that shit and let me go." Carlos pleaded.

Petey smacked Carlos upside his head with his pistol and yelled, "Shut the fuck up nigga I'm doing the talking, now drive!"

"Where to?" Carlos asked.

"Go up Georgia Avenue." Petey said.

Carlos drove up Georgia Avenue still not knowing his fate.

Chicken Wing started talking, "Los, where the money at and don't play no games. I ain't talking 'bout that punk ass two hundred thousand in the trunk either, take us to ya'll stash."

"Slim, we ain't got no more money, the Feds got everything when Bilal got locked up." Carlos said.

Carlos knew that if he told them where the 5.3 million was at then not only would he be dead, but Bilal and Meeka would also die.

"So you ain't tryna give that shit up, huh?" Petey said.

"Man slim, that's the truth, I swear to God on everything I love that's all we got." Carlos said, pleading for his life.

"Pull over in this alley." Petey said, as he kept his gun stuck in Carlos' rib cage.

"Man Petey, don't kill me, I swear that's all we got man!" Carlos pleaded, with tears in his eyes.

"Shut the fuck up and pull in the alley!"

Meanwhile, Bilal went around Trinidad to pick up his money from Petey. When he drove up to Petey's stash spot, he didn't see Petey or Chicken Wing's car, there were only two dudes out front talking.

Bilal rolled down his window and said, "Hey what's up youngin, ya'll see Petey?"

"Naw, we waitin' on him now." One of the dudes said.

"How long you've been waiting?"

"We just got here slim."

Bilal parked his car and figured he'd wait for Petey since he had his clientele out front waiting on him, he knew Petey wouldn't be that long. But usually when Petey wasn't around to serve these niggas then Chicken Wing would. Bilal paged Carlos and when he didn't call him right back, Bilal sensed something was wrong. Usually when he paged Carlos he would call him right back.

Why the fuck wasn't Carlos callin' him back, I hope that dude Lil Manny ain't wit the Feds. Bilal paged Carlos again and after about 45 minutes of waiting on Petey and Carlos to call back, Bilal grew impatient. Petey's customers left and Bilal went looking for Carlos. First Bilal went around 9th Street where Carlos runners were. He pulled up on Lil Kenny and Raymond.

"Hey Kenny." Bilal called out to him.

"What's up Bilal." Lil Kenny said.

"You seen Los?"

"Naw, he ain't come through yet and I have been paging him all day."

"Look, when you see him tell him to call me."

"Ok Bilal."

Bilal then drove around Orleans Pl. where he was supposed to meet Carlos after he picked the money up. Bilal pulled up around back and saw Cat, Soup Bone and Lil Short Dog.

"Ya'll seen Los come through here?"

"Naw Bilal, but I saw him earlier when I was coming out the Madness Shop, he was going up Georgia Avenue and he had Petey and Chicken Wing wit 'em." Short Dog said.

"Petey and Chicken Wing?" Bilal said, with a disturbed look on his face.

"Yeah slim."

"You sure it was Petey and Chicken Wing?"

"Yeah." Short Dog said.

Bilal instantly got nervous and as he was headed toward Georgia Avenue, all he could think about was Carlos and how he loved him like a little brother. He knew that if he was with Petey and Chicken Wing something was wrong, plus Carlos had never called him back. As he raced up Georgia Avenue, tears started forming in his eyes. If something happened to Carlos then those niggas was gonna pay, pay with their lives.

Bilal looked up and down Georgia Avenue but there was no sign of Carlos' car. When he turned onto Webster Street, he passed an alley and as he was driving by he caught a glimpse of a car sitting there. Bilal put his Benz in reverse, pulled into the alley and saw that it was his friend's car.

He got out with tears swelling up in his eyes and looked in Carlos' car, saw that it was unlocked and opened the door, Carlos' keys were still in the ignition. Bilal knew something had happened to Carlos. Bilal took the keys outta the ignition and went straight to the trunk of his car. When he opened the trunk, he saw Carlos' body curled up like a baby with two holes in his head the size of a half a dollar, instantly Bilal dropped to his knees.

Ring, Ring, Ring. "Hello, law offices of Rohon & Robinson." Cindy said.

"I'd like to speak with Jovan Price." Bilal said.

"Please hold." Cindy said. She then buzzed Jovan. "Jovan." She said.

"Yeah Cindy." Jovan said.

"You have a call on line one."

"Ok, thanks Cindy."

"Jovan Price here." Jovan said, answering the phone.

"Hey Jay, come over my house now!" Bilal said, with anger.

"What's up Lal, you alright?"

"Fuck no I ain't alright, I need you over here now!" Bilal yelled into the phone.

"Ok slim, I'm on my way." Jovan said, hanging up the phone.

Jovan then went into Mark's office and said, "Hey Mark, I gotta make a run, family emergency."

"Is everything alright Jovan?" Mark asked.

"I don't know yet Mark."

"Look, go 'head and take the rest of the day off."

"Ok, thanks Mark."

As Jovan drove out to Bilal's house, he couldn't stop wondering what was going on. Bilal had called him at work and it sounded like he was crying and angry, what the fuck coulda happened. As he pulled up Bilal was out front, his eyes were red and swollen.

Jovan got out of his van, walked over to Bilal and asked him, "What's up man, you a'ight?"

"Naw Jovan, come round back."

"What the fuck is going on man?"

"Jay, they killed Los man!" Bilal said, his eyes filling with tears.

"What?" Jovan asked him, not sure he heard him correctly.

"Man they killed Los, they killed my man Jay!" Bilal cried, as the tears gushed outta his eyes.

"Who, who killed Los?"

"Petey and Chicken Wing!" Bilal yelled.

"How you know that Lal?"

Bilal laid the whole thing down to Jovan. Jovan had just met Carlos and this nigga had brought him an 850 BMW for a present. This nigga was a good dude and he was Jovan's best friend's partner and comrade. The whole time Bilal was telling the story he was breaking down how much he loved Carlos. Jovan could now see the pain that he had held back when Mal-Mal died, he had held onto that pain by loving Carlos.

Damn, shit done got fucked up and there's only one way to get it back right. Petey and Chicken Wing were some cruddy niggas and they had to get what they deserved, but first Jovan had to calm Bilal down so that he wouldn't make any dumb moves that could get them life in prison. Jovan's loyalty to Bilal was concrete, so there was no way he was gonna let these niggas get away with this shit. They had pulled a fucked up move and Carlos died for some bullshit ass two hundred thousand. They had just talked about getting outta this game last night, but as he saw it, once you're in there's no way out because every time you try and make that step out, something always pull you right back in.

"Look Bilal, this the move but first you gotta calm down. Is Meeka in the house?" Jovan asked Bilal.

"Naw, she's at work."

"Good, then let's go in and have a drink and plan this shit out perfectly."

As Bilal tried to calm himself down, Jovan laid out his plan.

"Look Lal, you know that Madness party is tonight."

"Yeah Jay."

"Don't you got tickets to that joint?"

"I got two tickets, why."

"Good, I'ma need 'em. Most likely them niggas is gonna be there celebrating what they did, they got some free money and you know they're gonna be flauntin'. How many guns you got Lal?"

"I got three hammers, a .357 Desert Eagle and two 16 shot Smith & Wesson 9MM with black talon bullets. Yeah Jay, I got a silencer that fits both nines." Bilal said.

"A silencer, where the fuck you get that?" Jovan asked Bilal.

"My connect sent that shit up to me the last time I coped from him."

"Ok, that's perfect. Give me those two nines and the silencer."

"What you gonna do Jay?"

"What I do best, both those niggas will be dead within 48 hours or less."

"Hold up Jay, if you're gonna go to that party you gotta be right."

Bilal went upstairs and come back down with a jewelry box.

"Here you go man." Bilal said, opening up the jewelry box.

When Jovan opened up the box, the 18K Presidential Rolex and matching bracelet almost blinded him. Bilal's watch and bracelet had the biggest diamonds Jovan had ever seen.

"Man Bilal, what you tryna do get my arm chopped off tonight." Jovan said, still staring at all the diamonds on the jewelry.

"Naw Jay, that's yours now, it used to be Carlos but I know he'd rather you have it. That shit is worth almost three hundred thousand. You got an outfit for tonight Jay?"

"Yeah, I got a black Versace suit I brought from California that I've never wore and a black and gold Versace silk print shirt with Medusa heads all over it and some black Versace slip-ons with the matching belt."

"Damn nigga, you tryna kill 'em ain't you."

"Bilal, I'ma keep my van over here tonight and push the 850 to the party."

"Ok. Jay, how you gonna put in the work."

"I'll let you know everything after I do it, just stay home and wait for my call."

"Cool."

On Jovan's way home, he thought about Bilal and Carlos. Damn, shit was going sweet all we had to do was get this money and step-off. Now it's Bilal and me just like old times. Those niggas had violated my family, so in turn, they had violated me also.

When Jovan got to Grandma's house he called Sonya.

Ring, Ring, Ring. "Hello." Sonya said.

"What's up baby?" Jovan said to Sonya.

"Jovan, I was just thinking of you."

"You mean to tell me that out of the whole day, you just started thinking about me." Jovan said, smiling.

"No, actually Jovan I've been thinking about you all day."

"Me too Sonya, you been on my mind also, so what's up?"

"You, Mr. Jovan Price, you're what's up."

"Look, what are you doing tonight?" Jovan asked Sonya.

"Well, I promised my friend Germain that I would go to this Hair Show party with her downtown." She said.

"You mean the Madness Connection party?" Jovan asked her.

"Yeah, you heard about it Jovan?"

"Yeah, I was thinking about going, you got tickets?"

"Well, Germain only has one ticket, she's trying to get the other one now."

"Well guess what, you're in luck."

"Why you say that Jovan?"

"I've got an extra ticket that you can have if you want it."

"Jovan, are you going to the party too?"

"Yeah baby, I gotta come keep my eye on you, make sure you ain't getting too fresh with nobody." Jovan said, jokingly.

"Like I told you before you don't ever have to worry about that."

"I'm just joking wit'cha boo."

"Jovan, you're the one whose probably going to be talking to all them bitches." Sonya said, sarcastically.

"Naw boo, you ain't got to worry about that because I'm too focused on you."

"Well that's good that you're going, now I can keep my promise to Germain and see you at the same time." Sonya said, happy that Jovan would be at the party tonight.

"How you getting there?"

"Germain is driving."

"Good, then I can take you home after the party."

"That'll be perfect cause Germain lives all the way out in Oxon Hill, MD and if she takes me home, it'll be out of her way."

"You can come on over now and get the ticket and meet my Grandma at the same time if you like."

"Where does she stay Jovan?"

"812 9th St., NE." Jovan told her.

"First, I'ma call Germain and let her know about the ticket then I'll be over."

"Cool."

While Sonya was on her way over he was still thinking about a master plan on how to lay my demonstration down. Jovan took out his suit, belt and shoes and laid them out. He hasn't been to a party like this in a long time, so when he go he's gonna do it right.

Sonya came over and got her ticket and met my Grandmother, she didn't have a lot of time to stay cause she had to get back home and get herself together. Before she left we kissed as if we were together for years.

"I'll see you tonight Jovan and you better behave yourself."

"Like I told you, you ain't gotta worry 'bout that."

Sonya
Little did Jovan know I was all his and tonight I planned to look extremely good, so I got out my black Chanel dress, my Chanel shoes, my Cartier earrings, necklace and bracelet with matching watch. I let my long hair out so it could fall down my back. My dress was a perfect fit, I had never worn it before, it was strapless and exposed the crease of my back and it felt so good and smooth, like another layer of skin on my body. Germain is on her way to pick me up but little did she know she wouldn't be bringing me back.

Jovan
It was 10:00 o'clock and the party had just started and I was still at home contemplating my move. I showered and got myself together, I never went to parties when they first started, I always came in a little late to give that grand appearance, so I just laid back on my bed and thought about my plans.

After I kill these two niggas, I would take Sonya home and who knows what was gonna happen after that. I only hope Sonya don't be following me around because I gotta duck her for at least half the time we are at the party.

It was now 11:00 o'clock, so I put my clothes on and took

out my new Rolex and bracelet Bilal gave me, damn, this watch was hittin'. I looked at my fine ass imagine in the mirror and said to myself, "Jovan, you're a fly ma'fucka". I then grabbed about two thousand dollars out of my gym bag, all hundred dollar bills, got in my 850 BMW and headed to the party.

When I pulled up, I circled the block first to see if I saw Petey and Chicken Wing's cars, they wasn't out front which was good. As I turned the corner onto 14th Street, I saw Petey's Benz parked in the cut and it was kinda dark which was perfect. Then I looked down the street and Chicken Wing's Porsche was parked at least a half block away. I parked my car three spaces from Petey's, got out and went into the party.

As soon as I came through door, I heard DC's number one party anthem, "Before I Let Go" by Frankie Beverly. The joint was packed with females, gangsters and a few lames. As I made my way through the crowd, I could see bitches out the corner of my eye tapping their girlfriends as I walked by say, "girl who is that fine ass brother right there?".

I made my way upstairs to where everyone was chillin' and as I glanced through the party looking for Petey and Chicken Wing, I saw a few good men who were regarded as real niggas. In DC, when real niggas acknowledge one another we call it tilting our hat. The first MOBs I tilted my hat to was Don and AB, they were over by the VIP section poppin' bottles with some bad bitches, then I saw ED and Ty, the ones giving this party. Also I saw that paradise of MOBs, Block, Marlon, Pee-Wee and the number one super middleweight champion, Keith Holmes. Mark Johnson who was the flyweight WBC Champ was also in the house. Big Sweat and them Willington Park youngins were there also. I also saw young Ish, J-Rock, Rat Man, Rudy and Fat Troy, these young niggas were doin' it.

The dude Ish had a Rolex on his arm that looked so heavy it made him slow down when he walked. I respected these dudes ever since their man, Lil James, got double life for a crime he didn't commit. It was rumored that they stopped hustling and ventured their money into the music industry so they could pay for his lawyer legitimately. I hear they're tryin' to get him Johnny Cochran, damn, that's real. Then I saw Big Poo and Fats, they used to cop from me back in '91.

As I walked through the party, all these dudes tilted their hats to me and I returned the favor. Also a lot of bad bitches I know were coming up to me tryna get with a nigga, my Rolex was attracting bitches like a magnet. The first broad I saw was Peppa and she was looking good as shit. I wanted to tell her to meet me outside after the party but I had plans for something else, so we kicked it for a minute.

Then I saw Keda and she also looked good tonight. I haven't seen or talked to her since I had been home. I let her know how much I appreciated what she did for me when I was locked up and told her if there's ever anything she needed, I'd help her out.

Then I saw Big Titty Tracey and her crew. Cha-cha and Nicki came over to talk to me and Lil Shana and her cousins, Nicki and Toya were also there. I used to mess with Nicki back in the day and she was looking good as shit too. If I didn't have nothin' to do I'd would have taken her straight to the hotel. As soon as I finished talking to Nicki, my old piece Barvette walked up behind me.

"Hey Jovan." Barvette said, hugging me around my waist.

"Hey, what's up Barvette?" I said, turning around.

"I haven't seen you in years, boy where have you been?"

"I was away for a minute." I said to her.

"I can see nothing has changed."

"What do you mean?"

"You still fly and you got a watch on that looks like it cost more than this building."

"Yeah, you know me, shit don't stop cause the nigga got knocked." I said, laughing.

"Jovan, you still the same."

As Barvette and me were talking, I saw Petey and Chicken Wing with some bitches taking flicks and it looked like they were already drunk. When I saw them, I locked my eyes in their direction, not looking directly at them but I kept them in sight.

While I was peeping Petey and Chicken Wing, everybody rushed toward the stage where the Hair Show was. I didn't go down there but I looked off the balcony where everybody was. When I looked on stage, I saw the strangest shit ever at a party like this, there was Trina Boo and another girl modeling for a Hair Salon, I think it was Erotica. Trina Boo was behind this girl motioning like she was fucking her with a Dildo doggy style. The whole party was in an uproar, niggas were trying to get on stage and people were rushing up front to see what was happening. These broads were on stage acting out a lesbo scene. Throughout all the commotion, I still kept my eye on Petey and Chicken Wing.

After Trina Boo and her friend did their little lesbo trick, everything calmed down and that's when I saw Sonya and Germain downstairs by the bar. Sonya had a black dress on that look like another layer of skin and she also had on some pretty diamond earrings and necklace. You could see the shape of Sonya's ass through her dress and her hair was falling straight down her back, damn she looked so good, a straight dime piece and I mean a strong dime.

I went downstairs to greet her but I still kept my victims in sight. As I crept up behind Sonya, I whispered in her ear, "Damn you look gorgeous tonight."

She didn't even bother to turn around, she just said, "I see you finally got away from all them bitches that were hawking you."

"What are you talking about boo?" I asked her, innocently.

"Jovan, I just left the ladies room and every bitch that came in there was talking 'bout you."

"I can't help that Sonya."

"I know baby, you're just a smooth ass nigga and I can't get mad because other bitches want you, in fact that shit kinda turns me on."

Sonya then turned around and looked at me and said, "My God Jovan, you look very nice, I now see why all these bitches tryna get with you."

"And you mean to tell me all the time you been here, ain't none of these niggas try to talk to you." I said to Sonya.

"Yeah they have Jovan, but I batted that shit down."

"What'd you tell 'em."

"I told them that I was very involved with a man I hardly know."

We both laughed then Germain joined us.

"Oh, hi Jovan." Germain said.

"Hey Germain."

"You know we've only been here for a half hour and we've already heard a lot about you in the ladies room."

"Yeah, Sonya already told me." I said to Germain.

"Jovan, are you behaving yourself?" Germain asked me.

"Yes indeed." I said, smiling at her.

"You better cause if you make my friend mad, I'ma have to kick your butt."

"She know she doesn't gotta worry about that."

As I talked to Sonya, I could see that Trina Boo was on her way over. I didn't know Trina Boo personally, but I heard a few rumors that'll make a nigga want to get to know her fast and I do mean real fast.

"Hey cuz." Trina Boo said.

"Girl, don't hey cuz me, I saw you on stage acting like you don't have no sense." Sonya said to her cousin Trina.

"Girl, that was just as act for the shop. Who is that with you?"

"Oh excuse me, Jovan this is my cousin Trina."

"Hi Trina."

"Call me Trina Boo."

"No Jovan, call her Trina, her name is Trina."

"There you go acting like you somebody's mother."

As Sonya was talking to Trina, I saw that Petey and Chicken Wing were about to leave and they had that broad Pebbles wit 'em. This was my chance to make my move.

"Hey Sonya, can you excuse me for a moment, I gotta go talk to one of my clients in the lobby." I said to Sonya.

"Sure baby, I'll be right here waiting on you. Jovan, you sure take your work seriously, you at a party and you talking to clients."

"Gots to get that money Boo."

"That's right baby, go right ahead."

"Hey, you better behave yourself while I'm gone."

"Boy, I told you once before, matter of fact twice, that you definitely don't have to worry about that."

"Ok, I'll be back in about 20 minutes, maybe less."

As Petey and Chicken Wing were in the lobby still trying to talk Pebbles into leaving with them, I walked straight past them and out of the party. I looked around to make sure no one saw me as I went to my car and popped the hydraulic stash. I took out one of the 9MM that Bilal gave me and screwed on the silencer. I then got out my car and went over to Petey's Benz. I took my watch and bracelet off, put 'em in my pocket and crawled under Petey's car.

I waited for about ten minutes before I saw Petey and Chicken Wing walking towards their cars. Pebbles wasn't with 'em, which was good cause if she was then I'd have to whack her too and I ain't tryna kill no bitch who ain't got a damn thing to do with this. As they got closer, I could hear them talking.

"Damn slim, I told you we shoulda got that nigga Bilal first, he the one wit all the bank." Chicken Wing said.

"It's hard to get that bitch ass nigga because he don't even be coming out." Petey said.

"Yeah, I searched the fuck out that party for him."

As I heard these niggas talking about killing and robbing my best friend, my only family, I knew I had to kill these niggas. I wasn't nervous or anxious, I just wanted this shit to be done right. As Petey walked towards his car, Chicken Wing stepped off.

"I'll see you tomorrow, we can page that bitch nigga Bilal, tell 'em we got his money and get him then." Petey said.

"Yeah, that's what's happening." Chicken Wing said.

Chicken Wing headed down the street to his car, damn that nigga Chicken Wing was getting away, fuck it I can't let the cat outta the bag. If I jump out now, I'd have to kill Petey then chase Chicken Wing down the street and that shit would be real sloppy and for sure somebody would see me, so I stayed on Petey.

As Petey got close to the car, I positioned myself and as soon as he put his key in the door, I rolled from up under the car and placed my gun right up under his nut rack and said, "Nigga, if you still wanna make babies, then shut the fuck up!"

Petey was in shock, he couldn't move or scream, so he tried to negotiate. "Look man, all I got is my Rolex and about fifteen hundred on me, you can have the shit."

"Naw nigga, give it to your peoples for funeral arrangements." I said, then I shot Petey in the nuts three times, "pat-pat-pat".

As Petey stumbled back in shock holdin' his nuts, I got up and shot him three times in the chest, "pat-pat-pat", he then fell to the ground. I looked around for a second to see if anybody saw me, no one was in sight. I then stood over top of him and delivered four shots to his head, "pat-pat-pat-pat". I then spit on him and as he lay there dying I said, "You deserved that, you bitch ass nigga!" I wiped off the gun, took off the silencer and put it in my pocket. I put my Rolex and bracelet back on, threw the gun down the sewer and headed back to the party.

As I was walking up to the front entrance of the party I could hear the seductive melody of Teddy Pendergrass' voice penetrating through the speakers. On my way back in, I saw a good dude I knew by the name of Cat Eye Tony, on his way out.

"What's up Jovan?" Cat Eye Tony said.

"What's up Tony? Hey, the party over or what?" I said.

"Yeah Jovan, you know when they play Teddy Pendergrass' "Turn Off The Lights", that means it's time to roll."

"Yeah I know, I'll holla at you Tony."

"Ok, good to see you Jovan."

"Yeah, you too Tony."

While maneuvering my way through the crowd of people

who were leaving the party, I looked around and noticed that Sonya and Germain wasn't standing in the same spot I had left them, but after a few seconds I finally spotted them over by the picture booth talking to a few of their female friends. I walked over and slightly eased my hand on Sonya's waist pulling her away.

"What's up Boo, did I take too long?" I asked her, nibbling on her ear.

"No Jovan, you said you'd be gone 20 minutes, that was only 15 minutes." Sonya said, enjoying Jovan's tongue on her ear.

"So, you clockin' me now?"

"How can I clock a man that's always on time."

"Look, this joint 'bout over, you ready to go?"

"Yeah. Oh Germain, Jovan is gonna take me home tonight." Sonya said to Germain.

"What?" Germain said, looking at her with an evil eye.

"Like I said, Jovan taking me home, so now you can get back to your husband early." Sonya said, giving Germain the same evil eye.

"Sonya, you nasty!" Germain said, laughing.

"Shut up girl, you so silly."

"Jovan, take it easy on her." Germain said, winking her eye at Jovan.

"Bye Germain."

"Bye then."

"Germain, you want us to walk you to your car?" Jovan asked.

"Yeah Jovan, thanks."

We walked Germain to her car and said our goodbyes once again.

"You know something, ya'll two look cute together." Germain said, getting into her car.

"Bye silly, call me when you get in the house." Sonya said.

As Sonya and me were walking to my car, we saw a light crowd and the police up ahead.

"Look Jovan, something happened."

"Well Boo, it ain't none of our business, c'mon get in the car." I said, knowing that we had to get out of there fast now that the police had shown up.

"See Jovan, that's why I don't like going out, niggas always out trippin'."

"Yeah, I know, they always doing something stupid."

"Why can't they be more like you?" Sonya said.

"What do you mean Sonya?"

"I mean you gotta job, you don't be around a lot of niggas, you just be chillin' and you still got the same things these niggas out here hustling got."

"I guess that's the life they chose." I told her, but in my head I'm saying, "baby you just don't know, I'm the reason why everybody standin' there. I just gave 10 shots to a nigga who deserved it".

As we pulled off and made our way through traffic, I put in a CD that would fit the mood. Traffic began to flow and the music began to take over our emotions. I played Jon B's & Tupac's song "Baby Are U Still Down". I looked out the corner of my eye and peeped Sonya staring at my watch as the street lights beamed down on its diamonds that reflected rays of rain-bows. As my 850I BMW glided up Connecticut Avenue in the cool summer night like a space ship taking off, I placed my hand on Sonya's thigh and rubbed it softly as if I was rubbin' a lion's fur. I could see that just from me touching her like that, I put her at ease to a point where she placed her hand on top of mine and closed her eyes.

When I pulled up to Sonya's condo she was sleeping lightly.

"Hey Sonya, we're here." I said to her, gently waking her.

She woke up in amazement and said, "Oh, I'm sorry Jovan, I guess I got caught up in the music and fell asleep."

"So Sonya, am I going to see you tomorrow or what?"

"Sure Jovan." Sonya said.

"Would you like me to walk you to your door?" I asked, hoping that she would invite me in.

"Sure Jovan, that'll be nice."

I parked my car and walked Sonya to her door. Once we got to the door, Sonya turned around and planted such a wet erotic kiss on my lips that I couldn't hold back, I kissed her passionately and held her soft body close. We kissed for what seemed like an eternity then she placed her key in the door. As I turned around and began to walk away, Sonya stood in her doorway and watched me as I walked down the hall, then I turned around once more and looked at her staring at me.

"What's wrong Boo?" I asked her.

Sonya looked at me with those pretty eyes and said, "Jovan, please stay with me tonight."

That's all she had to say because as soon as we got in her apartment, Sonya grabbed my hand and directed me to her bed-room. All at once I pressed my tongue deep into her mouth and slid off her dress with one stroke. As she took off my jacket and shirt, I admired her perfect body, her titties were round, not too big not too small, but perfect and she wasn't wearing any panties and I saw that her pussy was neatly shaved. I caressed her lips while she continued to unbutton my pants and soon we both were completely naked.

As I placed her on the bed and kissed her more passionately than the last, I began to run my fingers over her hard nipples and lightly sucked on them as if I was sucking on a fresh strawberry. I then ran my wet tongue all over her breast down to her navel and then to her thighs. As her moans of ecstasy grew, I caressed her thighs and gently ran my tongue teasingly around the outside of her pussy. I could feel her body ripple and tense as I continued. I didn't move too fast or too slow, I patiently took my time exploring Sonya's sweet pussy. As I kept going, I could feel her hands reaching behind my head trying to get me to crush my face into her pussy, eager for me to lick more of her but I wasn't going to make it that easy for her. Instead, I grabbed her hands and held them back and continued to tease her sweet throbbing pussy never penetrating her, only dabbing and rubbing it slightly. She moaned as I felt her body shudder and all at once, I pressed my tongue deep into her pussy and she gave a soft cry.

"Oh my God Jovan!"

I motioned my tongue in and out of her pussy as if it was my dick. Then I started licking on her clit as if it was an ice cream cone, up and down, side to side. While licking on her clit, I pressed one finger inside her wet pussy and as her moans got louder, I placed two fingers deep into her pussy and positioned them in a motion as if telling someone to come here until I felt a spongy spot of flesh. I continued to lick Sonya's clit until I found her "G" spot and then her moans were no longer soft they became a loud cry.

"Oh my God Jovan, what are you doing to me? Oh Jovan, Jovan, Jovan!" Sonya screamed.

I could feel her body tremble and her legs shake as she closed her eyes tightly and let the waves of her orgasm rush through her body. After Sonya had came repeatedly, I caressed her thighs for about 10 seconds, letting her catch her breath. I laid on top of her in the missionary position and gently stuck my hard dick into her wet pussy and Sonya held me so tight I could feel the rate of her heartbeat. As I stuck my dick deep into her pussy, Sonya pushed forward toward my dick letting her clit rub up against my flesh as we joined in rhythm.

I ran my tongue around her nipples, kissed her neck and enjoyed her moans as she whispered in my ear, "Oh Jovan baby, don't stop, don't ever stop. This dick is so good baby, oh Jovan, you don't know what you're doing to me!"

Again, I could feel her body tense and tremble as she came all over my dick, pussy juices flowing, again I laid there for 10 seconds letting her recoup, then I turned her around, massaged her back and ran my tongue all over her body. I grabbed hold to Sonya's ass, which was soft and pretty and rubbed it for a few seconds, then pulled her up in a doggy style position, spread her ass cheeks apart, positioned myself behind her and slowly put my full length hard throbbing dick into her wet pussy. Sonya's pussy clung tightly onto my dick, her pussy gripped my dick as I deeply penetrated her slowly with long deep strokes and our rhythm came together at once. As I begin to move in and out of her faster, her moaning got louder as her orgasm began to build.

"Oh Jovan, you're fucking me so good baby! Why are you doing this to me?"

My rhythm began to move faster and faster and the more strokes I made, the wetter her pussy got, Sonya's pussy was so wet that her juices were dripping off my balls.

"Oh yes Jovan, fuck me boo, fuck me boo!"

As she cried out in pleasure, I began to pound harder into her. I pounded Sonya's pussy and caressed her ass at the same time with a ferocity that was sending her over the brink. Sonya's body tightened and her squeals of pleasure became sobs of ecstasy.

She looked over her shoulder into my eyes and moaned, "Jovan, I'm about to cum, Jovan I'm cumming boo! Oh boo, I'm cumming! Boo, oh Jovan I'm cumming!"

Sonya's pussy exploded on my dick as she sunk her head into her pillow trying to hide her tears of joy, pain, pleasure and lust, lovemaking and fucking, all wrapped up in one.

As she got herself together, I laid down beside her and placed her head on my chest, ran my fingers through her hair and gently kissed her on her forehead and lips.

"Jovan." She said

"Yeah Boo?"

"Please don't leave me, I need you, Boo."

"I ain't going anywhere." I said, stroking her breasts gently.

"You promise?"

"I promise."

With that, Sonya began to rub my dick and kiss my chest at the same time, she kissed all over my body while stroking my dick hard. She grabbed my dick and played with it before easing down and taking it into her mouth. Her tongue moved around the head of my dick slowly as she stroked it up and down, damn that shit felt good. She then began sucking it slowly as the blood continued to swell my dick. Sonya was bobbing her head up and down sending me to a place of ecstasy no woman had ever taken me before.

As I was about to cum, Sonya stopped sucking my dick and got on top and rode my dick moving her hips back and forth, up and down and harder and faster until we both came and exploded a load that was built up from the moment we met. Sonya laid on top of me with my dick still in her pussy and buried her face in my chest.

"Jovan, you don't know what you just did to me, please don't hurt me baby."

I made love to Sonya all night and all morning. After we took a shower together, I looked over at my pager and saw that Bilal was paging me. I called him back while Sonya was cooking breakfast.

Ring, Ring, Ring. "Hello." Bilal said.

"Lal, what's up nigga?"

"Man, why you ain't call me back last night, I got a little worried."

"Worried for what? Nigga, I'm like James Bond 007."

"Did everything go alright?" Bilal asked.

"Well yeah and no, but I'll fill you in when I get there."

"You're ok though Jovan, right?" Bilal asked, afraid that Jovan may have been hurt.

"Most definitely nigga, I told you I'm like James Bond 007."

"Yeah ok."

"What time you coming over?" Bilal asked.

"Soon as I eat my breakfast."

"Where you at anyway nigga?"

"I'm over a friend's house."

"Who?"

"Her name is Sonya."

"You talking about that female you met in the courthouse?"

"Yeah."

"Damn slim, you work fast don't you."

"I wouldn't call it that, I'd just say it was something destined to happen."

Triple Crown Publications presents

CHAPTER 20

"The Tightest"

After Jovan got off the phone with Bilal, he ate the veggie omelet Sonya cooked and drank some freshly made orange juice and Sonya just sat there looking at him.

"What's wrong?" Jovan asked her, enjoying my breakfast.

"Nothing." She said, smiling.

"Then why you looking at me like that?"

"You just don't know Jovan."

"Know what?"

"You don't have a clue what you're doin' to me."

"Yes I do and I feel the same way about you." Jovan said.

"I hope so."

"Look, I've got some business to take care of this morning then I'm going to the gym. What are you going to do today?" Jovan asked.

"Germain and me were gonna go to Chevy Chase Pavilion and do a little shopping."

"So am I gonna see you later on?"

"Jovan, you can see me whenever you want."

"I'ma call you after the gym, maybe we can repeat last night." Jovan said, grinning.

"I like that idea Jovan."" Sonya said, also grinning.

We laughed, kissed and said our goodbyes.

"Oh Jovan, I forgot to tell you that's a nice watch you have."

"Yeah, I had to confiscate it from a client who couldn't pay his bill." Jovan lied.

On Jovan's way over to Bilal's house he was putting his plan together on how he was going to deal with Chicken Wing. Only thing he knew about Chicken Wing was that he loved hood rat bitches, he didn't know where he lived at or nothing, he didn't even know if this nigga had a baby momma or not. Only thing Jovan knew was that he hung around Trinidad and drove a black Porsche, damn he had to think of something quick. Even though Petey was dead, Chicken Wing still may have something planned for Bilal.

Before Jovan got on the highway to Bilal's, he stopped in Georgetown and went to "Up Against The Wall". He saw this nice blue and white DKNY spandex gym suit with a matching baseball cap and thought it would be perfect for Sonya. Even though mostly hood rats wore this he brought it any way. Jovan also brought a pair of thick DKNY shades. He went down to the sex store beside Houston's Restaurant and brought a few things then got back on the highway and headed to Bilal's house.

When Jovan reached Bilal's, the only cars he saw sitting out on the lawn was his MPV van and Meeka's Lexus Coupe. Bilal greeted Jovan at the door.

"Hey Lal, what happened to all your cars?" Jovan asked him, looking around.

"I went out to Eagle Motors this morning and sold all that shit back to 'em."

"What'd they give you for them?"

"Four hundred fifty thousand all together."

"Damn Lal, they got over on you." Jovan said, amazed that he had settled for such a low price.

"Not really Jay, only by like about fifty to seventy-five thousand."

"Well, anyway I'm glad you got rid of all that shit."

"Me too Jay, I'm serious 'bout this Atlanta thing."

Jovan went into his van, got out the Hugo Boss sweat suit and New Balance 996 tennis shoes he brought the other day and then Bilal and him went downstairs to talk. Jovan told him about everything, about how he had hid under Petey's car and how he heard them talking about robbing and killing him. About how he had shot Petey in his nuts first and the way he was looking at him when he did it.

"Damn Jay, you shot him in the nuts?" Bilal said.

"I had to make him know not to ever fuck with my family."

"Yeah slim, from what you telling me you straight punished that nigga."

"Yeah and guess what Lal, the whole time I was doing this shit, my broad was in the party thinking I'm in the lobby talking to a client."

"Damn Jay, you smooth as shit!"

"I told you Lal, I'm like James Bond!"

"Yeah and outta of all the killers in the city Jay, can't none of 'em fuck with you. Now I've heard of niggas doin' similar shit, but none of it was as smooth as yours and what makes your work tighter is nobody never knew you did it and besides that fact, you're a fuckin' lawyer."

"Not yet Bilal." Jovan said, reminding him once again that he was not a lawyer yet.

"Yeah, but soon though Jay. Anyway this is what's up, while you lay the demonstration down on Chicken Wing, I'ma send this money down to Mexico. We got six million now and I'ma cop with three and hold the other three back. I want you to take the other three with you and put it up over Grandma Price house.

"Why?"

"Cause I'm 'bout to sell the house."

"Good idea."

"After I get these bricks, it may take me about three weeks to get rid of 'em. Jay, we can make 8.5 million on this and I sell the house for a cool three and a half, plus the three you holdin', that's fifteen million altogether."

"Man Lal, I got a suggestion."

"What's up Jay?"

"Look, we already got six plus the house, why don't we just sell the house and keep the six, that's 10 million and we can step off with that, fuck the extra 5 mil. You know the Feds tryna get at you and ain't no sense in keep hustling slim. We can get the money and step off, go somewhere and do this shit legally man." Jovan said to Bilal.

"Jay, I already got all my clientele waiting for me to get down. Shit Jay, I already got at least three million as soon as I get the shit, these niggas out here hungry. Niggas ain't got nothing and the ones who do can't beat my prices, so everybody coming straight to me. Two to three weeks top Jay and we're gone. Remember, I'm the hustler I know what the fuck I'm doing. I've been doing this shit since '91 and look how far it got us."

"Ok Lal, whatever you say it sounds good. Three weeks for

an extra 5 mil I can't argue with you on that. When you say you coping again?"

"I got these two suitcases full of money I'm taking 'em to my carriers today. My shit should be here first thing in the morning."

"I need to take a shower Lal."

"You ain't take no shower over that girl's house?"

"Yeah, but I really wasn't washing up, I was laying down the pipe."

"You a trip Jay. Use the shower upstairs it got a Jacuzzi in it too."

"Naw, I don't need all that, but I can use a razor."

"Just look in the cabinet, there's some brand new razors in there."

After Jovan took his shower, he shaved off his goatee and mustache, put on his clothes and headed for Trinidad. Before he left he paged Sonya and she called right back. Jovan thought damn, I musta really put it on her, but little did she know she put it on me also. Sonya was the baddest and sexiest female he ever had and to be honest she had the best pussy ever.

"Hello."

"Baby, what's up sweetheart?"

"You." Sonya said.

"Is that right."

"Yes sir Mr. Price."

"Hey look, what time you gonna go up Wisconsin Avenue to Chevy Chase Pavillion?"

"What time is it now Jovan?"

"Almost 12:30."

"We should be finished by 2:00 o'clock, you wanna meet me somewhere?"

"If you want you can tell Germain to drop you off at the gym, I'll be finished working out by then."

"Which gym are you going to be at?"

"Finley's boxing gym on 10th Street."

"Oh I know were that's at, my lil brother Tony used to box for Mr. Finley."

"Ok Boo, I'll see you then."

"Oh Jovan."

"What's up baby?"

"Don't be letting anybody mess your handsome face up."

"Boo, you must not be hip to my work, I'm like Mike Tyson when it comes down to that." Jovan said, laughing.

It was one fifteen when Jovan got around Trinidad. He pulled his van up around the corner at the top of 16th Street and looked around for a second to scope the scenery out. After he saw that there were no spectators around, mainly because it was still early in the day, he jumped in the back seat of the van, pulled out the binoculars he previously had from when he killed Fat Mike and focused them perfectly.

As Jovan looked down 16th Street, he spotted Chicken Wing's car. He looked over to the left and saw two guys standing in front of their stash house, Chicken Wing was nowhere in sight. A gold 4-door Acura Legend pulled up and rolled down their window to talk to the two guys out front. One guy yelled towards the house and Chicken Wing came out front. The dudes in the Acura got out, they looked familiar and as Jovan beamed in closer he could see that it was Big Poo and Fats, they were talking to Chicken Wing. Then Poo reached in his car, pulled out a bag and gave it to Chicken Wing, it was obvious this was a drug transaction taking place.

After Poo and Fats left, Chicken Wing stayed out front and sat with the other two guys. Jovan assumed that Chicken Wing had gotten everything Petey left behind and was selling the remaining bricks before he put his lick down on Bilal.

As they sat out front, Jovan was changing his clothes in the back of the van. He put on the DKNY spandex suit he brought from Up Against the Wall, also he put on the ass pads and fake tittie bra he brought from the sex store. Jovan then put on the ponytail wig he got from the costume shop in Georgetown and the matching DKNY baseball cap pulling the ponytail through the hole in the back of the cap. He looked in the mirror at his disguise and wasn't satisfied, so he put on Meeka's bright red lipstick that he had taken from the cabinet when he took a shower at Bilal's. Jovan then placed the big shades on that covered most of his face and looked in the mirror again, this time he was satisfied with what he saw.

It was 1:45 and for the next ten minutes, Jovan was going be a certified hood rat. He popped his stash spot, opened it and retrieved the 9MM and screwed the silencer on it. He placed it in Meeka's coach bag that he had also taken from Bilal's house. Jovan got out of his van and walked around Bladens Burg Road, came through the cut on 16th Street and walked by Chicken Wing and his crew. Jovan knew Chicken Wing was on hood rats hard as hell and this butt pad made his ass look like Mary J. Blige's. Although he felt humiliated wearing this costume, he knew it would serve its purpose, so he did what was necessary. As he walked pass Chicken Wing he started switching and Chicken Wing came off the porch and fell right into his trap.

"Damn, she phat as shit, girl come here!" Chicken Wing yelled.

As Jovan walked faster up the street, Chicken Wing began to follow. He put his hand into his bag and held onto the gun like glue. As Chicken Wing got closer, Jovan looked around and saw three little girls playing jump rope. This was his chance and he couldn't blow it, he needed to get this nigga. As the little girls were playing, Jovan started walking faster to get them out of reach.

Chicken Wing started a light jog saying, "Hey, hold up for a minute let me holla at you."

Jovan slowed down and when he heard Chicken Wing's foot steps getting closer he waited for a second until he was right behind him, about 2 feet away. Jovan didn't panic he was going to give it to a nigga who truly deserved it. When Jovan felt Chicken Wing's breath damn near on the back of his neck, he turned around and shot Chicken Wing four times in the solar plex part of his stomach "pat, pat, pat, pat", that way he would instantly lose his breath and wouldn't be able to holla for help.

As Chicken Wing clutched his stomach on the way down to the pavement, Jovan shot him once in the forehead "pat" and quickly put his gun back in the bag. He didn't run from the scene, he just began to walk away fast.

As Jovan was walking away, he could hear the little girls laughing, "Ooh, aha, you see that, he tried to touch that girl's butt and she turned around and punched him in his stomach. That's what he get!"

As Chicken Wing was curled up on the sidewalk dead, those little girls thought he was punched in the stomach for touching Jovan's ass, this came out better then he planned. Jovan headed back to his van and no one saw him get in. As he drove off, he could see Chicken Wing's crew walking towards him laughing, not knowing he was through, finished, done like a hot turkey on Thanksgiving.

It was just turning 2:00 o'clock and Jovan pulled up on 9th Street, took off his costume, wiped the lipstick off of his lips, wiped the gun down, placed everything in Meeka's big coach bag and placed the bag in the dumpster. Jovan walked in the gym through the back way on the 9th Street side and came out front on the 10th Street side.

Sonya and Germain were just pulling up when he came out on 10th Street and when Sonya got outta the car, instantly Jovan was aroused and pleased at what he saw. She had on a pair of tight Moschino jeans and t-shirt with some open toed sandals. She had her long hair in a ponytail, Sonya looked good even in regular gear. Her beauty was natural, she didn't need make up or nothing she was a natural queen ready to claim her spot.

"Hi Jovan." Germain said.

"Hi Germain." Jovan said.

"How you doing?"

"I'm fine."

"That's good, how'd you like the party last night?" Germain asked.

"It was cool."

"What about the after party?" She started laughing.

"What after party, Germain?" Jovan asked, even though he knew she was insinuating about the explosive sex that Sonya and him had.

"The one on Connecticut Avenue." She said, still laughing.

"Bye Germain, you talk too much, open the trunk so I can get my bags." Sonya said, as she tried to hide her embarrassment.

Sonya got her bags and Germain and she said their good-byes.

"Bye Jovan."

"See you later Germain. Sonya, let me get them bags for you.

Damn girl, you got a lot of shit." Jovan said, getting her bags out of Germain's truck.

"Wait til you see what I got."

As they walked to Jovan's van Sonya started looking at him funny.

"Jovan, you look different boo." She said, still not sure what was different about Jovan.

"What you mean, what I don't appeal to you no more?"

"No silly, it's just something different about you, you're still fine but I'm sure you know that already."

"Naw, I only know what you tell me. Now what's different about me?"

"You look younger."

"Younger?"

"Yeah."

"Oh I know what you're talking about."

'What?"

"My goatee is gone."

"Yeah that's it, what you do shave it off?"

"Naw, I went to a different barber shop this morning and they fucked my shit up so I told him to shave it off. Don't worry it'll grow back in two days."

"I didn't say anything was wrong with it, you're still handsome, but?" Then she laughed.

"But what?"

"You look so young."

"Ok, so now you calling me a youngin?"

"No baby, you still look nice, I'm just playin'. You ain't mad at me are you?"

"Naw, I ain't mad."

"Cause if you were then I got something to cheer you up, but we gotta go to my house to get it." She said, with a sly grin on her face.

"Well, in that case I'm mad as hell." Jovan said, laughing

"I bet you are Jovan."

Sonya kissed Jovan once they got in the van and said, "I missed you all day."

"Me too, but before we go over to your house, I gotta go down the street to my Grandma's first."

"Ok baby."

Jovan's Grandma only lived a few blocks down the street from the gym. He still had the three million in the suitcases Bilal had told him to put up. When they got to his Grandma's house, he pulled out the suitcases and began to take them in the house.

"What's up Jovan, you packing up and moving out?"

"Naw Sonya, this is just some old things I had in storage while I was in school." Jovan said, lying.

Jovan went upstairs and put the suitcases in his room. When he came back downstairs, Sonya and Grandma was kicking it like old friends, Grandma liked Sonya which was cool because Grandma usually doesn't bond with just anybody. Jovan kissed Grandma, told her he'd be back later and they left.

On the way to Sonya's, they stopped at a 7 Eleven and Sonya went inside and got a few things. When they got to Sonya's condo, Jovan cooked dinner which was baked fish and baked potatoes and a toss salad. They ate, cuddled and watched TV, but after a while, they went right back to what they were doing last night.

This time Jovan was less aggressive and more gentle as they made love in the living room first, then the kitchen, the bathroom and finally, they found ourselves on the bedroom floor dripping from sweat and lovemaking. Jovan held Sonya deep in his chest as she gave him little kisses and rubbed her hands over his chest.

"Jovan, you're a king you know that?" Sonya said.

"If I'm a king, then what that make you?" Jovan asked.

"I don't know if I want you to say it." Sonya said, as she playfully pulled the hairs on his chest.

"I rather not say it, I'll just show you."

"You already have baby, you already have. You treated me like a queen from day one."

"Visa versa."

Sonya then got up and Jovan loved watching her walk around in the nude with her ass jiggling and titties bouncing. She went into the living room and came back with her shopping bags.

She gave Jovan one and said, "Here."

"What, what's this?"

"It's yours, open it."

Jovan reached in the bag and pulled out a black and silver Giovanni Versace sports jacket. First thing he did was look at the tag, which was $2,750.

"Sonya, this is nice but where you get the money to buy this?" Jovan asked her.

"Jovan, stop playin' with me."

"Ok, then how you know I don't have this jacket already?"

"That jacket was just brought in today, they didn't even have it on the rack and the faggot, Author, that works in there said that it wasn't going to be on sale until two weeks from now. You were at the gym all day, it would have been impossible for you to go all the way up Wisconsin Avenue and meet me back at the gym by 2:00 o'clock. Shit Jovan, I damn near had to pitch a bitch for him to sell it to me."

"Well boo, thank you very much, I like it, come here give me a kiss." Jovan said, pulling Sonya into his arms.

Sonya got back on the floor with Jovan and they kissed and made love all night long.

CHAPTER 21

"Against All Odds"

Bilal sent his carriers down to Mexico by plane and he was to get a call from them as soon as they landed. At 8:30 p.m., Bilal's connect called and told him that no one had exited the plane with the briefcases. Bilal then called the airport to see if there was a delay in the flight, he was told there was no delay but another flight was to land at 2:00 a.m. in the morning. Bilal called his connect back and told them that another flight was to land at 2:00 a.m. and that his carriers, which were two women, Meeka's and Carlos cousins, probably missed the flight, the connect said that they would call when they arrived.

Bilal was at home wondering what the hell had happened to Meeka and Carlos cousin, but he didn't panic even though he was going through a lot. Carlos had been killed, Meeka was pregnant and his pager was blowing up from niggas who was tryna spend money. Bilal had to keep calling niggas telling them to hold fast, that shit would be ready soon.

At 12:00 o'clock Jovan called Bilal from Sonya's.

Ring, Ring, Ring. "Hello." Bilal said.

"Damn Lal, you picking shit up on the first ring."

"Oh hey what's up Jay?"

"I'm just trippin' right now." Bilal said.

"What's up?" Jovan asked Bilal.

"You know my people ain't get there yet." Bilal said, worried as shit.

"What time was they supposed to be there?"

"Around 8:15-8:30." He said.

"Well, they mighta had a delay, you call the Airport?"

"Yeah I called, there wasn't any delay but another flight is due to land around 2:00 am."

"Cool, then they're probably on that joint."

"Jay, where you at?"

"Over Sonya's."

"You over there again?"

"Yeah."

"Damn nigga, that pussy must be good, don't let me find out you fallin' in love nigga." Bilal said, laughing

"Go head wit that shit Lal."

"Jay, did you handle that?" Bilal said, referring to Chicken Wing.

"Most definitely like a pro."

"Yeah."

"My smoothest one so far, I'll give it to you raw when I see you."

"Ok slim, you coming by in the morning?"

"Naw, tomorrow's Monday, you know I gotta work in the morning man."

"Oh yeah, I forgot you a big show lawyer." Bilal said, once again jokingly.

"Not yet Lal, but soon." Jovan said.

"I see you later Jay."

"Ok Lal." Jovan said, as he was about to hang up the phone.

"Oh Jay."

"What's up Lal?"

"I love you nigga"

"I love you too Lal."

It felt good talking to his best friend, even though he been through a lot lately, he sounded better, like everything was going as planned. Jovan would be glad when Bilal got that shit and dump it off fast so they could get the fuck away from here and do their thing legally. He could finish school in Atlanta, start his own law firm and have a few other businesses on the side.

While Sonya was still asleep, Jovan tried his new jacket on. This joint was tight as fuck. Jovan was going to wear this tomorrow with his black Versace slacks and white Versace mock neck shirt. Jovan knew Cindy want a nigga to slam meat up in her cause every time he came in she was always looking at him, complimenting him and shit. But Jovan wasn't gonna go at her though, shit Sonya was enough and right now she's all a nigga need.

As Jovan went to get a glass of juice outta Sonya's refrigerator, he didn't hear her creep up on him.

"So you couldn't wait to try it on, huh." Sonya said, smiling

Jovan turned around fast butt ass naked with his jacket on and said, "So how does it look on me boo?"

She laughed and said, "It would look better if you had on a pair of pants on to go with it."

"Yeah, you're right but right now since you're up, let me do something that'll make you smile."

"What's that?"

Jovan took his jacket off, blindfolded Sonya, fed her some fruit then smothered her body with chocolate and licked it all off not missing a spot. He could tell Sonya loved every bit of his lovemaking because no matter how he gave it to her she accepted it with multiple orgasms.

Jovan woke up the next morning around 8:00 a.m. Shit, he had to go to work and his pager was blowing up but he was in too much of a rush to look at it. Sonya was taking the day off so she cooked breakfast while he showered.

After Jovan got out the shower and looked at his pager, it was Bilal hitting him 911. Jovan immediately called back.

Ring, Ring, Ring. "Hello," Bilal said.

"Lal, it's me Jovan." Jovan said.

"Yeah Jay, look you gotta get over here fast."

"What's up Lal, you sound worried?"

"I can't talk on the phone, shit's looking fucked up."

"You a'ight?"

"Physically yeah, but mentally I'm fucked up Jay."

"Look, I'm on my way but first I gotta call the office."

Jovan called the office and lied to Mark.

Ring, Ring, Ring. "Good morning, law office of Rohon & Robinson." Cindy said.

"Cindy this Jovan, is Mark in yet?"

"Yes Jovan, he just came in."

"Mark, Jovan on line one." Cindy said to Mark.

"Jovan, what's up buddy?" Mark said.

"Hey Mark look, I'ma be a little late today."

"Ok Jovan, what time will you be in? You know we have a new case."

"Yeah I know, I'm going to be working on that while I'm out anyway."

"What are you going to do?" Mark asked Jovan.

"Well, you know the case we got where the guy was supposed to be selling drugs within a thousand feet of a school?"

"Yeah Jovan, that's the new one."

"Well, I don't think he was within that distance so I'm going to go out and measure it and take a few pictures." Jovan said, lying to Mark.

"That's good Jovan, take your time."

"Ok Mark, I'll see you later."

"Alright buddy."

Jovan kissed Sonya and told her he was in a rush and that he wasn't gonna be able to stay and eat breakfast. She kissed him and told him how proud she was of him for taking such pride in his job. Little did she know Jovan's duty right now wasn't to the law firm, it was to and for his loyalty to his truest friend, Bilal, his nigga for life.

As Jovan drove to Bilal's house faster than normal speed, he got there around 9:00 o'clock. As soon as Jovan came through the door, he knew something terrible had happened.

"C'mon downstairs Jay." Bilal said, heading downstairs.

Bilal eyes were bloodshot red and you could tell he didn't get any sleep.

"What's up Lal?"

"Jay, shit done got twisted, I should have listened to you from the jump." Bilal said, pacing.

"What happened?"

"Well last night, you know my carriers missed the first flight, or at least that's what we thought."

"Man Lal, don't tell me them bitches rolled out with the money."

"Naw, Jay just listen man. I stayed up all night and at 2:00 a.m. the second plane landed and my connect tells me ain't nobody get off the plane but some old people."

"What?" Jovan said, still not understanding.

"So what I did was called around looking for my carriers and nobody gave me any information, so I stayed up pacing the fucking floor all night wondering what the fuck happened, I even called Customs to see if them bitches had gotten locked up. Then I get a call around 7:30 this morning from the Precinct and come to find out these bitches never made it to the airport. That bitch ma'fuckin' Detective Tony Bridges, was following me when I gave them bitches the suitcases." Bilal said.

"Man Bilal, I told you that ma'fucka wasn't playing."

"I know Jay, that white cracker had it out for me ever since I took Orleans Pl. over."

"Did the bitches tell?"

"Naw, not yet but who knows what they'll do."

"Lal, we gotta go."

"I know Jay, but now ain't the time."

"The fuck you mean now ain't the time!!! Man in the next 24 hours, them peoples gonna be swarming the streets looking for your ass. Nigga fuck that, pack your shit and let's go!" Jovan told Bilal.

"Jay I gotta, I mean we gotta, do something fast."

"What, we already got 3 million and I know you still got something stashed in the cut for hard times, let's go Lal, I know how these people play."

"Yeah, I got like three hundred thousand over Meeka aunt's house, but that's around Orleans Pl."

"So fuck it, we'll send for it when we get to Atlanta."

"Jay I can't leave now, Meeka's pregnant and I still gotta get that money and..." Bilal said, but Jovan cut him off.

"And what, and what Lal?"

Lal looked Jovan straight in the eyes with all the sincerity he had ever seen and said, "Jay, you gotta kill Detective Bridges."

"What!" Jovan said, shocked at Bilal's request.

"Look Jay, I ain't never ask you for nothing, I've never asked you to kill nobody for me, you killed them other niggas outta your love for me. Jay, I'm asking you outta love and loyalty, if you want me to do it with you, I'll do it but you already know I ain't no killer Jay. This ma'fucka stole our dream from us and if we don't take care of him now then he'll haunt us forever."

"Lal, you trippin', that's a fucking police officer. Do you know the Feds will be on your ass for that?"

"Jay, I know we can get away with this, I know we can man."

When Jovan looked at Lal, he had tears in his eyes and he was looking at the tattoo on his arm which read, "In loving

Memory Of Mal-Mal, My Truest Love", and at that moment a sense of guilt came over Jovan.

After all these years, Jovan still felt responsible for Mal-Mal's death. Bilal showed his loyalty to Jovan at the tender age of fifteen and he failed him when he let his little brother die. Jovan always wanted to do something in return, he always wanted to fix that void in their relationship because deep down in Bilal's heart, he knew he held him responsible for Mal-Mal's death, he just loved Jovan too much to show it. Bilal and Jovan never talked about what happened that night when Mal-Mal died, but Jovan knew Ms. Cookie went to visit Bilal before she died and whatever was said on that visit Jovan would never know. He owed this nigga, he stand on principles of loyalty and honor and plus, he loved this nigga, he was his only friend they're like brothers. They made a vow at a young age that would never be broken.

"Ok Lal listen good, I'll make a deal with you."

"What Jay?"

"Look, after I handle this business, we're getting the fuck outta here, fuck that waitin' around to see what happens shit, we're taking the three million plus the two hundred thousand I got and we're going to Atlanta, you and. We'll leave Meeka up here to sell the house and get the three hundred thousand from over her aunt's. Let the house go for three million to get an easy buy, altogether that's six and a half million plus assets. We sell the 850, that's about fifty thousand plus the jewelry, that's about two hundred, and I know you got some jewelry too."

"Yeah Jay, I got about half a mil in jewelry."

"Ok, altogether that's seven point two million, we take that shit to Atlanta, legalize all of it and live comfortable and peaceful for the rest of our lives. Lal that's a one shot deal and if you ain't tryna do that, then I'm gone." Jovan told Bilal, seriously.

"But Jay, the Feds don't even know who you are, why you tryna leave."

"That's good they don't know who I am and I ain't tryna stick around so they can find out either. So, you in or what?"

"Nigga, you're my best friend and I love you. Jay, you my only family and I got no choice but to be in." Bilal said.

"Ok and Lal when we get to Atlanta ain't no hustling." Jovan said to him.

"It's a deal Jay."

"Ok now, I gotta put this shit together."

"How you gonna do it Jay?"

"I dunno yet, where's that desert eagle .357?" Jovan asked Bilal.

"It's upstairs in the room."

"Go get it."

Bilal went upstairs to get Jovan the gun and when he came down, Jovan was still in a daze wondering why the fuck he had just commit himself to do this crime. Damn, Bilal trippin' like shit, but Jovan laid the deal on the table and Bilal agreed with his plans. If everything went as planned, then they wouldn't have nothing to worry about and plus Bilal was right, if they left now Detective Bridges would track them down, he had to be dealt with.

Bilal came downstairs with the biggest gun Jovan had ever seen, a silver .357 Desert Eagle, one shot one kill.

"Jay, this here is my house gun, I keep it at home for protection."

"How many bullets does it hold?"

"Ten."

"This big ass gun only holds ten bullets?" Jovan asked, amazed.

"Yeah Jay, but that's the most powerful gun out there, one shot will send a ma'fucka straight to la-la land."

"Ok Lal, you got any money on you?"

"Nigga my name is money, how much you need?" Bilal said.

"About five thousand in big bills."

"You got that Jay."

Bilal went upstairs to get the money and as Jovan was downstairs still contemplating my next move, he heard Bilal and Meeka upstairs arguing about something. Jovan knew Meeka wasn't trippin' about the money Bilal was giving him, if so then Bilal didn't have his people in check.

"Here you go Jay, that's six thousand in case you need extra."

"A'ight thanks. Look Bilal, I'ma lay these demonstrations down proper, tomorrow morning get all your things together and when I call you be ready to leave."

"Ok Jay, oh Jay." Bilal said.

"Yeah what's up Lal?"

"What's up with that girl you've been spending all your time with?"

"Man Lal, for real I'm diggin' the shit outta her, but right now I got a more serious situation to deal with and if I gotta leave her behind then she's staying behind."

"Damn slim, I wish I could leave Meeka behind but she's pregnant."

"Bilal that's your decision, if you think it'd be better for her to stay then don't bring her."

"I'll think about it Jay."

"Yeah well by tomorrow morning I hope you come up with an answer. Look I'm gone I'll talk to you later."

It was 10:00 a.m. when Jovan left Bilal. He drove back to the city so fast that he got there in half an hour. Jovan went straight to Sunny Surplus Uniform Supply Store and purchased a blue police department t-shirt and hat, he also brought two metropolitan police stickers and two envelope folders.

Jovan drove down Benning Road to the automobile shop that sells old taxicabs and unmarked old police cars with the big spotlight on the side. The dealer was an old man who didn't care if you had ID or not, he just wanted to see cash. Jovan brought a late model 1986 Caprice Classic white with black interior and shinny hubcaps for $4,000. He parked his van on the side street next to Club Chateau and took out all of the things he had brought from the Supply Store. He put on the t-shirt and hat, took out an ink pen and wrote Bilal Davis on both folders. Jovan then placed a Metropolitan Police Department sticker in the back window and one in front on the left side by the spotlight.

Jovan was about to drive around to Orleans Pl., but before he did, he rode through 18th and D's drug market to test his disguise When Jovan rolled through the strip, niggas immediately scattered like roaches and he was satisfied with his disguise. He rolled through Orleans Pl. looking for any signs of Detective Bridges because he knew for sure he was out here looking for Bilal. Jovan spotted an unmarked police car sitting in the alley, he rode pass and entered the alley from the other side so that their cars would be opposite of each other and that both driver sides would meet.

As Jovan drove up he could see that everything was working out perfectly. Detective Tony Bridges was sitting in his car looking at something in his lap sipping on some coffee.

Jovan pulled his hat down and pulled up along side Detective Bridge's car and said, "Hi, how are you, I'm Detective J. Newman from the seventh district."

"Well Newman, what brings you into my territory?" Detective Bridges said.

"Well, I'm investigating a case of some big drug dealer who's controlling drugs in certain Southeast neighborhoods."

"What's his name?"

Jovan held up the two folders with Bilal's name on them.

"Bilal Davis, don't know much about him though." Jovan said.

"Well Newman, I think you just hit the jackpot. I'm here looking for the asshole, I just popped two of his carriers this morning." Detective Bridges said.

"Are they talking?"

"Well yeah their cooperating, but I think I need a little time with 'em."

""How long you been out here Detective 'huh' "Bridges is it?"

"Tony Bridges. Well, I just came out here about ten minutes ago." He said.

"Yeah me too. I've been cruisin' up and down these streets, I haven't even stopped to get a bite to eat yet."

"Well Newman, the best thing I can do for you is a Snicker's bar." Detective Bridges said.

"Well hell yeah, that beats nothin' at all."

As Detective Bridges went into his glove compartment to get the candy bar, Jovan pulled the .357 Desert Eagle from up under his leg. This was the only time he was paranoid and nervous with butterflies creeping in his stomach, he was in a state of oblivion. Detective Bridges was bringing the Snicker's bar up and as soon as he turned back in Jovan's direction exposing his face into the barrel of the gun, Jovan shot him one time right between the eyes. "Boom", the impact of the bullet was so powerful you could practically see brain matter scattered all over the inside of his car. Jovan then wiped off the gun and threw it in Detective Bridges' car. He pulled off slow and headed back down Benning Road at a normal speed.

Once Jovan got back to his van, he parked the car, took off the temporary tags and set the title and registration on fire because even though it was in a bogus name, he still didn't want to take any chances. He took off the t-shirt and hat and threw everything in the garbage. He then parked the car right behind the dealership so that if the police were ever looking for a white caprice, they wouldn't bother to look at this one because the dealership has about twenty white caprice classics. Jovan walked across the street to his van and drove back to work.

"Hello Cindy." Jovan said, walking into the office.

"Hi Jovan, how are you?" Cindy asked.

"Fine thanks. Cindy is Mark still in his office?"

"Yeah."

Jovan left Cindy's desk and walked into Mark's office where he was sitting at his desk going over some paperwork.

"Hey Jovan." Mark said, looking up from his work.

"Hey Mark, how you doing?"

"Well, everything's going ok but I still gotta get this kid's motion straight. Did you measure the distance?"

"Yeah and from where they're saying he was standing was definitely within a thousand feet, it was more like seven hundred feet to be honest."

"Shit Jovan, we gotta find some kinda technicality for this kid because if not, he's a goner."

"Don't worry 'bout that Mark, just give me a little time in the library."

"Ok Jovan, do your thing."

Jovan went into the library but he could hardly work because the thought of what he just did and the anticipation of going to Atlanta, was putting him in a state of confusion. He sat back for a moment and got his thoughts together. He then realized what he had just done was for the better and that from now on his life would be at peace.

Jovan got all the motions ready for Mark, it was a rush job, but it was complete. Mark read over Jovan's motions and asked him to change a few things, so he went back and put his all into them and delivered the best motions he had ever put together, just like the motion that helped set him free when he was in Lewisburg. Mark liked the motions so much that he made copies and placed them on the desk of all the associate attorneys. Before Jovan left work, he called Sonya at home. He missed Sonya bad and he wanted to ask her to leave with him but he couldn't.

Ring, Ring, Ring. "Hello." Sonya said.

"What's up baby?" Jovan said.

"You Jovan, I miss you so much."

"Sonya, I've only been out of your sight for a few hours."

"I missed you the moment you walked out that door this morning and I've been thinking about you all day." Sonya said, seriously.

"Me too, you've been on my mind so much I couldn't even work."

"Jovan, we gotta do something about this."

"Ain't too much we can or do you got any suggestions?" Jovan asked.

"Yeah, come stay with me tonight." Sonya said, hoping Jovan would agree to spend another night with her.

"I was planning on doing that anyway."

"I bet you were. What time you coming?"

"I'll be there right after work."

As soon as Jovan got off from work, he went straight to Sonya's condo. When he came in, Sonya was butt ass naked with a pair of red pumps on, his kinda girl, she wanted it morning, noon and night and he gave it to her. While Sonya and Jovan were lying together cuddled up after a long session of lovemaking, they began to talk.

"Hey my King." Sonya said.

"Yeah my Queen." Jovan answered.

"Have you ever felt something but was scared to address it because of what the outcome may be."

Jovan wanted to say yes in relation to what he did earlier, but instead he said, "No boo, if there's something I feel that needs to be addressed, then I'ma shoot my shot."

"Well Jovan, in that case I don't know what the outcome of what I'm about to say is gonna be, but I'm prepared."

"Is it something that I need to know?" Jovan asked, curious about what Sonya was about to tell him.

"Maybe, maybe not depends on how you take it."

"Well, go head and shoot your shot."

"Jovan C. Price, I think I'm falling in love with you." Sonya said, smiling.

"Well Sonya C. Dunkin, I feel the exact same way about you." Jovan said, taking her into his arms.

They hugged tight and kissed as Jovan wiped tears from Sonya's eyes, he knew that he was filling in that missing spot in her life and he accepted it. They made love again and fell asleep in each other arms.

The next morning Jovan called Bilal's house and when he didn't get an answer, he thought he must be out getting shit together so they could leave. The more Jovan looked at Sonya the worse he felt because last night she told him she was in love with him and she doesn't even know that he's leaving and she'll never see him again. As bad as he wanted to tell her he was leaving, he couldn't because he was in love with her also. Jovan tried to call Bilal's house again and still there wasn't no answer, "where the fuck is Bilal at?" Jovan wondered.

Jovan waited a few more minutes then decided to call Mark and tell him he would be leaving his job and going back to school.

Ring, Ring, Ring. "Good morning, law offices of Rohon & Robinson." Cindy said.

"Cindy, get me Mark." Jovan said.

"Oh, hello Jovan." Cindy said.

"I'm sorry, how you doing Cindy." Jovan said, apologizing for his rudeness.

"I'm fine thank you, hold on. Mark, Jovan's on line one."

Mark didn't pick up the phone instead he put Jovan on the intercom.

"Hey Jovan." Mark said.

"Hey Mark."

"I got some good news Jovan?"

"What's that?"

"I've got an old client who just got locked up this morning and he's got plenty of money to give us."

"Who's that?"

"Remember Bilal Davis?"

When Mark said that, a sharp pain hit Jovan in his heart. Jovan asked Mark, "What, who Mark?" He knew he did not just say Bilal had been arrested.

"Bilal Davis, the guy we just got out, he's back in trouble again and guess what the fool did Jovan?" Mark said.

"What Mark?" Jovan said.

"Do you remember the cop who walked up on us in court that day?"

When he said that Jovan damned near dropped the phone, this shit can't be real. Instantly, Jovan started to get dizzy and after a few seconds, he finally pulled myself together but was still trembling with fear for what he was soon about to hear.

"Well yesterday, that cop was killed on one of Bilal's drug strips and the gun that was used was left on the scene."

Jovan was saying to myself, I wiped the gun off, but he said to Mark, "Were there fingerprints on the gun?"

"No Jovan, no prints, but there was something worse than that."

"What?"

"The gun is registered in his fiancée's name."

Fuck, why the fuck didn't Bilal tell him that shit. Wait Bilal did say that this was his house gun, but hell he still didn't tell him it was registered in Meeka's name. Maybe that's what he and Meeka were arguing about. Fuck, shit all fucked up now for real.

"Mark, when did they get him?" Jovan asked.

"This morning, they locked him and his fiancée up. This is some major money for us Jovan. You coming by the office?"

"Yeah, I'll be there in a few."

After Jovan hung up with Mark, he kissed Sonya and got in the shower while she went downstairs to cook breakfast. While Jovan was in the shower, he started getting his thoughts together. Damn, Bilal shit's all fucked up. Jovan knew he had to leave now for sure. He knew Bilal wasn't saying a word but Meeka knows he gave him that gun and you know how scared females can get, they ain't used to this shit, plus she's pregnant, so he knew she's gonna tell. Jovan had 3.5 million, his van, the 850 BMW and two hundred thousand worth in jewelry, what he was gonna was do was leave Mark a retainer fee, tell him that it's from Bilal's family, pack his shit and head to Atlanta or maybe California. Wherever he went, it had to be far the fuck away from DC.

Jovan got out of the shower, ate a little something and told Sonya he had to leave for work. When he got to the door, he grabbed Sonya and held her tight. Jovan gave her the most passionate kiss ever, he put his heart and soul in it because this was the last time he was ever gonna touch her again.

After Jovan kissed her, she looked at him and said, "Damn Jovan!"

"What boo?"

"You just kissed me like this is the last time we're ever gonna kiss."

"Naw boo, I ain't going nowhere, I'll be back later on to finish it up, bye."

As Jovan walked down the hall he was crushed that he was lying to Sonya, cause if there was anybody he wanted to be with, it was her and he knew he wouldn't find no one else like her.

CHAPTER 22

"The Unforgiven"

Jovan went straight to Mark's office when he got in because he wanted Mark to fill him in on everything before he packed his shit. Mark told Jovan everything about their old client Bilal Davis. He said that he wouldn't be able to see him until about three days from now, after all the processing.

"Ok Mark, before I get too deep into this case, I first gotta go take care of something at home." Jovan said.

"Ok Jovan, but hurry back, I'ma need your special services on this one."

"You got it Mark." Jovan said, leaving Mark's office.

As Jovan was leaving out of the building, cars pulled up from everywhere. Uniformed and plainclothes officers, even the FBI, had their guns in Jovan's face.

"Don't fuckin' move, you're under arrest!" Someone with a gun in Jovan's face, yelled at him.

"What?"

"Put your hands on your head!" Another one yelled.

Now, as Jovan was putting his hands on his head, the Channel 5 news van pulled up. At that time, Mark came out of the building and said, "What the hell is going on?"

Mark knew some of the agents who were arresting Jovan and one of them said, "Mark, it's a long story, come on down to Homicide and I'll fill you in."

"Homicide?"

"Yeah Mark, it's a real messy situation." The agent said to Mark.

As Jovan was being handcuffed and hustled past the TV Reporter with his head down trying to cover his face from the camera, I heard the Reporter say, "Jovan Price, is being arrested for the murder of DC Police Narcotics, Detective Anthony T. Bridges."

Jovan was taken to the Homicide Division downtown and interrogated. They knew he was in the legal field so they did everything according to the law. Once Jovan was arrested, he was read his Miranda rights and while attempting to interrogate him again, they asked him he wanted to exercise his rights.

Jovan replied, "Yes, I wish to exercise my Fifth Amendment right to remain silent. I also would like to request an attorney from the law offices in which I'm employed." Jovan said.

At that moment, Michelle Robinson walked in and said, "Excuse me gentlemen, it is obvious that my client wishes not to speak with you and may I ask that you leave so I can converse with him in private."

The Feds were mad as fuck but they couldn't do anything, everything was according to the law.

"Jovan, what the hell is going on?" Michelle asked him once the Feds had left the room.

"I don't know Michelle, that's what I'm trying to figure out." Jovan told Michelle.

"They said they got an indictment on you in two hours and you know with all the publicity in this case, it's gonna be hard for me to get those Grand Jury Transcripts."

"Yeah, I know but work your way around and try and get them as fast as you can."

Jovan really didn't need the Grand Jury Transcripts cause he already knew that it was gonna say that Meeka snitched. She probably told the police that Bilal gave him the gun and that she argued with Bilal not to give it to him. She's gonna say Bilal was at home with her when the murder took place and that left only one suspect, him.

Jovan's main thing now was that outta all the murders he had committed, he didn't set up an alibi for this one. Fuck, his tightest job ever turned into his sloppiest work overnight.

"Look Jovan, I'm gonna take the case. Mark can't be your attorney because you're his employee and he also can't take your co-defendant because it would be a conflict of interest issue." Michelle said.

"So it's you and me Michelle?"

"Yeah and we're gonna ride this thing out until the wheels fall off Jovan. Well, there isn't too much we can do right now but go 'head and let 'em process you and when you get over to the DC jail, we can get everything together. Is there anyone you want me to call?"

"Yeah listen."

Jovan told Michelle to come closer so he could whisper in her ear, she understood everything he said very clearly and she shook her head in a yes motion and left.

Sonya
While I was still at work, Germain came running downstairs as if a bomb was about to go off in the building screaming, "Sonya, Sonya!"

"What Germain, what's going on?" I asked her.

"Oh my God Sonya, look!" She said, pointing to the television.

"Look at what Germain, you're scaring me." Sonya said, full of fear that something terrible had happened.

She then grabbed my hand and led me to the television and when I looked at the television, I saw Jovan's face. Instantly my whole body went numb as I listened to the news reporters. As I collapsed on the floor, Germain and another co-worker had to literally pick me up and shake me back to reality.

"Oh my God, please tell me I'm having a nightmare please! This can't be true, not Jovan, it can't be, Noooh!" I cried out loud as I covered my face with my hands and slid off the wall onto the floor. "No, not the man I'm in love with, this shit ain't supposed to happen to me!" I said as I continued to cry my heart out.

I cried so hard that the pupils in my eyes began to swell, nothing in the world could explain what I was feeling at that moment, and I mean nothing! I was so much in a daze that Germain had to wave her hand across my face as if to awake me from a hypnotic spell.

I took off work and went straight home to wait for Jovan to call and tell me what to do. For him to tell me that this wasn't him, that someone is trying to frame him, some type of lawyer scheme, tell me anything, but just don't tell me that it was him. Hell no, not Jovan, not my boo, I wouldn't believe it if it wasn't on camera because that's not his style.

While at home I cried so much that I cried myself to sleep without eating or drinking anything. I fell asleep in my living room with Jovan's t-shirt on smelling his scent. I was missing my man, wondering when was he gonna call and tell me to come visit him. Whatever Jovan wants me to do I'll do it, if he needs money for a lawyer, I got that, every visiting day I'll be there looking fly representing for my man. If he needs me to run errands, then I'll take all my leave from my job to be at his aide, I'll do anything for Jovan, anything.

Jovan

I was fingerprinted and processed at central cell booking then transported to the DC jail, also know as the Lion's Den. I was given an orange jumper, some blue karate shoes (that's what they call 'em) and a bedroll. I was sent straight to the hole and placed on special handling lockdown mainly because of the publicity in my case. As I was being transported handcuffed and shackled through the hallway and escorted by a white shirt lieutenant, I could hear dudes talking as I went by.

"Slim, ain't that the lawyer dude that was on TV today?" One inmate said.

"Yeah that's him, they say he put in that work on that police-man." Another inmate said.

Normally, other dudes would take that as a compliment of honor but me, I was ashamed, I never wanted my work to be known. As I was led to my cell and locked in, I could see everybody standing in their cells looking at me, some was whispering to each other, others were asking the CO what time would they be able to come out for their one hour of recreation. You could use that time to take a shower or use the phone, play basketball or just go around and talk to other inmates through the bars.

As I was making my bed, I heard someone call my name, at first I thought it was Bilal but the voice was different.

"Jovan, hey Jovan." The voice said.

"Yeah, who dat?"

"Chaz."

"Who?"

"Lil Chaz, from the Valley!" He said, as he screamed through the bars.

"Yeah nigga, what's up youngin?" I said, remembering the youngin.

"Ain't shit slim, I saw you come through the door."

"Then why you ain't say nothin'?"

"I was gonna let you get your shit together first. Look, I'm on detail and I come out in about ten minutes, I'ma come down and holla at you cause I ain't tryna scream through these bars you know how the walls got ears around here." Chaz said.

"Yeah I'm hip." I said, knowing that niggas were eaves dropping.

Chaz was from Valley Green Southeast. When I was doing shit on Whaler Pl. back in the day, shorty was my number #1 youngin, he used to pump coke and plus he wasn't no dummy. I had always liked this youngin, but the thing is his ass stayed locked up. After hearing Chaz tell me he was on detail, I was somewhat glad because even though this is a lockdown block, they still have at least two detail workers who clean up and in return they get to come out of their cells for a few extra hours and walk the tier or use the phone. I figured when he comes out I'd get him to make a phone call for me.

When Chaz came out for recreation, he came straight down to my cell and started sliding me shit through the bars. He gave me a bag of soap, toothpaste, lotion, peanut butter and crackers and some cigarettes so I could buy food off of other niggas trays and a big ass knife with rigids on the side. In DC jail, it was a must that one kept a knife on him, and if not on him, somewhere close by. I put the knife up in a good spot and shorty and me kicked it for the next hour.

"Yeah Jay, I saw that shit on TV earlier." Chaz said.

"Yeah you know that's some bullshit." I said, looking him in the eye.

"Whatever it is I know you can handle it."

"Hey Chaz, you see them bring my man Bilal in here?"

"Naw, but I heard they got him in the intake block."

"The intake block?"

"Yeah, you know Bilal got that power in here, these ma'-fuckas do whatever he says."

"How long you think they gonna keep me on special handling?"

"Most likely until the publicity dies down. Look Jovan, I've only got like twenty minutes left you want me to call somebody for you?" Chaz asked.

"Yeah, hold up." I wrote Sonya's number down and gave it to Chaz. "Tell her I said to call my grandmother and comfort her and to come see me tomorrow on visits."

"Ok slim, is that all?"

"Oh, tell her I said I love her."

"A'ight slim."

"Oh Chaz." I said, before he left to make the call to Sonya.

"What's up Jovan?"

"Why you in here on lockdown?" I asked him, curiously.

"Cause I had to put that knife in one of them bitch niggas upstairs who wasn't hip to my work."

Sonya
At 10:00 p.m. I received a collect call from the DC jail. The operator said, "You have a collect call from a Jovan, press 5 if you accept."

"Hello baby, please tell me that wasn't you." I said, anxiously.

"Hold up, this ain't Jovan." Chaz said.

"Then who the hell is this?" Sonya said.

"I'm a friend of Jovan's, he asked me to deliver you this message."

"Ok, I'm sorry." I said.

"I understand. He wants you to call his grandmother and comfort her, he also wants you to come visit him tomorrow and he told me to tell you he loves you." Chaz said.

At that moment, tears gushed outta my eyes like a waterfall.

"Tell him that I'll be there and that I love him also."

"I sure will."

"Thank you and hey I'm sorry for cursing at you." I said, embarrassed.

"It's ok, like I said I understand." Chaz said.

The call I had been waiting for all night finally came through and it wasn't even Jovan. Even though it wasn't him, the message that he sent still rang in my ears like church bells.

Jovan
The next morning, I was told to get ready for a visit, visiting hours didn't start until 1:00 p.m., and it was only 9:30 a.m. It must be Michelle coming to talk about the case, well whoever it is, I'm ready because I got to get a message to Bilal to get me outta this hole. The Lieutenant cuffed and walked me to the visiting room and when I came through the door they led me to the same conference room I interviewed Bilal in, it was Michelle and Andy, Mark's investigator.

"Hey Jovan, how they treating you?" Michelle asked me.

"Like shit, they got me locked down because of all the publicity."

"Don't worry 'bout that, I'll call the jail and pull a few strings for you." Andy said.

"Ok Andy thanks."

"Now Jovan, this is it, the Prosecutor says she got some concrete evidence on you but she's not gonna disclose that information to me. She and I don't get along that well, so I'ma have Mark try and pull it outta her no later then within the next couple of weeks so we'll have it." Michelle said.

"Good."

"Also, I called the number you gave me, everything is ok on that end."

"What 'bout the Lab reports on the gun?"

"I have that, there are no fingerprints and only one shot was fired and the gun is registered to a Ms. Tamneka Gonzales." Michelle said.

"That's all it says?" I asked Michelle.

"Yes Jovan." She said.

"What 'bout the Grand Jury Transcripts?"

"We're still working on it. Have you seen your co-defendant Bilal Davis yet?"

"Naw, they got him in the intake block."

"Don't worry, you'll get to see him soon, maybe in a week or so."

"Yeah, try to work that out."

"Ain't too much we can do right now but wait for this evidence the Prosecutor has and the Grand Jury Transcripts." Michelle said.

"Ok Michelle, oh how's Mark handling this?" I asked, afraid to hear her answer.

"He's pissed because of how he used to brag on you and how he's now got a few dick heads clowning him about you."

"Tell him I'm sorry, but this is something that didn't happen, it's some type of mistake."

"I'm sure he knows that Jovan. Oh Jovan, Cindy ain't taking it to well either." Andy said.

"What do you mean Andy?"

"She's been crying, asking about you all day." Andy said, laughing. "Hey, tell me something Jovan, did you tap that ass?"

"Naw Andy I, don't confuse work with pleasure."

CHAPTER 23

"6 Months Later"

Sonya came to visit Jovan every visiting day, but today was the most intense visit they had. Jovan's case was still at a stand still and his trial was not going to start for two weeks. The Prosecutor was still holding back on evidence and Michelle couldn't get her hands on those transcripts. Jovan was prepared because no one could place him at the scene not even Meeka, the only thing she knows is that Bilal gave him the gun and he could argue that because she wasn't downstairs when Bilal gave it to him.

Jovan has only seen Bilal once and that was in the infirmary and he said everything was cool on his end and that they should get a severance on their case. Jovan had already done that because wasn't no sense in both of them going on the same trial, they each had a better chance going in there alone.

Jovan talked to the Lieutenant today and he said that the publicity on his case is down and that he'd let him out into population tomorrow. When Jovan talked to Sonya today on the phone he asked her not to come to his trial and to stay home and wait for his calls. She wasn't tryna hear it though, but Jovan being the man, he had to put his foot down.

At 12:00 o'clock, the Lieutenant came to Jovan's cell. At first, he thought he was coming to tell him to pack up so he could go to population, but instead, he said get ready for a visit. Now

Jovan had already seen Michelle and Andy yesterday and Sonya visits didn't start until 1:00 p.m., a whole hour from now, so who the hell could it be, he knew it wasn't the Homicide Division cause they already knew he wasn't talking.

Jovan got ready for the visit and was escorted to the visiting room. When he came through he saw Mark, Michelle and Andy. This was the first time Jovan had seen Mark since he was arrested. When Jovan entered the room, everyone was quiet Mark did the talking.

"Look Jovan, I had to sell my soul to get you this." He said.

There was a big yellow envelope on the table, and as Jovan reached for it Mark grabbed his hand and said, "Don't look at it in here, take it back to your cell and when you finish make sure this envelope and its contents self-destruct."

They got up to leave and Jovan asked, "That's it?"

"Yeah Jovan, trial starts in two weeks so get ready to rumble."

Jovan was so eager and curious to open the envelope, he pressed for the guards to take him back to his block.

"CO, hey CO, my visit over wit I'm ready to go back!"

"Ok here I come, hold up you're on special handling you gotta wait for a white shirt." The CO said.

Lazy bitch. As Jovan began to get mad, a Lieutenant was walking pass so he said, "Excuse me LT, my visit is over with can you take me back to my block?"

"C'mon, you're Price right?"

"Yeah."

"Well you know you're going to population today." The LT said to me.

"Oh yeah." Jovan said, glad to be getting out of solitary confinement.

"Have your shit packed by three o'clock."

"Ok LT."

As soon as Jovan was placed back in his cell, he opened the envelope. There were only two pages, the first one read:

On May12, 1994 Defendant Jovan C. Price was Indicted in Washington, DC Superior Court for the following murders in the 1st degree.

Count 1 Michael A. Jones aka Fate Mike

Count 2 Peter C. Milligan aka Petey

Count 3 Corey L. Washington aka Chicken Wing

Count 4 Anthony T. Bridges, Detective MPPD 6th District

Additional Summary
It is also known that Defendant Jovan C. Price committed several other murders dating back at least to 1985.

As Jovan read off his indictment his heart started beating so fast he thought he was gonna have a heart attack. He hurried up and moved to the next page. It read:

It is May 21, 1994 and this is the interrogation and debriefing of Bilal Ali Davis. Mr. Davis informed that he was the head of a multi-million dollar drug operation and that Mr. Jovan C. Price was his hit man. Mr. Davis said that most of the weapons used in the murders committed by Mr. Price were discarded and that Mr. Price was an extremely careful professional. Mr. Davis gave extreme detail of most crimes Mr. Price committed, but acknowledged that he was not present at any dating from 1992 on up. But he informed us that Mr. Price committed a murder in 1985 in his presence and that he, Mr. Davis, was arrested

and did time in Cedar Knoll and Oak Hill Youth Division for that crime.

At that very moment, Jovan didn't think there was any definition in the place of words that could describe his pain. He dropped to his knees, the same knees he dropped when Bilal got Juvenile life for a crime he had committed, the same knees he dropped when Mal-Mal and Ms. Cookie died. Jovan couldn't stop the tears from coming down his face because he realized that Bilal had tricked him because he still held him responsible for his little brother's death.

As Jovan got up off the floor, tore up the envelope and papers, he washed his face and when he looked in the mirror he saw a reflection, a true resemblance of his father. Then those jewels that were handed down to him as an innocent child came back, "trust no one", "master your condition", and "keep the suckers within the bounds of moderation". Those precious jewels were given to Jovan at a tender age, preparing him for the future. He always knew that he'd have to live by them but when it came down to Bilal Ali Davis, they didn't apply when they should have.

It was now 1:00 o'clock and Sonya was like clock work when it came down to Jovan's visits. She'd be the first one in line outside, she told 'em that she comes at least an hour early just so she could get in first and get her full visit.

"You got a visit Price!" The LT called out to me. "Cuff up." He said.

When Jovan got into the visiting room, Sonya was looking good as shit. She always came fly representing her nigga to the fullest and she had the deepest glow ever. Jovan knew this woman loved him and knew he loved her, but it would break her heart to know that he's a cold blooded killer, that he killed outta loyalty and love and that his best friend whom he killed for was now doing a whodini trick.

"What's up boo?" Jovan said picking up the phone to speak,

while at the same time looking at Sonya and wishing that they were able to touch each other instead of speaking on these damn phones.

"I love you Jovan." Sonya said, picking up her phone also.

"I love you too."

"Good then, now that we got that outta the way Jovan, I wanna ask you a question."

"What boo?"

"Why don't you want me to come to your trial?" She asked still not understanding why he would not her there by his side.

"I have my reasons and that's it, I don't wanna talk about that." Jovan said, not wanting to reveal the real reason why he didn't want her at his trial. "My trial starts in two weeks and everyday after trial, I'll call to inform you of what's going on, I promise."

"Ok Jovan but I miss you, I miss you so much." Sonya said, not wanting to spend the little time they had together arguing.

"I miss you too Sonya."

We talked for a while and then all of a sudden, Sonya got up out of her seat.

"Jovan, I love you very much, probably more then you'll ever know."

"I love you too baby, now sit down." Jovan said to her, wondering why she was standing up all of a sudden.

"No Jovan, I have something to ask you." She said, still standing.

"What is it and why can't you ask me sitting down?" Jovan said.

"Because Jovan, what I have to asked you is very important."

"Ok boo, go 'head ask your question."

"First, I want you to look at me in my eyes and know that what I'm saying is true and from the of my heart."

As they talked through the glass, Sonya got down on one knee in the visiting hall in front of everybody.

"Jovan Conrad Price will you marry me?" Sonya asked.

Jovan thought, what the fuck is she trippin' off of, he was facing life and she's proposing to him, he had never seen or heard of this shit before.

"Sonya, get up off the floor everybody's looking at you, you're embarrassing yourself." Jovan told her.

"So what, I love you and I want to be your wife and I'm not getting up until you give me an answer." Sonya said, refusing to get up off her knee.

"Look Sonya, there's a lot of shit about me that you don't know." Jovan told her.

"So what Jovan, I don't care about that. There's a history with me also but I love you so much that I'm willing to bury it for you."

"I don't think yours is worst than mine."

"Trust me Jovan, if it ain't, it's running neck to neck."

"Sonya if I marry you there are certain things you must do."

"Whatever it is Jovan, I'll do it. Whatever it takes I'll do it baby. I know you've got skeletons in the closet, who doesn't, I've got some too baby. Whatever you tryna do I'ma follow that pattern, you're the king baby." Sonya said, meaning every word of what she was saying because she loved Jovan more than life itself.

Sonya's eyes got watery as she stayed there on one knee. "Baby, can I get an answer?"

"Sonya, you sure you're ready for that?" Jovan asked her, still unsure of his answer.

"Yes baby."

"You know if I marry you, you gotta be down to the end?"

"Like I said Jovan, I'll do anything, even if it involved anything like Bonnie & Clyde and when I say that nigga, I mean it."

"Sonya, you gotta be down with the move."

"Baby, you lead I'll follow and if you fall down, I'm picking you up and carrying you the rest of the way even if it breaks my back. Now what's the move and can I get an answer?"

"Yes boo, yes I'll marry you." Jovan finally said to her.

Tears started gushing outta Sonya's eyes. "Baby you are my life and I vow with my life that I'll be by your side through any storm."

"Ok boo, I love you too. Now will you please get up off the floor."

After their visit was over Jovan was escorted back to his cell. It was two o'clock and since he had packed his shit earlier for population, he did about fifteen hundred pushups, a thousand crunches and a few bend and reaches. He was thinking about how he was gonna get out of this shitty situation. Jovan was hoping they would put him in the same block as Bilal then he could really figure it out. Jovan wanted to look him in his eyes because the fact that he did this to him made him feel like he's half dead, not his man, his best friend, his only family. Jovan had killed at will for this nigga, he had protected him and fed and clothed this nigga when his dope fiend ass mother wouldn't. How the fuck could he empty his brain and sell his soul like that, what Bilal did to Jovan was unforgiving, he had committed the greatest sin.

The LT came down to my cell and said, "Price, you got your stuff ready?"

"Yeah LT I'm ready. Where I'm going?"

"You're going to NE 3 Cell 63."

As soon as Jovan got to the block, the first people he saw were Lil Rat Man from Glass Manor and Lil Hog from down Southwest, they were running the block. These niggas had all types of tennis shoes, commissary knives, street food, weed and liquor. They said they had a cellular phone but the police took it when they got shook down last week. Damn, Jovan would have loved to use that cell joint right about now.

It was almost 2:15 and the CO came and started calling for Jumah (the Muslim prayer service).

"Jovan." Lil Rat said.

"What's up Rat?" Jovan said, while lying on his bunk.

"Look, if you tryna see your man Bilal you better get on that Jumah list."

Jovan went over and signed the Jumah list and asked Lil Rat, "When are they gonna take us up there?"

"They be back in 'bout five minutes, what size shoe you wear?" He asked.

"I wear a 9 ?."

"Hog, get Jovan a pair of them Jordan's out my room when you come up."

"Thanks youngin." Jovan said.

"Ain't shit slim, I got a lot of that shit and plus you a real nigga. You used to look out for me when I was a young nigga." Lil Rat said.

Jovan went downstairs to his cell and got the knife that Lil Chaz had given him. This was a big ass knife and it had rigids on the side like a hacksaw.

The CO came back into the block and said, "Everybody who signed the Jumah list let's go front and center!"

"Jovan, you got a joint?" Rat asked me.

"Yeah, I'm a'ight Rat."

"Stand on this side so he won't pat you down." Rat said, pointing to the opposite wall from where Jovan was standing.

Jovan stood on the side of the Sally-Port and watched the CO pat down all the dudes in front, then he crept back in like he had already been searched. On our way to Jumah, Jovan let everybody walk ahead of him so he would be in the hallway damn near by himself.

As Jovan turned the corner to where the Jumah services were held, he heard the most beautiful chanting sound ever, there wasn't a crack in the voice and it sounded milky and smooth. As he got closer he heard it louder, "Allah-U-Akbar", "Allah-U-Akbar". When Jovan peeped through the door, he saw where the sound came from, young Rico (aka Ali Katabb), was standing in the middle of the floor with his hands behind his ears singing this beautiful song. Rico was back from Allenwood Penitentiary on his appeal. Later, Jovan came to find out that this song isn't really a song it's a call to prayer for Muslims.

As Jovan entered the room, he looked around for Bilal and when he looked to his left he saw him in the corner making Salat (The Muslim Prayer). Jovan always knew Bilal was a Muslim but he had never seen him do the prayer. Bilal's father, Saleem, was Muslim and if Saleem knew that his son was a cold hoe he'd probably kill him himself.

At Jumah everybody came because this is where co-defendants met up to discuss their case. This is where niggas passed shit off or it was just something else to do other than be in the block. Only a few dudes in here were true Muslims, most of these niggas were faking it, just trying to be accepted and were punks for real, like Bilal for instance. Jovan went to the back of the room and found a seat.

When Bilal finished his Salat, looked up and saw Jovan in the back of the room, his eyes were like pop rocks, like he had just seen a ghost or something. He put his shoes on and headed toward Jovan with a fake ass smile, he had on his DC jail jumper, a black Kuffi, a platinum chain with the word "Allah" in Arabic writing, a pair of Cartier glasses and some brown suede Butta Timberland boots.

When Bilal came over Jovan greeted him. "Damn nigga, even in jail you lookin' slick."

"Yeah, you know me Jay, shit don't stop cause the nigga got knocked." Bilal said.

"That's right slim."

"So, what is your lawyer saying Jay?" Bilal asked me.

"Oh they bullshittin', they're saying that the Prosecutor got some damaging evidence on me." Jovan said.

"Did they give it to you?"

"Give me what?"

"The evidence."

"Oh naw, they ain't tryna disclose that info to me."

"So what else they say?"

"They said somebody gave the Feds some type of info on me or something."

At that moment Bilal tightened up. "Who they say it was Jay?"

"I don't know Lal, they won't tell me."

"You sure they ain't gonna tell you Jay?"

"Naw, they ain't gonna tell me, so who you think it is Lal?" Jovan asked him, already knowing the answer.

"I dunno Jay, but hey don't even worry about that, we're gonna beat this shit. Did they give you another indictment or anything?"

"Naw Lal, the only indictment I got said accessory or conspiracy to commit murder why you ask?"

"Cause I heard that they be tryna fuck with niggas and give 'em another indictment right before their trial."

"Oh naw, they can't indict me on anything cause you the only nigga I've ever done something with Lal and that was in '85, everything else I've done by myself with no witnesses. You're the only one I've told about my work Lal and I know your loyalty with me, so hell naw, they can't indict me on nothing."

"Yeah Jay, you're right."

As Lal sat there and lied to him to his face and tried to compose himself, Jovan smiled and said, "Lal, you know I love you right?"

"Yeah Jay, I love you too."

Jumah was now over and everybody was leaving, Bilal and Jovan stayed behind so that they could walk the hall and get a little extra time in.

"What block you in Jay?" Bilal asked me.

"NE-3, where you at Lal?" Jovan said.

"NW-3."

"Oh, we're going the same way then."

As they walked into the hallway, Jovan could see that it was only Bilal and him. As Bilal kept talking, Jovan knelt down as if he was tying his shoe and let Bilal walk in front of him. Jovan then reached into his jumpsuit and grabbed hold to his knife as if his palm was dipped in crazy glue, he held onto its handle with the tightest grip ever. Now Bilal is cut the fuck up, 200 pounds, big as a brick house and he also was the boxing champion down Oak Hill, so if Jovan made any mistakes he would capitalize on that and kill him with his own knife. No matter how many blows Jovan gave him, his first blow had to be his best most vicious and vital blow.

Bilal was positioned about 1 foot in front of Jovan on his left side and since Jovan was right handed, that was perfect. He wasn't nervous or scared, he was just cautious because he knew that this was a once in a lifetime golden opportunity. Jovan sent his first blow with the hardest hook shot he's ever took and the knife went straight through Bilal's jugular vein. As Bilal held his neck trying to stop the blood that was squirting out like a water fountain, Jovan's second blow went straight through his heart. Jovan pushed the knife with such force that when he pulled it out, tissues of flesh were hanging off.

Bilal fell to the floor with blood gushing out of his neck and heart, and when he hit the floor face first, Jovan already knew he was dead but he wasn't finished with him, he had to teach him a lesson. Jovan had to let him know that he lived and would be willing to die by the code of loyalty. He held his knife high in the air with both hands and drove it right in the middle of his back.

He then wiped the handle of the knife off and left it in his back and before he turned around he spit on him and said, "Now you know how it feels to be stabbed in the back ma'fucka!"

As Jovan walked back to his block, no one was in sight. He held back the tears, the pain and the hurt and held tight to the jewel his Pops gave him, "trust no one".

CHAPTER 24

"The Cruelest Lie"

Sonya
Trial started today for my fiancée and I've been up all night anticipating this day, and now that it was finally here, I eagerly wanted it to go away. Jovan had asked me not to come to his trial he said he had his reasons. Like I told you before, I'm from Trinidad NE and there isn't too much you can get pass me. Obviously, Jovan was hiding something from me and I wanted to know what it was. Is it that he has another woman, maybe a wife and child? Is it that something may come out in trial that would hurt me or make me ashamed of him? I don't know what it is but Jovan needs to know that no matter what, I still love him to death and want to be with him for the rest of my life.

CHAPTER 25

"Get Ready to Rumble"

Jovan

Today my trial started and I couldn't sleep all night long. I'm back in the lockdown special handling block cause when the Lieutenant came to my block and told me that my co-defendant had been killed in the hallway, I immediately told him that I wanted to go back to lockdown cause if anybody wanted to do something to Bilal for whatever reason, then they might try to do something to me.

He understood and escorted me back to special handling. While in lockdown I still exercised every day, I did pushups, crunches, sit-ups and jumping jacks and I also got my trial strategy together. I subpoenaed everyone I felt necessary that would aid in my defense. I knew that the Government's star witness was Bilal and his earlier Grand Jury testimony, but with him not here to testify to that, if they try and use it all I have to say is the he lied about everything he said I did, he was really the perpetrator and he wanted to destroy me because I wouldn't take his case on the murder of Detective Bridges.

As I prepared to go into the courtroom, my attorney Michelle bought me a suit that Sonya dropped by the office for me the day before, it was a black silk Armani suit, white shirt and tie to match. She also brought me a pair of Armani glasses that would give me that distinguished innocent look. I was brought in by the Marshall and sat at the table opposite the Prosecutor.

At my table was my attorney Michelle Robinson and Andy, sitting there with their briefs reading notes. Mark was in the audience seated right behind us because if there was any suggestion he had, he'd be able to reach over and say it. The courtroom was packed with all types of lawyers, paralegals and secretaries. The trial was cut off from the public at my attorney's request and only a few important people were allowed in. I told Sonya and Grandma not to come and that I'd fill them in daily about the trial.

As I sat down, I acknowledged Mark first and he winked and gave me a thumbs up.

"Good morning Jovan." Michelle said.

"Good Morning Michelle."

"Hey Jovan." Andy said.

"How you doing Andy?"

" Are you ready to rumble?" He asked.

"Yeah, let's get this mess over with."

"Ok buddy, put on your hard hat."

"I had it on a long time ago Andy."

The Bailiff stood and said, "All rise, this is the Courtroom of Judge Patricia A. Queen."

After Judge Queen came into the room and was seated, she motioned for everyone to be seated.

"Thank you, you all may be seated. Prosecutor, Debra White, do you wish to proceed in this case?"

"Yes I do Your Honor. First I would like to present to the court and the jury that Mr. Jovan C. Price is the sole perpetrator in the murders of Michael A. Jones a/k/a "Fat Mike", Peter C. Millegan a/k/a "Petey", Corey L. Washington a/k/a "Chicken Wing" and

Anthony T. Bridges, a Detective for the Metropolitan Police Department." The Prosecutor stated.

"Ok Miss White, is that all?" The Judge asked.

"Yes Your Honor." The Prosecutor said.

"Ok, now would the defense like to say something?" The Judge asked Michelle.

Michelle stood and said, "Yes, Your honor in fact I do, I would like to present to the court that my client is innocent of all charges and that if there's any physical evidence linking my client to any of these crimes, I ask that it be known to the court now."

"I would like to ask that the Government produce its evidence that's requested by the Defense." The Judge requested.

"I call into evidence the Grand Jury testimony of Bilal Ali Davis." The Prosecutor said.

The Judge asked, "Is Mr. Davis here today?"

"In fact no Your Honor, Mr. Davis was subsequently killed two weeks ago while incarcerated at the DC jail." The Prosecutor answered.

"So you're saying you're ready to proceed in this trial with only the transcripts of a Grand Jury proceedings." The Judge said.

"Well yes and no Your Honor, I have certain witnesses that will corroborate Mr. Davis' testimony transcripts." The Prosecutor said.

"Ok you may hand that discovery over to the Defense." The Judge said.

When the Prosecutor handed over the discovery, I read all the testimony Bilal gave. He told these people our life story, but as I read more I could see that the only physical evidence that Bilal gave was the 1985 murder and I wasn't even charged with that one. Also he said that he gave me the .357 which was registered in Meeka's name, but that's argumentative, that doesn't prove I killed Detective Bridges, that only proves he gave me the gun that was later used in a homicide and I can twist that.

Also in discovery was the witness sheet. The only witness the Government had other then Bilal was Tameeka Gonzales, the prosecutor was lying, saying she had other witnesses. All day long the prosecutor and my attorney presented their opening statements. Michelle was on point with everything she told the jury, that there's no physical evidence that would link me to Bilal, no photos together, no phone taps, no fingerprints, nothing but the fact that I was hired as a Paralegal on his previous case. I was proud of the way Michelle handled things today.

Sonya
I went into the courtroom and grabbed a seat all the way in the back, outta Jovan's sight. It wasn't that hard for me to get in, I told the guard at the door that I was a paralegal working in this case and he let me in. When Jovan came out he looked nice, he didn't look like he was on trial for murder he looked like the attorney representing a client for murder. I could see that the Armani suit and tie I picked out looked very nice on him and he looked conservative with those glasses on.

As the prosecutor was saying all these terrible things about my fiancée, I knew they wasn't true, Jovan couldn't done all those things, he didn't have time to because most of the crimes they said he committed was on dates and times when he was with me, so I know for sure it wasn't true.

Jovan
As soon as I got back to the DC jail, Cinquan came down to my cell.

"How it go today Jovan?" He asked me.

"It went okay Chaz."

"That's good to hear Jay, by the way you need anything while I'm out?" Chaz asked.

"Naw, the CO suppose to let me out for my rec in about ten minutes."

"A'ight I'ma holla at you later."

"Ok Chaz."

When the CO let me out I went straight to the telephone and called my fiancée.

Ring, Ring, Ring. "Hello." Sonya said.

"You have a collect call from 'Big Daddy', if you wish to accept press 5." The operator said.

Sonya pressed 5 and said, "Yeah, I got your Big Daddy."

"What's up boo?" I said to her.

"Nothin', I'm just sitting here missing you." She said.

"Yeah me too."

"So how'd it go today baby?" Sonya asked Jovan, like she was not in the courtroom earlier.

"Oh everything went smooth, I'll be home to you in no time."

"I wish you hurry up cause my pussy is throbbing for your dick."

"How do you think I feel?"

"I don't know Jovan, but if it's anything like me then I know you're in misery."

"You miss a nigga like that?"

"Hell yeah boo!"

"So how was your day at work?"

"Baby I took off for two weeks, I'm thinking about not ever going back."

"You can't just quit like that Sonya, you gotta have something to fall back on."

"I know baby but I'm just so frustrated."

"Pull yourself together boo, everything's gonna be fine, you're my Queen remember?"

"Yeah and you're my King."

Sonya
Jovan called me at 6:00 p.m. and we talked for a while, it was good to hear my baby's voice. I wanted to tell him how good he looked today in the suit I brought him, but I couldn't cause he didn't know I was there. Jovan had told me not to worry and to pull myself together. How can I not worry when he's been charged with four murders, three of 'em I'm not supposed to know anything about. Why was he hiding them from me when I knew he was innocent? He was with me when those crimes were committed, well not all of 'em, but the first three he was with me.

Damn, Jovan told me there are things I don't know about him, well there's something Jovan doesn't know about me, but regardless of that, I still love him no matter what.

Jovan
It's the fifth day of my trial and everything that the prosecutor has presented has been batted down by my attorney, Michelle has been doing a tremendous job. Today the Government said they had a witness to corroborate Bilal's Grand Jury testimony and my attorney said they have witnesses that can prove I was some-where else during the time of these crimes. The judge informed them that she would hear the Defense first and then the Government could call their witness.

Judge: Ok Ms. Robinson, would you like to call your first witness?

Michelle: Yes Your Honor, but first may I have a brief moment with my colleagues.

Judge: Go right ahead.

Michelle: Ok Your Honor I'm ready to call my first witness in the Defense case.

Judge: Ok call your witness.

Michelle: I'd like to call to the stand Ms. Kathy Morris.

Bailiff: Ms. Morris, do you swear to tell the truth the whole truth and nothing but the truth so help you God?

Kathy: Yes I do.

Michelle: Ms. Morris can you please state your full name and occupation.

Kathy: My name is Kathy Marie Morris and I'm employed as a waitress at Phillips Restaurant.

Michelle: Ms. Morris, were you working on the day of May 8, 1994?

Kathy: Yes I was.

Michelle: And what were your hours?

Kathy: From 11:00 a.m. to 7:00 p.m.

Michelle: Ms. Morris, at anytime between the hours of 12:30 p.m. and 3:00 p.m. did you see my client, Mr. Jovan C. Price enter the Restaurant?

Kathy: Yes I did.

Michelle: And what time did you notice this person?

Kathy: A young lady and he came in around 12:30 p.m. and I was assigned as their waitress and I seated them out on the patio.

Michelle: How long did the couple stay at the Restaurant?

Kathy: They stayed awhile and it was obvious that they were in a heavy conversation because they stayed longer than the normal customer would stay.

Michelle: Do you know what time they left?

Kathy: Yes, it was exactly 3:00 p.m.

Michelle: Ms. Morris, at anytime did you see the Defendant here get up and leave the Restaurant?

Kathy: No, not at all.

Michelle: Thank you Ms. Morris, that'll be all.

Judge: Ms. White, do you want to cross-examine the witness?

Prosecutor: Yes Your Honor, if I may.

Judge: Go ahead.

Prosecutor: Ms. Morris, do you know the Defendant?

Kathy: No, I do not.

Prosecutor: Well, can you tell me how outta all the customers you see and after months, how could you be exact with the time and identity of this person?

Kathy: First of all, I was their waitress and Mr. Price was kind when they came in. He asked to be seated while I was still telling them the menu, also he's a very handsome man and I was attracted to him, it's hard to forget a face when you're attracted to them.

Prosecutor: Thank you, that's all Ms. Morris you may step down.

Michelle: Your Honor, I would like to ask that the Government strike the murder of Michael A. Jones off the Defendant's indictment. The Government hasn't met its burden of proof and it is clear that the Defendant wasn't at the scene of the crime.

Judge: If the Government doesn't have anything con crete to meet its burden I'll have no other choice but to strike the charge according to the law.

Prosecutor: Well Your Honor, my star witness is deceased and no I don't have any other witness to meet the bur den, but as the trial continues I'm sure I can find something.

Judge: Well Ms. White, we're in the middle of trial now and you haven't found anything yet so 'm not going to waste anytime on this, I'm gonna strike this charge and if you find some concrete evi dence in the near future, you can always bring the case back before this Court.

Prosecutor: Thank you Your Honor.

Judge: Now Ms. Robinson, do you have any other wit nesses to call?

Michelle: Yes I do Your Honor. I would like to call a witness to clarify that on the weekend of May 16th my client was in Orlando, Florida in Disneyland with his girlfriend and child. There is no way pos sible he could have murdered Peter C. Milligan and Corey L. Washington.

Judge: Ok Ms. Robinson, you may call your witness but first let me tell you something, I'm not going to keep striking these charges all day, this is a trial and in the middle of trial anything can develop.

Michelle: Ok Your Honor, I understand completely. I would like to call my second witness for today, Keda Jones. Ms. Jones, please state to the Court your full name and occupation.

Keda: My name is Makeda Ivory Jones and I'm an employee at Erotica Hair Gallery.

Michelle: What is it that you do at the Erotica Hair Gallery?

Keda: I'm a hairstylist, as well as a manager.

Michelle: Ms. Jones, can you tell the Court how you know the Defendant, Jovan Price.

Keda: Yes, he's the father of one of my sons.

Michelle: Ms. Jones, were you with your son's father during the weekend of May 16th.

Keda: Yes I was, in fact my son and me were with his father on my son's Birthday, which was May 16th.

Michelle: And where did you go for your son's birthday?

Keda: Jovan took us to Disney World in Orlando, Florida.

Michelle: And how long did you stay?

Keda: We stayed for 2 days, Friday and Saturday, we left Sunday morning.

Michelle: Your Honor, I'd like to exhibit Ms. Jones' testimony in showing that my client wasn't even in the city of Washington, DC during the time of these crimes.

Judge: It is excepted, but first let's see if the Government wants to cross examine.

Prosecutor: Well, yes I do Your Honor, and I'd appreciate it if the Defense let's me do so before entering any kind of showing to the Court.

Michelle: You can do whatever you like Ms. White I'm just being a lawyer.

Prosecutor: I'm sure you are.

Judge: Ok knock it off! We won't be having any catfights in my Courtroom.

Michelle: Sorry Your Honor.

Prosecutor: Sorry Your Honor. Ms. Jones how long have you known Mr. Price?

Keda: 8 years.

Prosecutor: And how old is your son?

Keda: Seven.

Prosecutor: Would you say Mr. Price is a good father?

Keda: Yes I would.

Prosecutor: Ms. Jones, do you love Mr. Price?

Michelle: Objection Your Honor, the Prosecutor is badgering the witness.

Judge: Overruled, she can answer the question.

Keda: Well yes, I love him for the fact that he's an excellent father and he does for his child.

Prosecutor: So, would you lie for the man you love?

Michelle: Objection Your Honor, Prosecution is leading the witness.

Judge: Overruled, she can answer that.

Keda: No I wouldn't lie I wouldn't lie for no one.

Prosecutor: Ms. Jones, other than your testimony, do you have any proof that Mr. Price was with your son and you on the weekend of May 16th?

Keda: Well yes I do, I have the stubs from the flight and I also have a few pictures.

Prosecutor: Well Ms. Jones, I can see that the stubs are valid, but Mr. Price isn't in any of these photos.

Keda: He was the one taking them.

Prosecutor: I see, thank you, you may step down.

Michelle: Your Honor, I'd like to ask at this time her testimony be accepted.

Judge: Well, I'm not going to accept it just yet. If the Government can't prove Mr. Price's whereabouts then I'll consider it.

Prosecutor: Your Honor, I'll need a little more time.

Judge: Look Ms. White, I'm not going to be giving you all this time, but what I will do is adjourn the trial over the weekend and you can pick back up on Monday.

Jovan

When I got back to the jail I came out for recreation and went straight to the phone to call Keda. Keda was my gangsta and she had came through like a soldier for me. When I first got arrested and Michelle came into the interrogation room, I whispered in her ear to call Keda and give her the alibi. Keda wasn't even in Florida over the weekend, her sister Carla took her sons to Disneyland and before they left Keda took a few pictures of them.

Damn, Keda was a soldier she had lied for me and said I was one of her son's father. Even though I looked out for her son, I'd never think she'd say I was his father. Keda did shit right and for that I was going to bless her with something real nice when I got out. I dialed Keda's number.

Ring, Ring, Ring. "Hello." Keda said.

"You have a collect call from Jovan, if you wish to accept, dial 5 now." The operator said.

Keda pressed 5 and said, "Hello Jovan."

"Hi Keda." I said.

"Yeah what up boy, how I'd do?" She asked.

"You did good, thanks baby, I'll never forget that."

"That white lady was a bitch." Keda said.

"Yeah I know. Now look, don't talk too much on this phone."

"Ok."

"This what I'ma do. I really, really appreciate what you did and for that you will forever have my loyalty. You're more real than some of these bitch ass niggas out here."

"Jay I fucked wit you, I know we ain't together but the shit you did for me and my sons I'll never forget, and for that if I can do anything for you I will."

"Ok shorty thanks again. Look Keda, I'ma call my Grandma, I want you to go over there she's gonna give you a gym bag."

"What's in it?"

"It's a present for you?"

"Ok Jay."

As soon as I got off the phone with Keda, I called Grandma

and told her to go upstairs and grab the gym bag, not the suit-cases and give it to Keda when she came by. "Ok baby, when is she coming?" My Grandma asked.

"She should be ringing your doorbell anytime now."

After I got off the phone with Grandma, I called Sonya.

"Hey baby what's up?" I said to Sonya.

"Nothing." She said.

For some reason Sonya sounded upset.

"What's wrong Sonya?"

"Ain't nothing wrong with me." Sonya said.

"Damn, you sound like you mad with me 'bout something."

"Why, am I supposed to be mad at you about something?"

"Naw, look I see you got a bad attitude so I'll call you some other time."

"Oh, so now you don't wanna talk to me no more, what you gonna call one of your other bitches?"

"Man, what you talking 'bout Sonya?"

"Nothing Jovan nothing."

Sonya
When I was in court today everything was going good until I saw that bitch get up on the stand and lie for Jovan. I didn't care about her lying, but the fact that Jovan has a son and didn't tell me fucked my head up. Now from her testimony I know Jovan committed those murders, he wasn't in Florida he was at that party and that night was the night we first made love. That was the night my soul took flight, if anybody remembers anything about that night, it would be me.

Also, the next day Jovan was at the gym, or at least that's what he told me, he probably was somewhere laid up with that bitch Keda. But anyway, one thing I do know he wasn't in no damn Florida, he was at my house fucking my brains out. I don't care if Jovan is a killer or not, I know he has things in the closet, but so do I. That's not what I'm mad at, I'm mad because I'm his fiancée and I told him I was down for whatever and he still ain't tell me he had a child.

Jovan
Damn, it's Saturday and visits starts in 20 minutes. I doubt if Sonya's coming today even though she hasn't missed a visit yet, she's still probably mad I haven't called her since we last talked. Shit, she was trippin' for nothing, I told her that it was a lot she'd have to deal with by being with me. If she's frustrated by the whole thing and can't hold fast then she can go ahead with her life. I need a soldier, a gangsta who could weather the storm, don't get mad at me cause I ain't home yet, this kinda shit takes time.

The CO came to my cell and said, "Price, you gotta visit."

""Ok thanks CO."

After I got myself together, the Lieutenant escorted me to the visiting room. Sonya was sitting there looking mad as hell with her arms crossed. What the fuck is she trippin' off of? As I entered the booth, Sonya still didn't smile. I sat down and looked at her for a second, she still ain't say nothin'. She's probably still mad I ain't call her.

"What the fuck is wrong with you, why you looking so mean?" I asked her, picking up the phone to talk.

"Cause Jovan." She said.

"Cause what?"

"Look I told your ass I love you a million times! You act like you can't hear me, I got on my knees in this fucking visiting room cried my heart out to you and embarrassed myself. I asked you to marry me and you still ain't recognize. I done told you I was down regardless of anything and you still ain't realize nigga that I love you and will die for you." She said, crying.

At that moment, I was shocked at what she was saying but nothing was making any sense.

"Ok Sonya, what are you getting at and please make it plain so I'll understand."

"Jovan, I was in the courtroom Friday."

Instantly I knew what she was mad at. ""Sonya, I thought I told you not to come to court."

"Yeah I know, but baby I couldn't hold that back. Listen Jovan, I'm not mad at the shit you did, I know you're a good person and whatever happened, happened for a reason. You gotta do what you gotta do and the fact that you do it so well is even better. I understand you don't want me to know and I won't ask, that's not the problem. I'm down with you on that part all the way to the bloody end and will do whatever to protect you, and I mean whatever, but what fucks me up is that you got a fuckin' kid!" She said, getting upset again.

"Hold up boo, see that's why I ain't want you to come to court cause I knew you would take it like this." I said.

"Well Jovan, how else am I suppose to take it, you're about to be my husband."

"Look Sonya, listen that's not my son, it was part of the move. Look at you, you feel stupid don't you?" I said to her, now I was getting upset.

"Baby I'm sorry, but I thought..." Sonya said, but I cut her off before she could finish her sentence.

"Yeah, I know what you thought, but now you know everything so where do we go from here Sonya?"

"Jovan baby, I'm still here I ain't going nowhere, we're still gonna get married, have babies and all that, but now that I know about you it's time you know about me. We'll both have something over each other's heads and forever we shall remain loyal to each other."

Sonya told me some shit that I would never believe even if I saw it. She told me how she killed her father for cheating on her mother and that her little brother took the beef. She told me all about her past and about the day we met in the courthouse, she was going to see her Probation Officer, and how she did time in Federal Prison for being a drug carrier for that bitch ass Ray.

She told me so much shit that I knew for sure that I had the perfect one, the perfect soldier, a straight up real "bitch" down for the ride to the bloody end just like Bonnie & Clyde. So, I put her down with the move, the "Political" move and she graciously obliged.

Sonya

My visit with Jovan went well, we put everything on the floor. Now there was nothing for us to hide, no more lies. I knew that one day I'd have to stop living a lie but can't let the world know, only my man my love, my soon to be husband, who too was living a lie and no one else would ever know.

Jovan

It's Monday and after my visit with Sonya I felt unbeatable. I already got three bodies out the way, now I gotta get this last one over with then I'm a free man. Someway I gotta discredit Meeka's testimony. If I can do that, then I'm free. Michelle is doing a good job, but for real, I'm just tight like that, so any lawyer who would have taken my case woulda walked straight through it.

When I entered the courtroom, I looked in the back to see if I could see Sonya, she wasn't there. I told her she could come now since we had talked about everything.

"All rise!" The Bailiff said.

When I stood up for the judge, I was still looking for Sonya but don't see her. This is the last stage of my trial and I needed her support.

Prosecutor: You Honor, you gave me an extension of time last week to meet my burden. I feel that it's a shame for me to concede with the Defense in accepting Ms. Jones' testimony, and ask to strike the other two charges, but I do not have any other witness to corroborate the Grand Jury testimony of Bilal Davis.

Judge: Ms. White, so you're telling me to strike those charges?

Prosecutor: Well no, actually Your Honor I'd like to ask that they stay until the end of the trial.

Judge: Ms. White I'll hold these charges but if you can't get me a credible witness then I'll have to strike them.

Michelle: Excuse me Your Honor, I'd like to file for a mistri al on the basis that the Government has no phys ical or material evidence that can convict my client. In all actuality Your Honor, this is a waste of time and a defamationof Mr. Price's character.

Judge: I agree with you in part Ms. Robinson, if the Government cannot provide anything else, I may just consider your motion but until then let's pro ceed.

Prosecutor: Your Honor, I'd like to call my witness to the stand who will show that Mr. Price was the per petrator in the murder of the DC Detective Anthony Bridges. I'd like to call Tameeka Gonzales to the stand.

(Damn, Meeka was gonna fuck the whole thing up, hot snitch ass bitch, just like her man. Look at her all fat and pregnant.)

Prosecutor: Ms. Gonzales, will you please state your whole name and occupation.

Meeka: My name is Tameeka Marie Gonzales and I work for Geico Insurance Agency.

Prosecutor: Ms. Gonzales, do you know the Defendant, Mr. Jovan C. Price?

Meeka: Yes I do.

Prosecutor: And how do you know him?

Meeka: Through my fiancée, Bilal Davis.

Prosecutor: Ms. Gonzales, did Mr. Price enter your home on May 19, 1994?

Meeka: Yes.

Michelle: Objection Your Honor!

Judge: Overruled.

Prosecutor: Can you tell me what he was doing there?

Meeka: He was talking to Bilal about something.

Prosecutor: Do you know what they were talking about?

Meeka: No.

Prosecutor: At anytime did you see Mr. David go back and forth upstairs?

Meeka: Yes I did.

Prosecutor: Did you see Mr. David give Mr. Price a gun?

Meeka: No I did not.

(At the moment, I was shocked that Meeka ain't tell, damn Meeka's a soldier, she's keepin' that shit on the street. It was Bilal the whole time who snitched. Meeka was willing to do some time for her nigga and he the one who snitched. Damn, that's fucked up. I shoulda known Meeka was down, she comes from a family of hustlers and they taught her well. Damn, I respect that shit to the fullest degree.)

Prosecutor: Excuse me, I'd like for you to repeat that answer.

Meeka: No, I did not see Bilal Davis give Jovan Price any gun, matter of fact, I didn't see Bilal Davis give Jovan Price anything.

Prosecutor: You may step down.

Judge: Ok, now would the Defense like to cross-examine?

Michelle: Most definitely Your Honor. Now Ms. Gonzales did you purchase a .357 Desert Eagle from a gun shop on Marlboro Pike?

Meeka: Yes I did.

Michelle: And where was that gun kept?

Meeka: Upstairs in my bedroom.

Michelle: Now, at anytime did that gun ever leave your home?

Meeka: Yes it did.

Michelle: When was that?

Meeka: Right after Jovan Price left the house. Bilal was mad that Detective Bridges had arrested his car riers with his money. This was the second time Mr. Bridges had done that and Bilal was mad at that, he said he was gonna kill Detective Bridges.

I tried to stop him but he knocked me down and took the gun and left. Before he left, he told me that if I called the police that he would also kill my family and me.

Michelle: Thank you Ms. Gonzales, you've did a wonderful job. Your Honor, surely this is grounds for a mis trial, not only that, but a judgment of acquittal would be the proper channel according to the law.

Judge: Now Ms. White, if you can't come up with some thing else, I have no other choice but to rule in favor of the Defense and Ms. Robinson there isn't enough material to put in for a judgment of acquittal. We still have the Grand Jury testimony of Bilal Davis, and according to law, a Grand Jury's testimony still can be used even if the per son is not present, it's more like a last will.

Michelle: I understand Your Honor. A mistrial would be fine, and if we gotta come in here again with the boxing gloves on then we will.

(Damn, fuck a mistrial I need that judgment of acquittal. If I get a mistrial, that means I gotta stay in jail until another trial and that may take about a year, and who knows, I might not even beat the next trial.)

Prosecutor: Your Honor, before you rule I have another wit ness, a surprise witness.

(Who the fuck could that be? A surprise witness, now they puttin' shit in the game.

"Hey Michelle, what the fuck is going on?"

"I don't know Jovan, this is all new to me, hold up I'ma try and do something.")

Michelle: Your Honor, we've already heard everything about the case, another witness wouldn't help the Government. I ask that you don't let the Government proceed and that you go ahead and rule for a mistrial.

Judge: Now Ms. Robinson, you heard the Government, they don't just have a witness but a surprise wit ness. Now Ms. White, if this witness doesn't help your case, not only will I rule, but you're putting me in a spot that I may have to rule in favor of judgment of acquittal.

Prosecutor: Ok Your Honor, but I believe this witness will do very well. Matter fact, I think this witness can bring those charges back that was stricken. I'd like to call to the stand Sonya Chanel Dunkin.

(What the fuck! Man, I know Sonya ain't going out like that, I'm fucked up. I told this bitch everything and this bitch done flipped the script on me. Naw not Sonya, I love this women. Damn, it seems like everything I love turns into hate.)

Prosecutor: Ms. Dunkin, please state your full name and occupation.

Sonya: My name is Kia Lynett Daniels and I'm currently unemployed.

Prosecutor: Hold up! Hold up, your name is what?

Sonya: My name is. . . .

Prosecutor: Yeah, I heard that but this isn't what we talked about.

Sonya: You asked me my name and I told you.

Prosecutor: You're supposed to tell the court how Jovan Price committed these murders.

Michelle: Objection Your Honor! Apparently the Government's witness is a surprise to the Government.

Prosecutor: Your Honor, I'd like to strike this witness.

Michelle: Before you strike the witness Your Honor, may I have permission to cross-examine cause maybe there's something the court needs to know.

Judge: Somebody do something in here, I'm totally con fused.

Michelle: Ms. Daniels, who are you?

Sonya: My name is Kia Daniels, I had my name changed in 1993 when I was released from Danbury Federal Prison for women.

Michelle: And why were you in prison Ms. Daniels?

Sonya: I was convicted in 1989 for being a drug carrier.

Judge: Ms. White, you just called a convicted felon as your Defense and you didn't even know it?

Prosecutor: Apparently not Your Honor, I don't know what the hell is going on.

Judge: Ms. White, I won't tolerate that language in this Court. And furthermore, your case is weak it doesn't even hold enough merit for a mistrial. The fiancée of Bilal Davis just proved to us that his testimony was a lie, and now this witness here just proved to us that the Government will try anything to convict someone, even if they're innocent. I have no choice but to rule in favor of a judgment of acquittal. The Defendant, Jovan C. Price, is cleared of all charges brought against him and it is further ordered that he be released from this prison immediately. Court is adjourned!

Michelle: Thank you, Your Honor.

Jovan: Thank you, Your Honor, you've handled this case fair and just.

Judge: Now Mr. Price, I think in the near future that you should be careful about the people you meet.

Jovan: I sure will Your Honor.

Everyone in the courtroom was clapping and Sonya got off the stand and left. I wondered where she was going and what the fuck she was doing up there in the first place.

Sonya

This time when I entered the courtroom, I sat way, way in the back so no one could see me. I saw that Jovan kept looking back for me but I had on a disguise, I was dressed as an old woman. I wanted to help my man, show him that I was down. The purpose for my disguise was for Meeka. If Meeka woulda fucked my man around, I was gonna follow her out the courtroom and put a knife right in her neck. But when I saw that she didn't snitch, I knew my baby was coming home. I knew I would hear the judge say that she may rule for a mistrial and not the acquittal. Shit, if Jovan gets a mistrial that ain't nothing, that only means he's gotta stay in jail and wait for another trial, and that may take at least another year. Fuck that, I need my man home now! And I mean right now, this was my fiancée, I can't let him go out like that.

So when they called for a recess, I went into the ladies room and took off my disguise and found the Prosecutor in the hallway. I told her I hated Jovan for what he did and that he had a child on me and that I knew everything he did. She instantly told me to testify. I knew if I got up there and told them my real name and how I went to jail, it would fuck the whole trial up and cripple the prosecution so much that the Judge would flip the fuck out and rule for an acquittal.

I had to do it I had to do something to free my man. I couldn't be a witness for his defense, they wouldn't have believed me because I was his fiancée and they knew I would lie for him, so instead I turned it around and still lied. The best lie ever.

Jovan

On my way outta the courthouse, I was still looking for Sonya and she wasn't nowhere in sight. Fuck it, she mighta left, rolled out. I'm still fucked up as to why she got on the stand, was it to help me or ruin me? As Mark, Michelle and me walked out the DC Superior Court, Michelle gave me a hug and told me I owed her some money. I told her to put it on my tab.

"So Jovan, what are you going to do now?" Mark asked me.

"I don't know yet Mark, maybe I'll go back to school, maybe I'll just chill." I told him.

"Well, whatever you do, you know you gotta be smooth about it."

"Yeah, I know."

"Hey Jovan, let me tell you something so you'll know lawyer strategy and stay two steps ahead." Mark said.

"What's up Mark?"

"I always knew that Bilal and you were friends, I just didn't say nothing."

"Get the fuck outta here! How you know that?" I asked him, amazed that he knew of our friendship.

"You gotta finish law school to learn that Jovan. Look you need a ride?"

"Naw Mark, I think I'ma go catch a cab, walk around a little, get some peace of mind and fresh air."

"Ok buddy, I'll see you around. Take care and Jovan finish school man."

"Ok Mark."

As Mark left and got in his car, I took off my tie and glasses and started walking down the street. Damn, I've done killed six ma'fuckas, well seven, who truly deserved it and got away with it. Damn, I lived a lie, a good lie my best lie ever.

As I got to the curb to hold my thumb out for a taxi, a black limousine pulled up. The light was green but the limo stopped. As the window rolled down, I still wasn't paying attention until I heard a voice.

"Looking for somebody?"

When I looked to see who it was, Sonya was smiling the brightest smile I've ever seen. I immediately jumped in the limo and we started kissing as the limo pulled off. She told me what she did for me and I knew I had the perfect one.

"Baby we lived a lie." Sonya said to me.

"I know Sonya, a good lie."

"Naw boo, a bad lie."

"Yeah baby, a vicious lie."

I put my finger on Sonya's lips to tell her to keep quiet and said to her, "It was a cruel lie Sonya, but yet it was told in silence!"

CHAPTER 26

"2 Years Later" (1996)

Jovan & Sonya

After we left the courthouse, we went pass Grandma's and got the suitcases with the three million, sold the 850 BMW, but kept the jewelry. Then we went to Sonya's and got all of her things, sold her car, packed up and headed to Atlanta. Now we're Mr. and Mrs. Jovan and Kia Price and the proud parents of an 18 month old boy named Jovan Jr. We have a seven bedroom house worth seven hundred thousand, three cars, a burgundy Range Rover 4.6SE, a green 500SL Mercedes Benz and the new black 600S V12 Mercedes Benz coupe.

Jovan went back to school for 2 years, he just passed the bar exam in Atlanta and now he's the youngest person ever to have his own law firm.

Kia is doing modeling and have a string of Hair Salons all over Atlanta.

THE END

"Dear Readers"

As you can see, I tried my hardest not to expose too much game. Although this book may give you a harsh sense of reality, it is my duty to let you know that

"This Book Is Not A True Story"

J. Rock

About the Author

Jason Poole was born and raised in (Southeast) Washington, DC. He's now currently serving time in Federal Prison under the harsh Crack Cocaine Law. However, since his incarceration in 1996, he has taken up several law courses while fighting his appeal acting as his own attorney. Also he is in the process of obtaining his paralegal diploma and starting his own legal company H.O.P.E. (House of Paralegal Effectives). Since then, Mr. Poole has had one of his previous convictions overturned and will soon be back in Federal Court attacking his illegal sentence under the United States sentencing guidelines. Proceeds from this book will go to the legal defense for some of those who were wrongly convicted.

Remarks write to:

Jason C. Poole #20617-016

FCI Manchester

P.O. Box 4000

Manchester, KY 40962

ORDER FORM

Triple Crown Publications
2959 Stelzer Rd.
Columbus, Oh 43219

Name:

Address:

City/State:

Zip:

		TITLES	PRICES
		Dime Piece	$15.00
		Gangsta	$15.00
		Let That Be The Reason	$15.00
		A Hustler's Wife	$15.00
		The Game	$15.00
		Black	$15.00
		Dollar Bill	$15.00
		A Project Chick	$15.00
		Road Dawgz	$15.00
		Blinded	$15.00
		Diva	$15.00
		Sheisty	$15.00
		Grimey	$15.00
		Me & My Boyfriend	$15.00
		Larceny	$15.00
		Rage Times Fury	$15.00
		A Hood Legend	$15.00
		Flipside of The Game	$15.00
		Menage'A Way	$15.00

SHIPPING/HANDLING (Via U.S. Media Mail)   **$3.95**

TOTAL $_____

FORMS OF ACCEPTED PAYMENTS:

Postage Stamps, Institutional Checks & Money Orders, all mail in orders take 5-7 Business days to be delivered.